The
ENCANTO'S
CURSE

The
ENCANTO'S
CURSE

Melissa de la Cruz

G. P. PUTNAM'S SONS

G. P. PUTNAM'S SONS

An imprint of Penguin Random House LLC

1745 Broadway, New York, New York 10019

First published in the United States of America by G. P. Putnam's Sons,
an imprint of Penguin Random House LLC, 2025

G. P. Putnam's Sons is a registered trademark of Penguin Random House LLC.
The Penguin colophon is a registered trademark of Penguin Books Limited.

Visit us online at PenguinRandomHouse.com.

Library of Congress Cataloging-in-Publication Data
Names: De la Cruz, Melissa, 1971– author.
Title: The encanto's curse / Melissa de la Cruz.
Description: New York: G. P. Putnam's Sons, 2025. | Summary: After the mysterious death of her father, MJ Robertson-Rodriguez, a half-encanto princess, navigates political intrigue, a possible curse on her realm's throne, and a mysterious knight, Sir Lucas, as she decides whether to open her heart to love amidst the turmoil of Biringan.
Identifiers: LCCN 2024012570 (print) | LCCN 2024012571 (ebook) |
ISBN 9780593533116 (hardcover) | ISBN 9780593533123 (ebook)
Subjects: CYAC: Fantasy. | Blessing and cursing—Fiction. | Kings, queens, rulers, etc.—Fiction. |
Mythology, Philippine—Fiction. | Love stories. | LCGFT: Fantasy fiction. | Novels.
Classification: LCC PZ7.D36967 En 2025 (print) | LCC PZ7.D36967 (ebook) |
DDC [Fic]—dc23
LC record available at https://lccn.loc.gov/2024012570
LC ebook record available at https://lccn.loc.gov/2024012571

Manufactured in the United States of America

ISBN 9780593533116 (hardcover)
ISBN 9798217003754 (international edition)

1st Printing

LSCC

Design by Suki Boynton
Text set in Adobe Caslon Pro

For Mike and Mattie, always

ISLAND OF
BIRINGAN

Recorded for the Council of the Courts with
accurate measure and in full accounting by
cartographer Gabriela Roxas, RBO, SMM.

AURORA
WETLANDS

LAMBANA
PALACE

LAMBANA
VILLAGE

OLD BUMARA WALL

SIRENA
PALACE

SIRENA
VILLAGE

1

I SPRINTED ACROSS the beach. My heart pounded in my ears, rushing like the ocean waves that lapped at my ankles. Salt water coated my lips, and my wet hair clung to my cheeks, stinging the skin on my face, but I couldn't slow down. I had to keep going. I had to hide.

A raised pier where boats would dock loomed ahead of me. It was empty now, all of the fishermen having set sail that morning. Birds squawked and took to the sky, startled and annoyed, when I charged under the dock to take cover in the shadows. It smelled like rotting wood and seaweed here, and I tried to quiet my breathing, but my lungs burned with the effort.

I crouched low, closed my eyes, and listened, but all I heard was the creak of the wooden pier, rocking with the ebb and flow of the ocean waves. I knew I didn't have much time, but I had to catch my breath. I grounded myself, focusing on what was real, to calm down.

I am Maria Josephina Robertson-Rodriguez, Mahalina Jazreel, princess—no, queen *of the Court of Sirena, ruler of Biringan.*

It'd been only a few months since I was crowned, and it was

still hard for me to get used to calling myself queen. Repeating who I was, what I was supposed to be, helped remind me that this wasn't all some dream, that I wouldn't suddenly wake up back in my bed in San Diego or have to go to school with all the other humans like everyone else. A nobody. I was a diwata, a spirit of the mountains and sea in the land of encantos, and the ruler of the hidden world. And I was hiding.

Heavy boots shifted in the sand behind me, and it made my stomach drop.

He was here.

I pressed my back against the pillar. The sound of boot steps grew closer, then paused, the wearer waiting or listening. Probably both.

I held my breath and my fingers shook, so I clenched my fist around the dagger at my side, a gift from my godfather, Don Elias. He had given it to me for this very purpose, and I was not going to fail. Not this time.

I leapt out from behind the pillar and cut down with my dagger.

But my opponent knew I was coming. He always knew when danger was near.

He raised his own dagger to meet mine, our blades singing off each other, then stepped back and had the gall to smile at me. Lucas Invierno, the most esteemed knight in all of Biringan City, the datu of Mount Makiling, and, oh—might I mention, my ex-boyfriend.

I swung at him, but Lucas was faster than me. He knocked away my dagger again, moving around me, fluid like smoke.

Frustration bubbled up inside me, and I moved to hit him

again. I was tired of losing. But Lucas had a lifetime of practice in the martial art of Arnis, whereas I was no better than a child swinging a stick. It was the only way I could learn to defend myself, as humiliating as it was. But it was all for a reason.

After the mambabarang attack before my coronation, Elias recommended I learn to better protect myself, both physically and magically. Being queen of Biringan, of all the encantos, I would be foolish not to think that other malicious forces might attack again, even if I had the protection of the entire Royal Guard. I couldn't rely entirely on other people. Without my approval, though, Elias had hired the best knight in the kingdom to help me. Lucas had just started to work full-time at the palace, stepping into his father's vacant role as head of security at the Court of Sirena. Of course, just my luck, the captain of the Royal Guard had to be the love of my life, soon to be married to someone else. But he was the best fit for the job.

I tried to summon my power, raising my hand toward Lucas, focusing on the magic coursing through my veins like Elias had taught me. I wanted to turn his dagger into something else—a snake, a twig, a palm frond, anything—but nothing happened. Lucas danced in, and I barely had time to catch his strike. It sent a shock wave through me; he was so strong. He was not hold-ing back.

Lucas came at me with his left hand and disarmed me with one move. I tried to throw my shoulder into him, but he used my momentum and tripped me. I somersaulted, suddenly seeing the blue sky, and landed on my back in the shallow water.

Lucas straddled me in a winning finisher and spun the dagger around, placing the dull handle against my neck, knowing better than to put a blade to his queen's throat. Sunlight sparkled in the water droplets on his hair, making him look like he was made of diamonds.

"Got you," Lucas said, a little breathless, with a hint of a smile. His words, smooth and low, had an air of flirtation to them. Like old times.

I bit down a retort. It was the first thing he'd said to me in months that wasn't strictly professional or hardly more than a "Good strike," "Go again," or "Your Majesty." Of all times to flirt, this was the least anticipated. And the least welcome. Did he know what he was doing? Or was it by accident? When it came to Lucas, it was difficult to tell. He was always so mysterious and knew exactly how to get a rise out of me, for better or for worse. I was not in the mood for his games, especially now.

He must have realized what he'd said too, because color rose in his cheeks, and the gold in his dark eyes glinted. After a heartbeat too long, he lifted the hilt of his blade from my neck and raised himself off me.

I stayed there in the shallow water, as if proving a point that I could get up anytime I wanted, but he extended a hand to help me. I ignored him and stood on my own. "Months of training, sparring with me every day, and all you can say is 'Got you'?" I asked, glaring at him.

He sheathed his dagger. Like me, he was dressed in twill pants and a loose shirt for sparring, and the tips of his pointed ears had turned the same shade of red as his clothes. Infuriatingly, he didn't say anything again, falling back into silence.

I almost wished I hadn't said anything. Exchanging a few strictly professional words was better than enduring this silent treatment.

Since the announcement of his engagement to my nemesis, Amador Oscura, Lucas had stopped talking to me. There had been no explanation, no conversation, not even so much as a goodbye.

No one tells you how much it sucks to find out that your boyfriend was planning on getting married to someone else the whole time you were together. Granted, we'd never officially called ourselves boyfriend-girlfriend because we were so busy with our respective duties—me being in the royal palace and him in the neighboring Court of Sigbin. But when I got a wedding invitation from Amador a month after my coronation, it was shocking, to say the least.

I almost hadn't bought the engagement, not until I saw the announcement in the news crystals—basically magical iPads—and realized it was true. Their engagement photo had been picture-perfect. The two of them arm in arm, dressed to the nines in silks and matching gold headdresses. The whole kingdom would be in attendance.

I went through the five stages of grief after getting dumped: laughing at the absurdity of it all, fuming for being delusional enough to think Lucas wasn't Amador's lapdog, wondering if Lucas was under some sort of love spell, and crying in the bathtub . . . I was still working on the acceptance stage.

Lucas didn't say anything more while I grabbed my wet ponytail and wrung it out, finding it covered in sand and seaweed. I knew Jinky, my lady-in-waiting, would have a fit about the state of my hair. All her hard work making it silky smooth and full, down the proverbial drain.

Everything would be so different if I were better at using my ability. If I could master my power like I was supposed to, maybe I wouldn't feel like such a failure.

Lucas's gaze was downcast while he waited for another sparring round. His finger traced the hilt of his knife in small circles, and the muscles in his jaw tightened. He brushed his dark hair out of his eyes, and when he gazed out across the sea, I couldn't help but admire his profile, sharp as glass, and his expression, just as cold. I hoped he would say something. The silence was slowly killing me. A part of me wanted to stay mad at him, but another part of me still wanted to kiss him. Lucas had that effect, infuriating to no end.

I missed him, and I still didn't know why he lied.

He'd told me that he and Amador weren't romantically involved, that she was just saying that at school to get under my skin. But once the announcement was released, he never denied it.

He'd used me, hurt me, lied to me. I refused to let him think all was forgiven. One thing was for sure: I was not going to be hung up on a cheater. He could rot for all I cared.

I diverted my gaze out across the water. I wanted him to know how he made me feel, but I also didn't know what to say. And then I thought, maybe he didn't, either.

I was going to be the bigger person, even if he didn't deserve it.

"I shouldn't have snapped earlier," I said. Out of the corner of my eye, I saw him shift, turning to me. "You beat me, fair and square."

"You're getting better," he said softly. "You almost had me."

I kept my gaze on the water, my heart sinking. *Almost.*

I was about to stoop down and pick up the dagger that Lucas had knocked from my hand, but he beat me to it. He held it out to me, handle first. "Thank you," I said automatically. I took it and wiped it clean on my shirt before putting it back in the sheath at my hip. Our eyes met, and I could almost trick myself into thinking he looked sorry. He opened his mouth like he wanted to say something, but he didn't. And that was all I needed to know.

"Well done, Datu Lucas," a voice called from the pier above us. Don Elias, my godfather and councilor to the throne, gazed down at us, a hint of disappointment on his face. "That is enough for today."

We jumped away from each other, startled, but Lucas regained his composure quickly. He snapped his heels together and bowed slightly to Don Elias, then to me, before he crossed the beach and disappeared into the jungle between the shoreline and the palace.

Elias waited for me as I joined him on the pier, and we walked together up the dirt path leading through the grounds.

"He caught you again," Elias said, like I hadn't been there.

"It's not fair. Lucas's power is sensing danger. It's like he has Spidey-sense."

Elias frowned at me. "Spidey-sense?"

Of course that would go over his head. He hadn't grown up in the human world like I had. I figured it wasn't worth explaining and just sighed.

"You must learn to control your power," Elias said. "Your alchemy is your greatest advantage. Do not rely on physical strength alone."

"I know," I said with a groan. "It's just not . . . working."

"You were able to summon your power to accept the scepter during your coronation."

"That was different. That was all adrenaline and—"

"You have used your power once. You can do it again."

The memory of that day, of the bugs and the hag called a mambabarang, came rushing back. My grand-auntie Elowina, who had wanted to claim the throne for herself, had almost killed half the court for it. I'd managed to use my father's protective amulet—an anting-anting—to create salt water to kill her. I'd been desperate then, and I was starting to think it had all been a fluke. But Elias sounded a lot more confident in me than I felt. Either he believed or *wanted* to believe in me, and I wasn't sure which put more pressure on me. I couldn't shake the feeling that I would let everyone down.

Elias escorted me in the same direction that Lucas had disappeared in, through the jungle and up a narrow stone staircase cut into the cliffside toward Sirena Palace. My body ached, my joints swollen and stiff from sparring, but I followed Elias without complaint. If he knew how hard I'd trained with Lucas, he'd probably call for a palanquin. Elias had become protective of me, especially after learning that his best friend—my father—had been murdered. But I was determined not to give him any more reason to fear for my well-being.

"We will do everything we can to protect you, but you must be able to protect yourself," Elias said. "Your power is a rare gift, one we haven't seen in an age, and once you can control it, you will not have to look up at anyone from the flat of your back."

Granted, most people in the kingdom wouldn't mind having to look up at Lucas from the flats of their backs. I forced myself to shove away the thought. I didn't want to be the jealous type. I needed to focus on controlling my talent. Apparently, my grandmother—my father's mother, the last queen before me—had had my gift too, but she had been able to master it because she had hundreds of years of practice.

According to scholars, magic should be easy for someone with my talent. At my age, I should be able to turn a flower into stone, a palm tree into gold, or sand into sugar. Everyone told me it was alchemy, the ability to turn one thing into another. It was how I'd turned fresh water into salt water to defeat the mambabarang. I was supposed to be able to control the very elements of nature. Emphasis on *supposed to*.

Idly, I tried to summon my power on a sampaguita flower jutting out from the cliff. My power burbled and buzzed beneath my skin like soda. But the flower simply shuddered under my command and snapped in half, its petals drifting through the air to land at my feet.

Changing nature felt about as possible as me sprouting wings and taking flight. It was like my power had a mind of its own, operating under someone else's will. I was never going to get the hang of this.

Still in lecture mode, Elias brought me through the garden, which was full of hibiscus and orchids. He rambled on and on about security and safety, but I had already tuned him out. I'd heard the lecture a million times. In the garden, the air smelled fresh and instantly settled my nerves, even though I was still annoyed from today's failures. This was one of the few places where I could find sanctuary. The palace staff rarely came out here. It was where I could be myself without having to be fussed over or advised. I felt like me, the same old MJ again.

"Princess—" Elias caught himself, just like I still did. "Er, apologies, my queen, you are bleeding." Elias's eyes fell to my knee, where I saw a smear of bright red blood through my ripped pants.

I hadn't even noticed. "It must have happened when I fell."

"You fell?"

"On the rocks. I took a shortcut on the beach to catch Lucas by surprise." I had been trying to use the rocks so he would have a harder time tracking me through the sand. Yet another failure.

Elias pursed his lips much like a father would and turned around, calling, "Nix!" There was no answer. The garden was quiet. Elias tried again, louder. "Nix!"

After a beat with still no sign of her, he sighed. "Where is that healer? I just saw her a minute ago."

Elias was about to call for her again when a pale face popped up from behind a garden wall. My best friend, Phoenix "Nix" Xing, looked startled, like we'd interrupted something. Knowing her, she had probably had her face buried in a book.

"Y-yes?" she asked, black hair sticking out of the braided bun on the top of her head.

"Your attention, please," Elias said, tipping his head toward me.

Nix disappeared behind the hedges once more, and I could hear her hurrying over. I tried to reassure the both of them. "It's no big deal, really."

But Nix appeared, straightening her robes, and asked, "What'd you do this time?" Instead of the shabby robes I was used to seeing her in, the crisp blue healer's uniform suited her nicely. Ever since she had learned she was a resurrector and started her formal training, she had skyrocketed to the head of her group at the Biringan Academy of Noble Arts.

"It's not that bad!" I said. "It's just a scrape. You're both acting like it's the end of the world."

"Scrapes I can handle," Nix said. "And a queen is not allowed to have scrapes."

Elias had me sit down on one of the garden benches beneath a mango tree. I hiked up my pants and stayed still while Nix looked me over.

She leaned in close and clicked her tongue. "This will be quick," she said, then hovered her hands over my knee, and a tingling chill seeped into my skin. It felt like the VapoRub my mom used to put on my chest when I had a cold. Nix's magic stitched the skin on my knee back together in seconds, leaving nothing but a fresh red splotch that would fully heal in a day.

"You're the best, Nix," I said, admiring her work.

Nix shrugged and smiled at me, dark eyes sparkling.

Ever since she'd come to live with me in the palace, we'd grown closer. She'd been my best friend since I was first brought to the island after my father's death, and she helped me figure out how to live as an encanto. Like me, she'd come from the human world, where she'd been hiding from her family—the *imperial* family of Jade Mountain—and sought refuge in Biringan, living in a shack on the outskirts of town while attending school with other encantos our age. But when I took over the official duties of being queen, the palace still felt too big, and I hated the thought of her living all alone in an abandoned building, so she moved into her own tower on the eastern wing. We'd spent every day together since.

We stayed up late reading romance novels and playing board games, spent days off shopping and eating, swimming in the ocean, sitting in the astronomy tower to watch the stars. Being with Nix was like one long sleepover. Growing up in the human world, I had never had a friend like her, and our friendship was something that I wanted to protect.

Being a queen can be lonely, but Nix never treated me any differently for it, and for that, I owed her everything.

"You should be more careful next time," Elias said. "Lucas is there to train you, not to injure you."

Oh, Lucas has injured me enough, I thought.

"Sir." A squeak of a voice made Elias turn. A dwende—beings akin to dwarves or gnomes, no taller than my hip—with a flaming red beard and a stovepipe hat stood at attention. "The accounts are ready for you."

"Ah, thank you, Toli. I'll be there right away." As chief councilor to the crown, Elias oversaw most of the administrative work and other official business. Sometimes I almost thought he preferred spending time in his office surrounded by towers of papers, like it was some kind of sanctuary from having to worry about me.

The dwende Toli left, expecting Elias to follow, but before he did, Elias turned to me and said, "You must try harder, anak." It was an affectionate term of endearment, yet I couldn't help but feel like it was a reminder that I was still inexperienced.

"I will," I said. And I meant it.

When Elias left, Nix stood up. "Training didn't go great?" she asked me.

I heaved myself to my feet, and we started walking toward the palace. The gleaming gemstone towers jutted into the satin-blue sky like a crown befitting a queen, but seeing it these days always made me feel like I wasn't good enough to set foot inside my own home. "What gave it away?" I groaned. I stared at the gravel path so I wouldn't have to see the palace. The gardens, though, were on the western side of the grounds, meaning the palace cast them in shadow at this time of day. I was appreciative of the breeze, despite my sour mood.

"You just have to practice," said Nix.

"I've been practicing! When I'm not being queen or when I'm not with you, it's all I do! I'm starting to think what I did at my coronation was a fluke."

"It wasn't! My training with the healers shows how hard it can be to control magic. It's about focus and determination. So something must be making you distracted."

"Hm, I wonder what it could possibly be," I said sarcastically.

Nix frowned. "Is this still about Lucas?"

Heat rose to my face. "No."

"Liar."

Only my best friend could get away with calling me out. "How can you tell?"

"Your heart rate accelerated, your body temperature rose, and your sweat glands have begun to produce more—"

"Okay, okay, I get it," I said, before she could go on one of her famous tangents. I nudged her with my elbow and couldn't help but smile. "You don't have to use your magic. Show-off."

Nix looked all too proud of herself. "You just need to give it time. You're too hard on yourself."

I let out a huff. I knew she was right—it would take time and practice for me to get anywhere with my power, but it still felt like I was running on a treadmill, going nowhere. Every time Lucas came near me, ignored me, pretended like I didn't exist, it felt like I was less than nothing. How could I focus on my magic when that was all I thought about? "I can't escape him," I said. "Seeing Lucas's face reminds me he's marrying . . . her."

Just at that moment, I spotted Amador Oscura. She was standing in the garden, gazing at her reflection in the pond, and smoothing out her blue-black hair. When she heard us coming, she whipped around, smiling brightly. "I was hoping you'd—" When she saw it was me, her smile dropped, but it didn't take away from her beauty. Her skin practically glowed against her soft peach Maria Clara dress, like she'd just stepped out of a fashion shoot. The only thing out of place was a smear of pink lipstick on the corner of her mouth, which she wiped away with the back of her hand. I imagined Lucas had been the one responsible for smearing her makeup, and it made my shoulders tense up.

Lady Amador Oscura was the grand duchess of the Sigbin Court, the same court Lucas belonged to. She was a royal, just like me, but of a lesser house, still bound to the council and an active member of the parliament. Royals came in and out of the palace, especially to see Elias, so I shouldn't have been surprised to find her here. And yet I was. She always found ways of undermining me, belittling me, making comments about my half-human lineage. I'd dealt with queen bees at school before, but she was on another level.

"What are you doing here?" I snapped.

Amador looked shocked for the briefest moment before she gathered her wits and straightened her shoulders. She scrunched her nose like she smelled something foul and lifted her chin. "Official business," she said.

"What business?"

Amador only lifted a shoulder and repeated, "Official."

What kind required Amador to be in the garden was beyond me, but then again, Elias oversaw so many meetings, I wouldn't be surprised if she had been told to wait outside while another meeting ran late.

I glanced at Nix, who was pretending to inspect a bed of purple peonies. Nix had never liked Amador, and they always butted heads. After all, Nix was the one who'd warned me about Amador from the start, and I had the feeling that Nix was afraid of her but chose to pretend like she didn't exist as a defense mechanism. Amador's eyes darted to Nix, too, and her expression narrowed, making her small mouth even smaller. She dragged her thumb against her mouth and glared at me.

"What are *you* doing here?" Amador asked, as if making a keen observation.

I almost laughed. "You're in *my* garden."

"Oh, *your* garden?" Amador asked innocently. "I didn't know our queen was so protective of her weeds."

I rolled my eyes. "The pigs are out back, rolling in the mud. You should join them. I'm sure you'd love it."

Amador's face soured. She looked me up and down, taking in my Arnis uniform coated in sand and still damp with salt water. Compared to her, I looked like something the fishermen dragged out of the ocean. Whatever she saw satisfied her, and a haughty smile curled her mouth.

From behind, the sound of heeled shoes on the stone path grew closer, and a feminine voice called out, "What is going on here?"

A tall female encanto with long pointed ears walked toward us, her hands clasped delicately in front of her slim waist. Her head tilted with curiosity. She wore a long Maria Clara dress in Sigbin blue just like Amador's, large diamond earrings, and an even bigger diamond necklace, which was cinched at her throat. It was like she was covered in diamonds, from the ones pinning up her dark hair to the ones on her fingers. In human years, she looked like she would be in her forties, but in encanto years, it was difficult to tell.

"I'm having a chat with the queen, Mother," Amador said.

This was Amador's mom?

The woman blinked, surprised. "Oh! Your Majesty, I didn't recognize you in your—" Like her daughter, her eyes went to my clothing, and she turned her head ever so slightly, as if she were trying to find the best word before she settled on: "State. Forgive me, I do not believe we've had the pleasure of introductions yet. I am Amihan Oscura, archduchess of Sigbin Court." She curtsied so smoothly, she could have been floating.

I was amazed I hadn't seen the family resemblance sooner. She and Amador had the same pinched expression, the same cold blue eyes, and even the same smile.

Amihan enunciated every word like it was a treasure she was gifting to the air. "I am simply thrilled I finally get to meet you in person. My husband, the archduke, has been away on business for some time, you see, and it has taken us simply *forever* to return to the kingdom. I am so glad that you and my daughter have become fast friends."

Friends? I looked at Amador, who fluttered her eyelashes innocently. "Oh yes, Mother. We are the *best* of friends."

A smile curled Amihan's lips, like Amador had said the thing she most wanted to hear. "Excellent."

I held my tongue; my head was buzzing so loud with anger. I wasn't sure what kind of game Amador was playing. "What brings you to the palace?" I asked, trying to divert the conversation.

"We are here to finalize our seal of devotion," Amihan said.

"It's a magical oath we signed when we got engaged," Amador added to me. She knew I needed the explanation and was using it against me like I was stupid. "A binding contract between me and my beloved, Lucas. The head magistrate oversees the promise we'll make to each other; we just need the official seal from Elias before we're wed. It's almost as important as the vows we'll take on our wedding day."

"That's . . . great." It felt like I'd been hit over the head.

"I'm looking for Lucas," she said. "Have you seen him?"

"He left," I said, my voice flat.

Amador pouted. "Oh. Shame. I'll have to keep scouring the

grounds for him. He must be here somewhere." She sighed and glanced at her mother. "Having a fiancé to escort me around is such a luxury, isn't it? I'm not sure what I would do without him."

"A matched pair, indeed," said Amihan, smiling all too proudly. "Ever since you were children."

Amador folded one arm over her stomach and raised the other to rest her chin on her delicate hand, showing off the gleaming diamond ring on her finger. The diamond was as large as her fingernail, the band a ring of golden ivy, as if it had been touched by Midas. No doubt a betrothal gift.

Something hot and sharp poked my rib cage. "You two will be very happy together," I said, clenching my jaw so hard, I barely opened my mouth. "My blessings to you both." My mom always said it was better to take the high road when dealing with bullies, and this was the best I could do.

"You will be in attendance at the wedding, I hope?" Amihan asked. Her eyes were bright but the skin around them was tight. It almost looked like she was nervous. "It would be an honor to have the queen in attendance."

"Of course she'll be at the wedding, Mother. She's my *best* friend," Amador said, her voice dripping in molten sugar.

A smile twitched its way onto my lips, but I couldn't say anything back. Amador was trying to get a rise out of me, and the worst part was that it worked. She knew Lucas and I had fallen for each other, and she was reminding me that he had been hers all along. I had never stood a chance.

"Sure," I said before I could stop myself. "I . . . Absolutely."

Amihan seemed thrilled. "Well, then! We can't be late! We

must see the royal magistrate." She clicked her tongue and added, "Must you smile like that, Amador? You're going to get wrinkles."

Amador, who had been grinning with self-satisfaction, stopped at once and lowered her head while Amihan curtsied at me once more before turning and leaving. Amador stayed behind and dragged her thumb across her lip line again, eyes lowered. For a moment, I wondered, *If Lucas wasn't the one who smeared her lipstick, who was?* But then I remembered I didn't care.

"Wrinkles?" Nix asked under her breath, baffled. "Woof, what a handful."

Like mother, like daughter. Now I knew where Amador got her superficiality from. But I got a smidge of satisfaction out of seeing her taken down a peg. A bitter, mean part of me wanted to see Amador get her comeuppance for everything she'd done to me, but it didn't actually make me feel any better. Not really. I still felt like I was losing.

My knees wobbled, and I barely managed to walk past Amador and head toward the palace entrance.

Nix leaned into me and whispered, "Are you okay?"

I could only nod. It was like I'd lost my voice; I was so angry.

Amador called after us so sweetly, I bet it made her teeth hurt. "I heard you're having difficulty honing your power."

I slowed to a stop.

Amador's voice was drenched in false compassion. "It's truly an embarrassment that our queen can't control her powers yet. Such a shame, truly. No wonder the other kingdoms pity us."

I didn't think I was doing a bad job as queen so far. I'd passed laws decreeing universal housing, full access to healers, free education. More equality, more equity. Some nobles criticized me, but most of Biringan City believed in what I was doing. Who cared if I couldn't use my magic yet?

A malicious voice inside of me, spurred on by my own pettiness, told me she was asking for it. I whipped around to glare at Amador and lifted my finger, pointing it right at her as I summoned my power. The temperature of the air rose around my head.

I wanted to give her zits, or make her puke, or make her diamond ring turn to charcoal. I didn't want to hurt her, but she needed to be taught a lesson—

My power surged and then, like a backfiring car, cracked.

Power shot back up my arm, making it tingle like it had fallen asleep. "Ah!" I gasped, and shook it out, annoyed. Amador merely lifted her chin and walked away from me, unaffected.

I regretted my reaction a second later.

Nix grabbed me by the arm and carted me deeper into the garden.

My arm still tingled and my blood boiled, but Nix's grasp on me was firm, and the farther we got from Amador, the better I felt. My power roiled out of me like waves, and the air around us smelled like sulfur, turning acrid as my bitterness ate away at my heart. I didn't mean to do it, but my power was erratic and unpredictable and something to be embarrassed about. Exactly like Amador had said.

I couldn't entirely blame her for what Lucas had done to me. She was the one who'd told me the truth, even if I hadn't wanted to hear it. She was the one who'd said from practically the moment

I met her that they were engaged. I might hate Amador, but she wasn't the one who broke my heart.

Nix waved her other hand in front of her face, dispelling the rotten-egg smell. If she hadn't known about my power, she would have thought I'd farted, but she didn't say anything about it.

By the time we reached the edge of the garden in the shadow of the palace, I was exhausted. Trying to use my power so much had drained me.

"Just ignore her," Nix said. "Leave Amador alone."

That took me by surprise. "You almost sound like you're defending her."

She rolled her eyes but didn't deny it. "It's just more distractions. Maybe you should think about moving on from Lucas. It'll only get worse the longer you think about him."

Deep down, I knew she was right. I may have been queen, but who was I to tell him who he could and couldn't marry? Wielding my authority like a leash, punishing those who didn't bend to my will—that would go against everything I believed in. If Lucas had loved me, he would have stayed true.

I forced myself to take another deep breath and gazed up at the shining towers of the palace. My home. The one place I belonged.

"I've never been dumped before," I admitted. "This sucks. I'm sorry I'm in a bad mood."

"I get it." She looked out across the garden, and then she said, "Could you imagine Amador rolling around in the mud with pigs?"

A smile made its way across my mouth. "If only I had the honor of pushing her in myself."

2

THAT NIGHT, IN the dark, starlit sky, I flew.

The stars shone bright, and the air was thick with the promise of rain. I soared, swooping and gliding above the palace towers. I was free, finally, and because of that, I knew that I was dreaming.

The crescent moon offered a little light, but I didn't need it to see. My dream-eyes could pierce through the darkness, seeing the world as if it were bathed in red. The world thrummed with life. I could sense it all around me, how it shifted like a ripple in still water. Biringan City was resting, but its pulse kept beating.

I spotted my shadow when it cut across the roof. There I saw the unmistakable shape of wings sprouting from my back, and I somehow looked smaller. My wings buffeted the air, carrying me into the sky, but all I could think about was the pain. It felt like I had torn myself in two. A hunger, desperate and furious, burned through me, and it made my limbs twitch and my throat seize up. I tried to cry out, but it came out like a mangled rasp. I could fly, but there was a price.

I was starving.

MY EYES SNAPPED open, and I was in bed.

It had only been a nightmare.

I held my head in my hands and curled into myself, waiting to calm down as the details of the dream started to fade, but my heart raced like I'd sprinted a mile. I forced myself to breathe.

Usually my nightmares were about school or running from a mambabarang, but this one had felt so real. It scared me.

I lifted my head and looked around, grounding myself in reality. I was in my bedroom fit for a queen. My four-poster bed draped with sheer lace; my settee, where I napped; my bookcase and vanity, all neat and organized; the privacy screen covered in painted jasmine flowers, where Jinky dressed me every day—nothing out of place. I was home. A relieved sigh melted out of me, but the dream had shaken me too badly to fall back asleep.

After another hour of twisting and turning in bed, I gave up and went for a walk. Naturally, I stopped by the kitchens to grab a snack, then navigated my way to the astronomy tower.

Scientists used to work here, foretelling the future in the stars, but a new astronomy tower had been built in Mount Makiling, leaving this tower abandoned. It was a perfect getaway from the hustle and bustle of the palace, where nothing ever seemed quiet and peaceful.

To my surprise, I wasn't the only one who couldn't sleep. Nix was already here. She was sitting on the tower's balcony, cocooned inside a down duvet and peering through a telescope, nestled in one of two beanbag chairs we'd set up here at the beginning of summer, our own little hideout. Her face brightened in the glow of the firefly lantern when she saw me come in.

"You're awake! Did you come to see the meteor shower, too?" she asked, pointing skyward. Sure enough, a handful of stars streaked overhead, leaving a glittering trail of stardust in their wake. Living in Biringan often reminded me just how far from home I really was.

"I'm here purely by chance, but what do the stars say?" I asked, taking a seat on the beanbag chair beside her.

Nix peered through the telescope. "Hmm," she said. "They say, 'Reply hazy; ask again later.'"

I laughed when she grinned toothily at me, and it made me feel immediately better, the remnants of the nightmare dissipating like smoke in the wind. I offered her some of the snacks I'd swiped from the kitchen, and she munched on some banana chips happily.

Instead of healer's robes, Nix was in her pajamas—an old Lakers jersey she'd kept from her time in the human world and yoga pants. She opened the duvet for me and wrapped me up with her, stamping out the chill of the breeze coming from the ocean. Because we were so high up, it was a lot colder than usual, but it was warm and cozy by her side. Sometimes life in the castle was so stifling.

Jinky had scrubbed me down within an inch of my life with sugar and salt, shampooed my hair with sweet-smelling nectar, and slathered me in oils and serums that made me feel like I was an eel, slipping and sliding around my room while I got dressed for bed. My conversations with Lucas and Amador had replayed in my head over and over as I fell asleep, and my arm still ached from my magic backfiring. No wonder I'd had a nightmare. Even Jinky's wonderful concoction of lavender-and-coconut sleeping oil couldn't calm me down.

At first being queen was a dream. It was nice to have all my needs anticipated, never have to decide what to wear that day, always have Jinky do my hair, and awake to a hot breakfast, served in bed. But the novelty had started to wear off. I couldn't so much as go to the kitchens to pour myself a glass of water without some dwende presenting one to me on a gold platter. Garnished with lemon and mint.

I knew I shouldn't complain. People would literally kill me for my crown. But I was still a girl. I needed some semblance of independence, and being in the old astronomy tower with Nix, I could pretend like I wasn't in charge of an entire island nation and act like a kid, even if it was just for a little while longer.

"Want to see what else I found?" I asked, grinning. Nix pulled her attention away from the meteor shower and raised her eyebrows expectantly. I didn't wait for her to guess and pulled out two crinkly bags of neon orange cheesy curls.

"Cheetos!" Nix let out a shriek and made grabby hands to get one, then cradled the bag to her chest like a baby. "From the human world? Are you kidding? I've missed these! Where did you get it?"

I laughed. "If I told you, I'd have to let you in on my black-market dealings. So then I'd have to kill you."

Nix tore into the bag and dug in, crunching loudly. I pulled my own open and savored every bite. If Ayo, my dwende butler, saw me eating junk food, let alone human junk food, I was pretty sure he'd have conniptions and start foaming at the mouth. You didn't hear it from me, but there was a thriving human junk-food market in Biringan City. It was entirely underground, seeing as most encantos rarely went to the human world without very good reason; otherwise they'd risk the safety of our people. But there were a daring few who ventured through the magical barrier separating our worlds to buy various human luxuries, like DVD box sets of American sitcoms and ballpoint pens. Most encantos kept them as collector's items, but I had a different use for them. What was that saying about taking a girl out of the human world?

Sometimes I missed it; most times I didn't. Growing up with my mom, always on the move, careful never to stay in one spot too long or risk my father's enemies finding us, made for a terribly lonely upbringing. We hadn't had a lot of money, and I hadn't had a lot of friends. I was always the new girl, the girl with the wrinkled clothes, the girl with her wardrobe in a suitcase. My mom did her best protecting me in the human world, and I owed her everything.

My mom had gotten comfortable living in Biringan City, especially since I lifted the decree about humans being tricked into servitude and trapped here. She became an art and art history teacher at BANA—Biringan Academy of Noble Arts—and taught pottery classes to young encantos of all social classes, even taking curious encantos, with a security detail, to the human world for extended field trips to better understand humans as a whole. And now for the summer, while school wasn't in session, she had taken her class to Paris, to see the Louvre and Parisian architecture. Before bed tonight, I had talked to her on the crystals—a kind of video call with gemstones—and she'd looked so happy. I often wondered if she wished my dad were still alive so they could spend time here together. But of course, even though there was magic in this world, it still couldn't bring back the dead. She'd only been gone a week so far, and I missed her.

I hadn't realized I'd eaten the whole bag of Cheetos until I reached the orange dust at the very bottom. I'd been eating on autopilot, lost in thought, and I mourned the fact that I had completely forgotten to actually enjoy it.

I folded up the bag and stashed it under the beanbag chair so it wouldn't blow away while Nix was still eating hers, gazing out across the roofs of the kingdom, colored blue in the moon and starlight. Strange—it looked so similar to my nightmare. But it didn't bother me. Being with Nix had comforted me the most.

"Do you miss it?" I asked her.

"Miss what?"

"The human world." I jutted my chin toward her Cheetos. "You know, the little things."

"Not really." She wiped her mouth clean with the back of her hand. "Being a runaway wasn't exactly the easiest." Like me, Nix had also been hiding from encantos. Though instead of them wanting to kill her, they were trying to bring her home. She'd fled the imperial palace on Jade Mountain and hidden in the last place anyone would look for her: high school. She wanted to be free, away from the confines of royal life.

Of course, like me, too, she couldn't stay in one place for long and found her way to Biringan, where she'd lived ever since. Maybe that was why we became fast friends; we were kindred spirits.

"I've made friends here," Nix said. "Met you. Met—" She stopped herself, and I thought maybe she was getting emotional, because she cleared her throat and said, "Met people I care about. This is my home now."

I was following her gaze out across the horizon when I spotted a dark shape on a balcony below.

It moved. Something was there.

I looked up, wondering if it was just a shadow from some flying animal. But as far as I could tell, there wasn't anything.

I scanned the nearby towers again, straining my eyes to peer through the dark, but then a different shadow moved on the tower next to ours, darting behind a balustrade and out of sight.

"Did you see that?" I asked.

"See what?"

I didn't know. I tried not to panic, but thoughts of assassins rammed their way into my brain. I was a queen. I was young. I was vulnerable. Elias had warned me of this exact thing.

I was a target.

There came a shrill birdcall from somewhere above us. Except it didn't sound like any bird I'd ever heard.

I didn't need Lucas's power to know something was wrong.

"Nix, get inside," I said.

"What? Why?"

"Just do it."

Nix leapt up and hurried toward the door. But a figure dropped down from the shadows and landed in front of her. Tall, broad-shouldered, bulky—a man, masked and cloaked.

"No!" Nix yelped and backed away.

Ice-cold fear lanced through me.

I'd left my dagger in my room. I was unarmed. The guards were downstairs, but by the time they heard anything, it would be too late.

Someone had come for me.

The man looked at us for one heartbeat, then in one move, he grabbed Nix by the wrist and threw her over his shoulder.

"Nix!" I yelled.

"Let me go!" she screamed, pounding her fists on the man's back and kicking her legs, but it had no effect. The bear of a man barely flinched. From within his cloak, he produced a silver gun.

He raised the weapon and aimed, though not at me. He pointed toward the garden below us and fired. A long cable shot out of the barrel, whipping into the night. He secured the gun to the floor with a solid clang, bolting it to the tower, and then he jumped.

Nix's scream fell away when she plummeted with him into the dark.

It all happened so fast, I didn't have time to move.

I watched as the assassin zipped down the line on a metal hook with Nix thrashing and kicking against him all the way, fighting with everything she had.

Before I could go after her, two more cloaked figures leapt down from above, blocking me. Their cloth masks hid the bottom halves of their faces, and their eyes were trained on me.

This was it. This was their plan. They wanted me alone before they attacked.

But they didn't move in. They simply stood, blocking the exit, waiting.

Nix's screams still carried all the way up here.

I called to my power, my blood pressure rising. I was going to fight.

I held out my hand to the assassins, commanding the elements to bend to my will. I wanted to turn their swords at their sides to liquid or melt their shoes to glue, but nothing happened. Nothing. It was like I didn't have any magic at all. I stared at my hand, stunned. My power failed me.

I'd have to do this the human way.

I grabbed a beanbag chair next to me and tossed it at one of the men. He caught it, but it hit him squarely in the chest, and he grunted. I rushed to the other, who was caught off guard. My fist connected with his nose, and he howled in pain.

It gave me enough time to grab the telescope off its tripod and use it like a bar, holding tight to both ends. Without thinking, I jumped after Nix. The wind whipped around me, and my stomach leapt into my throat, but I held on with everything I had as I plummeted down.

Nix and her kidnapper had already landed safely on the ground, but he was not alone. A handful of other cloaked figures emerged from the shadows, flanking him, and they took off into the garden. The whole time Nix was screaming, "Put me down now!"

I nearly tripped when I got to solid ground, but I kept running after them. Nix's screams were the only thing I could follow. The two men I'd fought on the tower landed close behind me, the zip of their hooks turning into solid footfalls as they got closer.

"Nix!" I cried. I'd lost sight of her, but I could still hear her. There was still time.

I sprinted through the garden. Where were the guards? We needed help. I tried to summon my power again, throwing my entire focus into anything that could slow the kidnappers down. I meant to turn the grass into wet cement, into mud, into tar, but nothing happened. I was left gasping, and my chest burned from exertion. I dropped my focus, and my head swam. I felt like I was going to faint. But I fought against it.

I didn't care about the garden when I broke through hedgerows, tearing across the flower beds and splashing across shallow fountains, sprinting as hard as I could after them, but they were getting farther away. I was going to lose them.

At the edge of the garden, I burst into the yard just in time to see Nix being carried toward the open front gate. She looked at me, tears shining on her cheeks, and my heart plummeted.

I was too late. I couldn't do anything.

Nix struggled and screwed up her face. "Put me down this instant; that is an ORDER!" she yelled. She raised her hand and slammed it into her captor's lower back. He went stock-still, stiff as a board, and fell forward with a yell. She'd locked the muscles in his legs with her power. With a solid thump, she and the man hit the ground. She got on her feet while he lay crumpled in a heap.

I caught up to them, fists raised. Magic or not, I was going to fight.

The other cloaked men had come to a stop after swooping in, ready to take her again, when she held out her hand once more.

"Stop this at once!" she yelled. "Or do you plan to defy a command from your princess?"

The men looked at her for a long minute before, one by one, they dropped to one knee and lowered their heads.

What was going on? Were these assassins working for Nix? I stood there, baffled, not quite sure what to do, when I heard the two men coming up behind me.

"Easy now," one of them said. He pulled his mask off. To my surprise, he was a boy, no older than me. His crooked nose was bleeding from when I'd punched him. He appeared to be East Asian, with straight black hair tied into a small ponytail at the back of his head. He wore a black shuhe and black trousers, similar to the Arnis uniform I had worn earlier.

"Relax, Phoenix," he said, his voice confident and low, though slightly nasally from his bleeding nose. "You know we wouldn't hurt you."

Panting, I still had my fists raised, sweat beading on my forehead. Nix stared at the guy with a stony expression, her eyes hard.

But to my surprise, he wasn't menacing. He was smiling.

I blinked a few times, not quite understanding. "Who are you? Nix, what's going on?" I asked.

Nix straightened, lowering her hand. "This is my older brother," she said. "Crown Prince Qian of Jade Mountain."

3

"ARE YOU HURT? I'm coming home right—" My mom's worried eyes took up most of the face of the crystal. Even through the illusion, her panic was palpable.

I interrupted her. "We're all okay, Mom, seriously. Don't worry. Don't come back. It's over now." I strode toward the grand hall, where the cloaked men from Jade Mountain were sequestered for the moment before I could meet with them properly.

"Of course I'm going to worry! It could have been so much worse! What if it had been an actual attack? What if someone had tried to harm you?"

"I know," I said, rubbing my sore eyes. I was so tired. "But they didn't. It's all under control. Elias is taking good care of us."

By now the whole palace had heard about Nix's attempted kidnapping. Guards had come to the scene shortly after to escort us back inside, and Elias ordered the rest to search the grounds for any more trouble. The moment I set foot back inside the palace, a footman shoved the crystal in my hands to talk with my frantic mother, who had been the first to be informed. Strangely enough, her freaking out made me calmer.

Mom frowned at me, her eyebrows scrunched, and shook her head, but she didn't argue. She trusted Elias, too. If anyone could watch out for me while she wasn't around, it was him.

"I'm going to talk with the prince from Jade Mountain now," I said, and stopped in front of the doors to the grand hall, flanked by two of my guards. "I've got this. I'll see you when you get back from your trip, okay?"

My mom sighed. "Fine. But if I catch so much as a whiff of trouble—"

"I know," I said, smiling. "I love you."

Her brow softened a little, and she said, "I love you, too. Be good."

"I will." I hung up and took a deep breath. I slipped the crystal into my pajama pocket and pushed through the double doors only to walk into an argument.

"—go back there, you can't make me!" shouted Nix. She was standing at the round table, her elbows locked as she braced herself against it, looking the angriest I'd ever seen her.

She was glaring at Prince Qian, who was sitting on one of the chairs on the opposite side, holding ice wrapped in a towel to his nose. He had shrugged off his cloak and was now down to a tight-fitting black T-shirt. He was shaking his head like he was frustrated.

The rest of Qian's entourage stood at the back of the room, masks lowered, arms folded across their chests like proper bodyguards. I wished I had an entourage like that. I was feeling vulnerable and unprotected despite the guards at the door. Qian's own guards looked around the room, though, taking in the decor and—specifically—me.

Qian's gaze darted to me with a raised eyebrow, and Nix turned in my direction.

"MJ," she said, her face pale. "I'm so sorry."

"*You're* sorry?" I scoffed. "I thought you were being kidnapped. They're the ones who should be sorry." I glared at Qian.

Qian shifted in his chair and lowered the ice. His nose was red, some blood still smeared on his upper lip. "Is it kidnapping if my little sister is being held captive here?"

"Captive? What are you talking about?"

Qian waved his hand. "Why else would a princess of Jade Mountain be so hard to find?"

"Because I didn't *want* to be found," Nix snapped. "And if you'd asked me before your general snatched me up, you might have known that."

"Heng was operating in your best interest," Qian said, tipping his head to the man scowling behind him. "Now, can you please fix my nose before we go home?"

"No!" Nix straightened up and folded her arms over her chest. "I swore to do no harm when I became a healer, but you can sit with that pain until you start to listen to me."

"'Do no harm'?" Qian laughed. It surprised me. He seemed a lot more at ease now despite everything that had gone down, and his eyes sparkled. He and Nix looked so much alike. "Tell that to Heng."

The general, Heng, stood behind Qian's chair and massaged his lower back, the spot where Nix had seized up his muscles. He was older than us, probably in his twenties or so, but who really knew when it came to encantos? He could have been four hundred.

Like Qian and the rest of the kidnapping party, Heng was dressed in all black, like a soldier, with combat boots and a tight T-shirt. Heng's dark hair was cropped short, revealing pointed ears that looked as sharp as the line of his jaw. He didn't look like someone I'd want to mess with, but then again, he had been no match against Nix. Something like pride warmed my chest. She had foiled their plan.

"Your Highness . . ." Heng started. He leaned down and spoke quietly in Qian's ear, too low for me to hear, but Qian hardly moved to turn his head; he was still watching me. Heat rushed up my face.

If Qian and his guards really had been assassins, if they really had been here to kill Nix, she would be dead by now. My power still failed me at the worst possible time. It was only luck that no one had gotten seriously hurt. I glanced at Nix, but she couldn't meet my gaze.

Qian said, "Heng seems to be of the opinion that Biringan has an odd method of diplomacy, and I can't help but agree." He dropped the ice on the table and sniffed, idly wiping away the remainder of blood that had dried on his lip. "Where does a queen learn such a right hook?"

"I could do much worse to protect my friend," I said through my teeth.

Qian, to my surprise, lifted an eyebrow again, and I swore his eyes lit up. It was almost like he was pleased. My stomach felt like it swarmed with butterflies for some reason.

The double doors burst open, and Elias strode in, followed closely by two dwendes, who had to sprint to keep up. Elias looked flustered but composed himself, one hand on his sword, standing equidistant between us.

Elias looked at Qian and then at me. Enunciating so I knew he was furious, he asked, "What. Happened."

Qian and I stared at each other for a long moment, waiting for the other to speak. In doing so, I took in the rest of his appearance. The features of his face combined in a way that reminded me of a deer, in a handsome, sort of otherworldly way. He had a long face with soft, dark eyes that were surprisingly warm but keen at the same time, clear and penetrating. His straight, shiny hair flopped down the middle, just barely brushing the top of his pointed ears.

I knew I'd been staring at him for a little too long when his full lips quirked up into a smile before he addressed Elias.

"I am here to rescue my sister and bring her back to Jade Mountain," Qian said. "We thought she was here against her will."

Nix tensed up when Elias turned to her. This was news to him. "You're from Jade Mountain?"

Nix's eyes shone and her mouth set in a line, but all she could do was nod. I spoke up for her because I knew she would have a hard time. "Nix and I were in the astronomy tower when they swooped in out of nowhere," I said. "They scared us. I fought back."

Qian bowed his head, gesturing to his nose. "And fought back you did. This is a royal gift."

I hated how hot my face felt, and I looked at Elias again. "I thought we were in danger," I said, then glared at Qian. "I thought we were under attack."

Elias asked me, "Why didn't I know a member of the Jade Mountain royal family was in this palace?"

"Is that a problem?"

Elias huffed, shoulders sagging, but didn't answer me.

"I'm not going home," Nix said. "I *won't*."

"Unfortunately, you do not get a choice," Qian said. For our sake, he addressed the rest of us. "We have very strict rules when it comes to the emperor's daughters. They are not to leave the kingdom unless they are married. It is for their own protection and our people's, should anyone try to use his daughters against him for political leverage."

"So she's a pawn," I said.

Qian's eyes flashed briefly before settling on me. "She's my blood. My kin. If that's what you consider a *pawn*."

"Then what happens if Nix doesn't go back to Jade Mountain?" I asked.

Qian tipped his hand, palm up, as if offering it on a platter. "War."

Everyone in the room fell silent. The idea alone sent a shiver down my spine.

Elias broke the silence. "That is a bold statement from a person who, may I remind you, trespassed on palace grounds in the middle of the night."

"Drastic measures were required. Phoenix Xing is under my protection. It took us months to figure out where she was. When she fled the mountain, many thought she was dead. But when we discovered her location, we had to act swiftly, fearing for her safety. We had no guarantee of what would be waiting for us when we came. We thought she was a prisoner."

"This was all a misunderstanding," I said. "She's perfectly safe here."

"I'm more of a captive in Jade Mountain," Nix said, clenching her fists. "I refuse to go back. Even here you won't listen to me, and it will be just the same there. I'm not one of your trophies to present to Father."

Qian sighed loudly through his broken nose. I could tell there was more here than I was clued in on, but I knew this conversation was getting nowhere.

"Is this how you treat all your siblings?" I asked Qian.

He inspected me again, and my chest felt tight when he did. There was a fire in his eyes, but it wasn't anger. "Forgive me, Your Highness, but I'm afraid we haven't been *formally* introduced."

"Mahalina Jazreel, queen of the Court of Sirena, ruler of the throne of Biringan."

"Ah, I see," said Qian. "That's why Nix calls you MJ."

"Only my friends call me that."

Qian nodded, like he'd gotten the message. He inspected me for a moment, his gaze softening. "Forgive me for asking, but . . . are you hapa?"

His question caught me off guard. I wasn't ashamed of my hapa identity—being half encanto, half human. When I'd first arrived here, those who were prejudiced against humans, like Amador, saw my half-human parentage as weak, something lower, something to pity. My mother was my whole family, and she made me the person I was. How could I ever be ashamed of that?

"Yes," I said, lifting my chin. "Is that a problem?"

"Absolutely not. In fact, I find it fascinating." Qian leaned forward, his eyes bright. "Because I am, too."

I didn't have time to ask him more because the door burst open.

Lucas strode in, pink-cheeked and hair a mess, as if he'd run all the way here. No doubt Elias had left him in charge of dispatching the rest of the security detail. His hand rested on the dagger at his belt when he took in the room, eyes lingering on Qian before meeting mine. His very presence sent my heart into my throat.

Lucas gave a quick, apologetic nod to Elias. "Perimeter secured," he said.

"Thank you, Sir Lucas," Elias said. "No need for further alarm."

Qian regarded Lucas with a casual grin and lifted his chin. "No need at all."

Lucas narrowed his eyes, but he didn't reply. He bowed and excused himself.

General Heng leaned in again and said something in Qian's ear, but he didn't give anything away on his face.

I cleared my throat. "Back to the matter at hand. There's no need to talk of war," I said. "But it's late—er, early." I had no idea what time it was, but if I had to guess, it was around three in the morning. Exhaustion was going to make me say something I knew I would regret. "I think that we should discuss this later. Get a few hours of sleep, have some breakfast. We can continue later. We'll speak more with full stomachs and clear heads."

Qian tipped his head, acquiescing. "As you wish."

"Elias," I said, "can you see to it that Qian and his companions have proper accommodations? Baths drawn, more food prepared, beds turned down—"

"Of course," Elias said.

"*Guests* of the palace are never in want of anything," I said to Qian, proving a point.

Qian met my gaze unwaveringly and smiled.

AFTER THAT DISASTER of a first meeting, I excused myself to bed and closed myself in my room. All I wanted was to be alone. I pressed my back against the door. My knees decided to stop working, and my chest tightened so hard, I thought maybe I should call for Nix in case I was having a heart attack. But I knew this was only delayed panic.

My hands trembled and I shook them out, trying to regain feeling in my fingertips as I made my way over to my vanity, still faintly lit with candlelight. I found a pitcher of ice-cold water and drank so much of it, I got brain freeze.

Fearing my legs would give out, I took the glass to the settee and fell into it, practically collapsing into a heap. I rested my forearm across my eyes, blocking out the light. It seemed like the weight of the world was pressing down on me.

Qian thought Nix was a *prisoner*. It took me totally by surprise. Of course her family had been worried about her, and they wanted her home, but she was adamant that she didn't want to leave. And I wasn't about to make the decision for her and force her to go back to Jade Mountain if she didn't want to. She had disappeared, been missing for months, hid in the human world far away from encantos for as long as she could to escape a life where she felt unseen and unwanted. I would be a terrible friend, not just a terrible queen, to send her back to a life she didn't want.

But if Nix didn't return home, it could start a war. It was a looming threat I couldn't ignore, especially with the fate of the kingdom being my responsibility.

In school, before I moved to Biringan City, I had a mythology class where I read *The Iliad* and about the Trojan War. It was a war between gods, demigods, and men, all because of one woman, Helen of Troy. The myths had been unkind to Helen. They'd blamed her for the war, when it had been those wanting to control her who had caused all the bloodshed. She was a scapegoat, someone to pin the blame on, when she had been nothing more than a pawn. The Trojan War was a tragedy, ruthless and long and entirely avoidable.

I couldn't let anything like that happen. I wouldn't let Nix's story turn out like Helen's. I needed to find a way to come to some agreement. If I failed, I could doom us all.

There came a swift knock at my door.

It was probably Elias coming to check on me, but when I opened the door, I took a surprised step back.

"Lucas," I barely managed to say.

Relief melted his face when he saw me. "Are you hurt?" he asked. Of course—he was here to do his duty as my protector.

"I'm fine," I said. I looked behind him at the empty hallway, wondering if anyone was nearby. It was a reflex at this point. "I'm okay." My heart pounded, seeing him in front of me again. Now that we were alone, did he feel like he could finally speak to me? "What are you doing—"

And then he rushed forward and kissed me.

4

TOGETHER LUCAS AND I stumbled back into my room, lips locked, and he used his foot to close the door. He held me close, squeezing my hips with strong hands. When he breathed me in, he took my breath away in the process. His lips were soft, full, and this was the first time we'd kissed—we'd *touched* beyond sparring—in months.

My eyes fluttered closed, and my mind went blank. All my worries melted away when he held me. Since I'd truly gotten to know him, Lucas was all I wanted. I'd missed the way he smelled, the way his hand felt in mine, the way he looked at me. We'd been at arm's length for months, and this felt like a dream. I'd had so many about him, I almost wondered if I would wake up from this one at any second.

I grabbed his shirt and pulled him toward me, feeling his heartbeat. He tipped my mouth open, deepening our kiss, holding me so tightly that I might have fallen over if it weren't for his strong embrace. The smell of him, the taste of him, overwhelmed me. He smelled like acrid wood smoke from being outside, and sweat, and steel—like *him*. I didn't want to let him go. His warm hands burned through my clothes as he traced the shape of my body, and desire pulsed through my veins. I let out a soft whimper, and Lucas sighed, as if in reply. It was so good.

I pulled back slightly.

"Wha-what are we doing?" I stammered, opening my eyes and catching sight of him in the soft candlelight. "We can't—"

His breath was hot and tickled my cheek. "I was so scared something bad had happened to you. When I saw you in the grand hall with them, I almost lost my mind—"

"You shouldn't be here; what if someone sees—"

He kissed me again, and it stopped me short. I didn't mind. I couldn't help myself. I cupped the back of his head, twirling the soft silk of his dark hair around my fingers as he placed small kisses on the corners of my lips.

Lucas let out a sigh, and this time his kiss turned urgent, desperate to close the distance between us, like he didn't want to spend another second away from me. I wanted him so badly, I would have torn myself apart to feel him everywhere at the same time. My fingers fluttered over his cut-glass cheekbones and traced over the sandpaper stubble on his jaw. The smallest touch sent me spiraling. He was *here*. This was real. It was like nothing had changed at all between us. He was in my arms again, and I had to keep him.

We stumbled as one, my back knocking into the vanity, and Lucas pressed against me, breathing hard. Those gold flecks in his dark eyes glimmered through cracked eyelids when he looked at me, maybe wondering if I was real, too. He moved down my neck, kissing my throat and grabbing my hands.

I angled my neck into his touch, counting the heartbeats so I could remember to breathe.

One . . . two . . . three . . .

We were together. We were alone. And it was perfect. He licked my skin, nipped at it with his teeth, and sent a shudder of pleasure down my spine.

But what about Amador? I was kissing her fiancé, her betrothed. What did that make me? A horrible, terrible, evil person for wanting him, that's what. I hated Amador, but she didn't deserve this.

I pulled away from him, gasping, and put distance between us, but Lucas looked at me with such softness, I almost regretted ending the moment so soon.

But why did it take a potential assassination attempt for him to come here now? Of all the times I'd wished he would talk to me, to muster up the nerve to tell me the reason why he broke my heart . . . Why did it take so long?

My desire for his touch was snuffed out like a candle's flame in a strong breeze.

"Lucas, I'm . . ." I started to speak, but I didn't know what to say, like he'd stolen my voice. He stepped in close and rubbed his thumbs in circles on the bare skin of my arms. At one time his touch might have been comforting, but now I was so mad, I could explode.

"I can't do this," I said, barely above a whisper.

He looked like I'd slapped him. Him! Of all the people to feel hurt, he was the last one who deserved it.

"What?" he asked.

I stepped away, breaking his hold on me once more, and

put a hand to my forehead. My skin was hot and clammy, and I felt flushed.

"I had to see you, MJ. I had to make sure you were all right."

"Is that how all knights treat their sovereigns?"

Lucas let out a breathy laugh, and I turned to see his face. Even in the dim candlelight, I could see him so clearly. He looked so infuriatingly handsome. "We can make it a thing if you want."

On any other occasion, the temptation to laugh would have been almost impossible to fight against. I wanted it so badly—to have him be all mine—and in another time, I might have agreed, but him being here now reminded me why I was so angry. Not just at him but at myself. It took me by surprise how strong the feeling was, like I could combust and burn everyone around me.

"You're engaged, Lucas," I said. "You can't just barge in here and act like nothing has changed . . . And this is all I get, a stolen kiss in the night behind closed doors? Is that some kind of consolation prize?"

Lucas's smile dropped, and he bowed his head, his hair flopping into his eyes. "My engagement doesn't change the way I feel about you."

I snorted, incredulous. "How is that better? I'm assuming Amador doesn't know about us—about what you're doing here right now. And that's not okay. You told me your betrothal to Amador wasn't real! Remember?" Lucas winced, but I needed answers. "Back then, when Amador told me you were together, you said she was lying. You said you wanted to be with *me*, that I was the one you chose. So then what happened? Why, Lucas? Why are you marrying her? Why did you lie to me?" My words felt ragged on my tongue.

I didn't stop Lucas when he brought his hands up to the sides of my face, anguish collapsing his handsome features. "I know," he said. "I remember what I said, I just . . . I can't talk about it. Not yet."

"Why?" I asked again. My fingers circled his wrists, seeking assurance. I hated how pathetic I sounded. It was like I was a spoiled girl who didn't get her way, but I wanted to know. I *needed* to know. Why was he doing this to me? Why would he come to my room and kiss me if he was promised to another? Why was he playing with my heart?

"It's out of my control," he said. "Marrying Amador, it's . . ." He trailed off, staring over my shoulder. "It's not my place to say."

That's not good enough of a reason, I thought. *Not by a long shot.*

Tears stung my eyes. I wrenched his hands away from me. "You brought me flowers; you asked Elias for permission to court me," I said, my rage rising. If I wasn't careful, it would boil over. "I thought we were real." My voice broke, and I sucked in a breath, realizing just how deeply I hurt. It was like a hot knife was pressed behind my rib cage, digging into the softest parts of me.

I didn't want to cry, especially not in front of him, but tears blurred my vision. Months of not saying anything to each other had dammed up so many leaks in my chest, it was bound to burst.

And all the while, Lucas just looked at me. Not saying anything.

"Do you love her?" I asked, desperate for him to speak.

"Yes, I mean—" He shook his head. "No. Not like that, I . . ." He watched me for a long moment, then dragged his teeth on his full bottom lip, finding the words. "Amador and I have been friends since we were kids. She's one of the most important people in my life. What we have is . . . it's more than you think."

I screwed up my face. "What does that mean?"

Lucas rubbed at the back of his neck, wincing. "I know, it doesn't make sense, but I can't tell you any more. It's not just up to me, I swear, MJ. You have to trust me. Just a little longer—"

"Trust—ha!" My laugh sounded unhinged. "Trust you? After all you've done is lie?"

Lucas clenched his jaw. While he looked at me, a crease formed between his eyebrows. Color appeared on his cheeks like he'd been sunburned as he failed to speak yet again. I wanted to shake the answers out of him, grab him by the throat and wrench the truth out.

The violent urge diminished as quickly as it came, the fury in my heart receding, leaving only pain behind.

"How can I ever trust you again?" I asked.

Lucas's eyes shone, bordering on glassy. Hearing the way my voice broke made him swallow thickly. "I know. But I can't . . ."

"Can't what? Be with me? Love me?" As I stared at him, my heart hardened in my chest. I had been so foolish. This whole time I'd been played. How could I believe him? How could I ever forgive him? "Go," I said.

"MJ—"

"I said, go. *Sir* Lucas."

Lucas clamped his mouth shut at the tone of my voice. It was an order from his queen, and he was bound to his duty.

He gave me a stiff half bow, heels together, then left. I stood in the middle of my room, watching until he closed the door behind him.

5

AT SUNRISE BREAKFAST was served on the terrace. I didn't see Qian and his men, and I assumed they'd decided to sleep in.

The cooks had gone all out making a lavish meal, stacking the table with fried eggs, tapas, mountains of garlic rice, pineapple-cured pork, sun-dried herring, and dessert tofu in a brown sugar syrup. I told one of the butlers to thank the kitchen and to let them know that they'd be compensated for their efforts tenfold. It was an impressive feast.

I was the first to arrive and practically collapsed into my chair. I hadn't slept after Lucas left. My eyes were still crusty and sore from lying in bed, staring at the ceiling for the rest of the night. This morning, while Jinky combed out my hair and dressed me in a casual patadyong, she had practically held me upright the whole time. I rested my elbows on the table, pressed my hands against my warm cheeks, and closed my eyes.

The morning was bright, and a slight breeze cut across the terrace, rustling the turquoise jade vines overhead and scenting the air with brine and cherry blossoms. The dappled light angled across my eyelids, and birdsong floated out from the trees. It should have been a perfect day, but rain was on the horizon. I could feel it. I could *smell* it. The air was dense, like a hair tie pulled taut, ready to snap. Not only could I smell rain but I could smell the goats and the pigs; I could hear the bees flying in the garden below, even *taste* the sea salt in the air. It was like my senses had been dialed way up.

There was something else, too, a steady *thump-thump-thump* resonating in my ears. It almost sounded like . . . a heartbeat. And it wasn't mine.

I was so hyperfocused on my heightened senses, I nearly jumped out of my skin when someone burst onto the terrace. I sat up and looked around blearily.

It was only Nix, though. Her dark hair hung loosely across her shoulders, and while she usually dressed casually despite her interest in fashion, today it looked like she had just rolled out of bed, too. I wouldn't put it past her to not have gotten a wink of sleep, either. She dropped into a chair next to me, tipped her head back into the sunlight, and let out a deep, beleaguered sigh.

Yeah, that about summarized it.

I chalked up my sensory overload to stress and rubbed my face, waking myself some more, then set a bowl of rice in front of Nix. A peace offering.

"Why didn't you say anything?" I asked, keeping my voice low.

Nix leaned over the table, resting her elbow and cradling her forehead in her hand. She stared at the rice bowl but didn't touch it, her gaze distant. "I didn't think they'd go that far."

"You don't sound too surprised. This is a common occurrence, then, for Jade Mountain?"

"I didn't think I was important enough for them to care."

"Clearly your family was worried about you."

Nix sighed again. She picked up a large spoon and stabbed it into the rice. "I ran away for a reason." She frowned at her food, a million things rushing behind her dark eyes that had suddenly lost their sparkle. "Growing up there, I was barely my own person. I couldn't choose my own clothes, what to eat, who to be. I'm one of fifty children . . . *fifty*. I didn't think they'd find me, to be honest, or even bother to look. I was just another face in the palace."

"And yet they sent Qian and an elite team of special forces to get you." I leaned toward her and said, "I meant what I said last night. I won't make you do something you don't want to do."

Nix finally looked up at me, and her gaze softened. "I know. Thank you. But it might be no use. Qian is the crown prince for a reason. Our people look to him for guidance, for inspiration. With him in charge, nothing can go wrong. He's exceptional at what he does, determined and cunning."

"What does he do? Besides being a prince?"

"He's a hunter."

"Oh? Of what?"

"Monsters, offspring of the Four Perils."

My eyes widened. "What's that?"

"They're four monsters that plague the world, causing death and destruction wherever they go. Our father, the emperor, will get reports from some nearby villages that are being tormented by a giant winged tiger that's eating people or terrorized by a sheep with a human face consuming an entire region's food supply, and Qian will be the one to find it and kill it. He's a hero. The entirety of Jade Mountain loves him. He's everyone's favorite, and I mean *everyone*—including me. He was my hero, too . . ."

The skin on my arms tightened. Her description brought to mind images of someone with singular focus, finding a target and pursuing it until it was dead. Tenacious to the end. No wonder he was popular. People expected the world from him, and he didn't let them down. Qian was a beacon for their kingdom, so of course he would be sent after the captured princess. But I couldn't picture Qian to be the hunting type. He had the casual swagger of someone who was in charge and knew it, but for some reason, I always pictured hunters to be flaunting it more. Human television taught me hunters were old guys with safari hats and pants tucked into their boots. Qian had changed my mind on that. Suddenly, Nix mentioning earlier that she wasn't some trophy to be brought back to their father made sense.

My heart ached. If I sometimes felt like the palace was suffocating, I bet Nix was feeling ten times worse if she ran away because of it.

"Well," I said, "you're not some trophy. I'm not letting him take you so easily. You're safe here."

Just then, Elias appeared and looked around the empty table. "Did Prince Qian not join you for breakfast?"

"Um, no," I said. "He didn't."

"It's a bad sign that he's not here." Elias gripped the back of an empty chair and sighed. He looked so tired. "Not a second should be wasted not talking. You must meet with them," he said to me. "Get them to sit down with you, negotiate."

"Negotiate makes it sound like we're kidnappers," I said. "Like we've done something wrong."

"In their eyes, you have. You're keeping their princess against *their* will."

Nix dropped her spoon and rounded on him. "But what about my will?" she asked.

"You are still a member of their house. They are responsible for your well-being, and if they see fit to bring you home . . . who are we to stop them?"

I knew, logically, that it made sense, but it still felt wrong somehow, like they were treating Nix as if she were property to be hauled away, to be carted around, to sit still and do as she was told. "Come on, Elias. You can't be on their side."

Elias took the other seat next to me and leaned forward, resting his elbows on his knees. Seeing him this close, I was struck by how much older he seemed. Gray flecked his short-trimmed dark beard, and the lines around his mahogany eyes were deeper, more pronounced, but his gaze was the same as always, soft and warm. "Queen Mahalina," he started, and I shot him a look.

"Please don't get all formal on me."

"I am not talking to my goddaughter; I'm talking to my queen. Jade Mountain is a neighboring kingdom, and despite what you might want to think, this isn't a minor squabble. Wars have been started over a lot less. The last time tensions rose between Biringan and Jade Mountain, your great-grandmother worked tirelessly to broker peace."

I wanted to snap back at him, say I wasn't a child, but by some miracle, I held my tongue. He was helping me. I didn't know why I wanted to fight.

"Forgive me, Elias," I said. "I don't have decades of experience with this kind of thing. How did she do it then?"

"She proved to Jade Mountain that she was an ally. She hosted them for diplomatic meetings at the royal jungle retreat in Mount Makiling, and together they signed the accords that still remain to this day, but peace takes work, and now Jade Mountain feels betrayed. One slip-up can shatter their trust, and this incident with Nix is placing peace on the edge of a knife. You must be careful. If you let Prince Qian dictate the rules, you are playing his game. You must set boundaries and offer to come to an agreement; otherwise you will not get what you want."

Encantos lived a long time. Grudges lived even longer. Like I'd been punched in the gut, I realized I'd been ignorant of how the balance between war and peace was so fragile. I still had a lot to learn about being queen.

I took in a deep breath and looked at Elias. He was my adviser, but he was also my godfather and my dad's best friend. He was the closest thing I had to a father now, and he was only trying to make sure that I was doing the right thing. I didn't hold it against him in the slightest. I knew I had an obligation to try, but at the same time, I wondered if I was capable of handling such a situation. Elias was right. I needed to at least do something. For Nix's sake.

I glanced at my friend, who was still picking away at her food. She hadn't eaten anything, her thoughts no doubt a million miles away. Was this how Helen of Troy had felt?

"I'm not what Qian thinks I am," I said to Elias. "I'm not an enemy. I'll talk to him."

WE CONVENED FOR another meeting in the grand hall later that afternoon.

Nix and I were the last to arrive. Everyone was already seated around the large round table, and my stomach fluttered with nerves. I couldn't fail Nix here. I tried to keep my head high, my hands placed delicately at my waist, but there was so much on the line.

Immediately, my eyes snared on Qian, who was deep in conversation with General Heng. Today Qian was dressed in the same clothes from last night. I couldn't help but notice the taut muscles of his forearms as they rested on the table. Even though he was still speaking with Heng, his dark gaze caught mine, and a small smile spread across his lips. Heat rushed to my face. He was remarkably handsome, all things considered. I tried to tell myself to get it under control. *This is about Nix,* I reminded myself.

When Qian finished his conversation, Heng nodded, and Qian stood up to greet us. "I was wondering if Her Royal Highness would arrive or if we were going to have to negotiate with one of the lesser houses."

I didn't know what he was talking about until I saw her. Amador was sitting on the opposite side of the room, with Lucas standing behind her. His eyes met mine briefly before he looked away, his fingers fidgeting with the hilt of the dagger at his side.

The skin of my hips burned with the ghost of his touch from last night, and my ears burned to match it.

Amador smiled, cupping her chin with her hand, making her engagement ring sparkle. "In typical royal custom, our queen prefers to arrive fashionably late." She eyed my more formal baro't saya—a long-skirt-and-blouse combo with a kerchief around my shoulders that Jinky was adamant about me wearing. I didn't put up a fight like the last time I came to the grand hall and made a fool of myself in front of the court. Today I wanted to put my best foot forward if that meant that I could get Qian to let Nix stay. I didn't think I looked half bad, but in Amador's eyes, I was always found wanting.

Qian, for what it was worth, seemed more impressed with my outfit. His gaze lingered on me, and his smile widened.

"Thank you for meeting with us," I said. Immediately after, though, I wondered if I should have thanked him at all. Did that inadvertently give him the upper hand, implying that he was the one who had to take time out of his day to speak with me? Elias wasn't here to help me maneuver the land mines of royal politics, and I forced the embarrassment heating up my neck to settle back down.

"Of course, Your Highness." Qian watched while Nix and I circled the table, and I did everything I possibly could not to glance at Lucas when I took my seat. I swore the taste of him had stayed on my lips from last night.

"What are you doing here, by the way?" I asked Amador. "You have a habit of wandering my palace whenever you feel like it."

Amador's lips twisted into an amused, self-righteous smirk.

"Seeing as my father is the ambassador for foreign relations, it's my duty in his absence to fulfill his role to ensure that relations with our neighbors to the north are upheld to the highest standard. I, the grand duchess of the Sigbin Court, offer anything I can to assist with these negotiations."

That word—*negotiations*—set me on edge. It felt like I was starting on my heels, taken off guard, and having to defend myself from something I hadn't even done.

Nix rounded on her brother. "Qian, seriously. Do we really have to go through all this?"

"Of course, little sister," Qian said. "Unless you're married, you're to be in Jade Mountain with your other siblings. No excuses. It's against our ways to have you living outside of our protective walls."

"What happened last night seems like it was a bit rash, don't you think?" I asked him.

Qian's eyes slid to me. "What if one of our enemies had found my sister first? Without the protection of Jade Mountain, she was vulnerable, alone, and no one would have known what had happened." He turned back to Nix. "Do you really expect Biringan to protect you? I wouldn't put it past them to protect themselves first."

"Hold on," I said, extending my hands. I remembered Elias's words, that we had to meet them where they were at, and tempered my nerves. "Nix isn't in danger right now, so we don't have to go that far. Instead, let's focus on what's in front of us. She's been living with us safely for the past year—without your knowledge, yes, but she is an independent person with her own desires. You want her to return to Jade Mountain, and I want her to do whatever she wishes."

"Are you saying that the queen of Biringan has more authority than the Jade Emperor?" Qian didn't say it with any accusation. Instead, he almost said it with mild amusement, as if he wanted to know what I truly thought.

I had to be careful about what I said. I could almost hear Elias reminding me to breathe. I took a moment to gather my thoughts and replied, "When anyone is within our borders, they are a guest of mine. It would be against every instinct to send a friend away. That same courtesy extends to you, Prince Qian."

Qian's eyebrows shot up, and he seemed somewhat appeased by that.

Amador, unprompted, added, "I am inclined to agree with the queen." I stared at her, bewildered, but she didn't look at me. "If the Jade Emperor himself walked through these doors, he would be welcomed like family."

That took me by surprise. I hadn't expected her to agree to anything I had to say. I'd always thought she wanted to contradict me for the fun of it, just to see it get under my skin, and my shock must have been all over my face, because when Qian looked back at me, he laughed.

"While it's sweet that you are so accommodating, Jade Mountain's enemies might feel welcome, too. What would prevent anyone from doing what we did last night and taking Nix?"

"Nothing," I admitted.

I think my honesty caught Qian off guard, because he leaned back, gently curled his hand into a fist, and tapped it on the arm of his chair. I wasn't sure if he'd ever met a royal who told him the truth outright.

Nix broke the silence, which made all eyes turn to her. "Why are you so worried about our enemies anyway, Qian?" Nix asked.

Qian took a deep breath, and I saw a flash of pink behind his lips when he licked them thoughtfully. It was a surprisingly endearing tic. But his expression darkened ever so slightly. "It's not just our enemies. Monsters have broken through our borders. Attacks committed by the offspring of the Four Perils have increased tenfold. You of all people, Nix, should know just how dangerous they can be."

Nix went pale, and her breath came out shakily.

Qian's voice was thick with emotion. "I thought you were . . ." He swallowed thickly. "I'd feared the worst, and then to find out you were here . . ." He gestured around the room. "Do you hate us that much to make us believe you were dead?"

Nix folded her lips between her teeth to stop herself from speaking. Turmoil, guilt, brewed in her eyes, but she clamped her hands into fists and looked at me as if asking for help.

When my father died, I wished I had been there for him. I'd never had the chance to get to know him because he'd sent me away to live with my mom in the human world for my own safety. But he was murdered. There was no goodbye, no last chance for either of us to say what we wanted. So not being there for him, especially in his last days, was a regret I carried with me. I never had my whole family together.

Nix tore her gaze away from me to look at her brother. "If I go, though, I'll never get to come back."

"Returning to Jade Mountain would mean returning to your family." Qian sighed. "You need to be serious. You're also coming to an age when it's time you started considering proposals. As one of the emperor's daughters, your role is vital to the kingdom, and it was bestowed upon you the moment you came into the world. You can't run from destiny."

Across the table, Amador shifted in her chair slightly, agitated, and her eyes darted up to Lucas, who remained stone-faced and at ease standing behind her. I wasn't sure why she looked so surprised, but I chose to ignore it. They, maybe more than anyone, knew what it meant to be betrothed, but at least they would have each other. If I lost Nix, I would be all alone here in Biringan City. I felt incredibly selfish for thinking that and squeezed my hands together more tightly in an attempt to get a grip. I had to remember this wasn't about me. Nix looked like Qian had said he would lock her in chains and banish her to a tower like a tragic princess from the stories.

"I don't believe in destiny," Nix said. "I don't want that life."

"Well . . ." Amador said, and clicked her tongue. She held out her hand toward Lucas, and he obediently accepted. It made my skin crawl. I had to dig my fingernails into the arms of my chair to stop myself from leaping to my feet in a rage.

"Forgive me, Prince—" Amador continued, but Qian interrupted.

"Please, call me Qian."

Amador's smile spread wide. "Of course. Qian. Forgive me for my ignorance, but I'm unaware of the customs in Jade Mountain. Must all of the emperor's daughters be married?"

Qian looked at Amador, hand in hand with Lucas, and he leaned forward. "I take it you understand the political importance of matrimony."

"I do," Amador said. "I've been betrothed to Lucas for most of my life, but we've known each other since birth. *Loved* each other since birth. Is there someone who has a similar history with Nix in Jade Mountain?"

Why did she want to know? What did she care? I thought bitterly.

"No," Qian said. "Nothing like the love you two have. But love is not a requirement for marriage. Though it helps." His gaze darted playfully to me, but I barely noticed.

Something ugly and boiling hot roiled inside my stomach, like I'd eaten a bowl of acid. Seeing Lucas and Amador together made my whole body feel too small to contain me. My heart drummed furiously against my rib cage, quickening with each passing second. The edges of my vision darkened, and what I could see turned red.

I wanted to kill Amador . . .

Then I snapped out of it, scared by how vicious my thoughts had turned. I let out a small gasp as cool air rushed into my lungs, and the darkness on the edges of my vision receded. Everyone looked at me, expecting me to say something, but a dull noise droned in my head like a hive, and I realized it was my blood roaring in my ears.

I'd never felt that angry before. I was clenching my fists so hard they were shaking, and the tips of my fingers had gone numb. When I looked down, I almost expected claws. Instead, I saw plain crescent shapes from my nails in my palms.

I stood up, bracing myself against the table, and took a moment to gather myself. Everyone was still staring at me, some glancing at one another as if they weren't sure I was in my right mind, but I cleared my throat and looked at Qian.

"Would you join me for a walk?" I asked. "I would like to speak with you privately."

Qian looked at me for a long second, eyes alight with interest, and nodded. "It would be my pleasure."

6

QIAN AND I left our respective parties behind and made our way outdoors. The garden in the afternoon was full of bees and hummingbirds flying among bright flowers and darting past our heads. Turquoise-colored petals from the flowering balafon trees flanking the path floated through the wind, littering the cobblestones beneath our feet like they were a carpet, making the air smell like cinnamon and peaches, summer and spice. It would have been a beautiful sight, but the angry droning in my ears remained for a few minutes even when we made our way down the garden steps and into the bright sunshine.

At least outside I felt normal again. My rage subsided like waves on the shore. It had come from the depths of my heart; it felt like I was drowning in it. I breathed deep, allowing myself to relax my shoulders.

Qian walked beside me, his arms clasped casually behind his back as I led him through the garden. At the edge was a private terrace with a pergola draped in sheer white curtains and two small chairs, which overlooked the blue water of Lake Reyna, the island, and the sea beyond. Gigantic thunderhead clouds loomed high in the distance, fluffy as cotton. Multicolored gulls cawed overhead and swooped through the air toward the Sirena village below. Qian went to the edge of the terrace and braced himself against the railing as the wind kicked up and made his hair flutter. It occurred to me how handsome he was, and in the wind, he looked especially regal and strong.

"Spectacular view," he said. He looked at me with a hint of mischief in his eyes, and I realized he wasn't just talking about the scenery.

"It's my favorite place," I said, tempering my blush with a distraction. "Nix and I come here often."

"I see no guards, no defenses. What's to stop a monster from lurking these grounds? Your borders aren't safe. Any number of them could have come into your garden and snatched my sister in a heartbeat."

"In these lands, creatures you'd deem monsters live among us, as equals and in peace," I said, knowing full well the manananggal was anything but peaceful.

"I heard that your court was attacked by a witch who deals in the black arts—a mambabarang, right? It slipped right in, killed your father, and then almost killed you during your coronation."

I shouldn't have been surprised that word got out about the attack. Everyone in attendance, including Nix, almost died. Qian watched me, gauging my reaction, but I straightened my shoulders and lifted my chin. "I stopped them. I protect the ones I care about." My heart hitched remembering that Lucas was included in that sentiment, and I cleared my throat. "I'm not weak."

Qian nodded as I spoke, tracing a finger along the intricate designs carved into the wood of the pergola, and smiled. "That I know." Was he flirting with me? Or was this just a way to play politics? I had to maintain my composure. Like Elias said, I couldn't let him dictate the rules.

"Yesterday you said you were hapa," I prompted.

Qian nodded again. "Nix and I are half siblings. My mother, my father's first wife, whom he married early in his reign, was human. Inevitably, due to the nature of us . . ." He gestured to me and then to himself. "I've outlived her by some margin."

Like humans, encantos could die, but they usually lived to be thousands of years old. The Jade Emperor himself was rumored to be nearly three thousand years old. I couldn't help but be reminded that someday I would stop aging, too, but I swallowed the lump that had formed in my throat, not wanting to think about how I could ever go on without my mom. "Nix and I bonded over being hapcantos when we first met. We became fast friends."

"And you've been treating her well? My Nix?"

Anger rose up in me again, though less so than when we were at the table. "I'm offended you think I wouldn't."

"Not every ruler in this age is so benevolent."

"Does that include yourself?"

Qian's eyes crinkled slightly when he smiled, and he took my jab lightly, more lightly than I might have expected of a future emperor. "I have my bad days. I am only encanto, after all. But I find locking people away in dungeons too medieval. Leave that to the Avalonians." I'd never met an Avalonian, but I think he meant it as a joke.

"Nix told me you're a good person," I said. "She seems to believe that you'll make a good emperor someday, too."

"A day I hope won't come too soon."

"You don't want to be emperor?"

"Not if I can help it."

My eyebrows shot up.

"Don't be so surprised," he said. "I'm in no rush to take the title. Any sane man doesn't want his father to die so he can take his crown."

At least Qian had one thing going for him: He wasn't power hungry like I initially expected of a crown prince. It was as if the light had shifted on his face, and now I saw him more clearly. Like me, he was just trying to do right. He was probably one of the only people who understood what I was going through.

A playful glint appeared in his eye. "What else did Nix say about me?" he asked.

"That you're a hunter, that you're patient and calculating."

Qian laughed. "She speaks too highly of me."

A bee landed on Qian's hand. He didn't flinch but simply raised it to his face, inspecting it closely before it flew away. He was a lot different from what I had expected. I needed to find a way to appeal to him.

"Neither of us wants war," I said.

Qian tipped his head. "On that we can both agree."

"Really? You seemed so blasé about it earlier. I figured you were out for blood."

Qian sighed loudly through his nose and glanced toward the sea. "First impressions are not my strong suit. And based on your reaction, they're not yours, either." He tapped on his broken nose.

"But I'm not opposed to finding a more diplomatic solution with you. War is a failure on all fronts."

"Good," I said. "I'm not your enemy."

Qian regarded me for a moment, taking me in with a slight smile. "No, indeed, you're not. Especially after I've had the pleasure of meeting you."

Even as I gazed across the seascape, I could still feel his eyes on me. It wasn't particularly uncomfortable, but at the same time, I didn't know what to do. He was making my heart race.

"I am sorry for what happened," he said. "Truly. I hope you won't hold it against us."

"A prince apologizing? I'm shocked." I didn't mean to say that out loud. I covered my mouth, but he laughed heartily at that. "I'm sorry. I'm not one to hold grudges, for too long at least. And I'm sorry about your nose. How is it?"

"Better. Nothing a healer can't fix. Do try and not make a habit out of it, though. I find I rather like the shape of it."

That got me to smile, and Qian seemed pleased with himself. I joined him at the railing and looked out across the water. Fishing boats bobbed on the horizon, and below, coming into view only when the breeze cut through the branches of the palm trees, we could see the market, teeming with activity and noise. Biringan City was a peaceful place, and I couldn't imagine war coming to its shores. It was the absolute last thing I wanted, but it didn't feel right handing Nix over to her family so easily.

"Nix feels at home here," I said. "She said she doesn't want to be caged. Isn't it fair to give her that freedom?"

"The world is dangerous. A cage in shark-infested waters is also protection." Qian tilted his head, curious. "How would your mother feel if you fled to another country? She'd probably think you were in danger or hurt. There'd be a million terrible things running through her head at all times, keeping her up at all hours, wondering if you were safe. And if she found you, would you blame her for wanting to take you home?"

"No," I admitted. "It's not too far off from what really happened, though our roles were reversed. I had to escape the human world and left my mom behind while she tried to protect me. She got hurt and was in the hospital while I was stuck here, trying to figure out the mess left by my father's passing. I felt so alone."

"Then you understand how protective I am of Nix. You see how I would move heaven and earth to ensure that she's safe." He came around to my other side, the scent of him catching the breeze and enveloping me. He smelled like bergamot.

"There's a fine line between wanting to protect someone and wanting to control them," I said.

"I disagree. Protection isn't control. It's only love. Nix is my favorite of all my sisters," Qian said. "When we were growing up, she was my shadow. I could hardly step two paces without finding her underfoot. When my father and I went on hunting trips, she'd cry and scream, wanting to go with us, but her nursemaids never let her, fearing it was too dangerous. Once, though, I found her stowed away in my luggage, and I pretended not to hear her giggling as we rode out into the forest. I circled the palace a few times until she started snoring and returned her to her room." His smile was warm—no doubt it was a good memory—and when he looked at me, there was only sincerity. "Nix means too much to me to let her go so easily."

"I understand. Really, I do. Nix has been a true friend to me since I arrived. I didn't have anyone except for her."

"But you can't keep her safe like I can."

The both of us wanted what was best for Nix, but neither of us felt like the other could provide it. Even though my opinion of him had changed ever so slightly, I still didn't think he knew what was best for her. But I didn't know what to do. I knew Nix should return to her family, but she was her own person who wanted independence. No matter if she were royal or not, would I be terrible to make her go back to Jade Mountain against her will? Would I be setting a poor example by letting Nix stay?

As I thought about it, Qian's hand accidentally brushed against mine. It was the slightest touch that made me flinch, so slight, I thought it had been an accident. And it seemed to be, because Qian simply rested his hands on the railing once more while he gazed out across the island. He wasn't a cruel person—at least, I didn't think so. He wasn't the enemy. But I had to find a way to get him to see things from my perspective.

I turned, squared my shoulders to him, and said, "Isn't it better that Nix live the life she wants? A family shouldn't hold her back." But I wasn't her family. Thinking that hurt more than I cared to admit. What was family if not the people we loved? But I wasn't family like Qian was hers.

Qian's gaze slid toward me, a hint of danger there, and my

heart skipped. "Nix is my top priority," he said. "Jade Mountain is where she belongs until she finds a suitable match."

Heat rose to my face. He was unswayed and being stubborn. The same roiling anger in my gut churned, and the bitterness in my mouth needed somewhere to go. "You don't know her at all. You only want to use her, but you're claiming it's for her own good. She doesn't deserve that."

Qian leveled his eyes at me again, and I met his gaze unwaveringly. We stood inches apart. I was fuming, but he remained calm and collected, tall and confident.

"You misunderstand me completely," he said. "My family's safety is more important to me than any power in the world. Nix knows this. Marriage between other kingdoms ensures it. She must put aside her selfish desires and think of the greater good."

"The greater good means nothing when freedom is sacrificed," I said.

"The greater good is nothing but sacrifice." He said it as if he were stating the obvious.

"I won't turn my back on my friend," I said defiantly.

"And I won't abandon my sister."

"Then we're at an impasse."

"I guess we are." Qian's dark eyes peered deeply into mine, but if he saw any anger in them, it didn't perturb him. To him, I probably looked like a flustered girl with a bad temper. Being this close to him, I noticed that his eyes weren't dark brown like I originally thought but a deep, almost impossible blue, like the deepest part of the ocean. After what felt like forever, Qian hummed, smiled, and said, "For now."

Qian took a step backward, then turned on his heels and headed back toward the palace. "My men and I will settle in for a while longer. Let's talk again tomorrow."

"You're not leaving?" I asked.

"Not yet. I'm coming to enjoy our one-on-ones," he called back to me. "I look forward to seeing more of you, MJ."

7

THAT NIGHT I dreamt again.

I flew fast, pleading for something, anything, to help my gnawing hunger, the pain of which was ripping me apart from the inside.

I wanted it to stop. I would do anything.

I beat my wings, soaring through the night sky, swooping over thatched roofs and the tops of palm trees, searching, hunting.

I crested another roof and came upon a row of merchant houses. I stopped to rest on a chimney and sensed a heartbeat. No—two.

In the warm light pouring off their house was a couple standing together under a palm tree, tending to their goats. While their herd grazed, the goats' cries bleating into the night, the couple kissed. They were both young, a man and a woman, too distracted by each other to notice me. The woman's red hair cascaded down her back, and the man's bright blue curls blew in the sea salt breeze as he held her hands so gently, tenderly tracing his thumbs over her delicate skin. The woman leaned into him, melting with bliss.

Young love.

But something inside me snapped, and jealousy, hot and acidic, exploded in my chest. My hands squeezed the chimney, snapping the stone. My mouth watered, fangs dripping, tongue lolling out.

My red sight beat with their hearts. How dare they love so freely? How dare they have it when I didn't? How dare they flaunt it? My pain spilled out, and it turned into a scream.

The couple looked up at me, terrified.

I leapt down from the roof and pounced.

"No!" I heard myself cry. But my voice was distant. "Stop!"

I blinked, and I was covered in gore. There were no bodies left, nothing recognizable. The air smelled of iron and salt. I dug my hands—*claws*—into a rib cage, and bones cracked. Warm blood soaked my hands like gloves. I was dressed in it. I wore it like a veil. Blood ran down my chin, down my throat, as I bit into flesh, and the pain went away.

Heart, liver, and stomach were the tastiest.

I JERKED AWAKE with a strangled cry. I was back in my room.

I threw the covers off myself and put my hands to my face, expecting to feel the slick, warm blood from my dream, but my skin was clean. My white nightgown was spotless. I was drenched in sweat, but there was no sign of any blood. I'd . . . I'd killed those people. Of course, it had only been a nightmare, but the way my hands broke bones—it had felt so real. A shudder rushed down my spine. The stress from dealing with Qian was taking its toll on me.

The curtains were still drawn, but I could tell it was already morning. A fierce storm rattled the windows. Thunder rolled overhead, and wind howled against the glass. It sounded just like my monstrous cry . . . My hands shook as I rubbed my eyes, trying to ease my mind.

What was wrong with me? It was like some wild thing had punctured its claws into my skin and refused to let go. But it was just a nightmare. It was silly to be bothered by something like this.

And yet the remnants of the nightmare clung to me like oil even as Jinky swept into the room with breakfast and dressed me for the day.

I wasn't hungry, even for tapsilog—plates heaping full of beef, garlic rice, and fried egg—with sweet puddings and cakes for dessert. Nausea threatened to make me puke, and I nudged the garlic rice away. I didn't want any of it.

"Are you feeling all right?" Jinky asked me. It was unusual that I'd turn down breakfast.

"I'm just anxious, that's all," I said. "Talking with Qian is proving more difficult than I thought." I massaged my stomach and sipped some water.

Jinky was a mountain spirit with pale moss-green skin, but her cheeks turned a shade of blue when she blushed, which she did now. "He's certainly dreamy, if I may say so."

"You're reading those romance novels again, aren't you?" I said with a teasing smile. It helped ease my stomachache. I'd managed to get my hands on some swoon-worthy reads from the human world for her after she'd shown an interest in books Nix and I had been reading one day.

"No!" Jinky squeaked. Then she realized she was lying to the queen, because her blush deepened, which made me smile more.

"I mean . . . Maybe. He does have a certain quality that is quite appealing."

I took another sip of water. "Good looks aren't everything."

"I suppose not," Jinky said, a little deflated. "Though his devotion to his sister is charming. He cares deeply for the ones he loves, doesn't he?"

"I'll give him that much." To his credit, it was a good quality. I wouldn't think highly of someone who didn't care about their family.

"Will you speak with him more again today?" Jinky asked. She started brushing my hair to put it into elaborate braids.

"I have to, for Nix's sake. Though I'm not sure what else I can do. We're both stubborn."

Jinky sighed thoughtfully. "I'm sure you'll figure it out."

"What would your romance heroines do in my position?"

Jinky looked taken aback. "Truly?"

"I'm looking for any help I can get at this point."

After thinking for a moment and pursing her lips, Jinky said, "I suppose they would spend alone time together someplace romantic, someplace remote, where they could open their hearts to each other . . ." Her voice got breathy as her gaze grew distant, dreamily staring into nothing, the brush hovering above my head. She snapped herself out of her daydream and continued doing my hair. "Though simply having a change of scenery would do the trick. A getaway."

"A getaway . . ." I remembered Elias mentioning Mount Makiling, the place where my ancestors used to make treaties with neighboring kingdoms, earlier. An idea started to form. "I could bring Qian to the jungle retreat in Mount Makiling, show him how guests are treated, prove to him that Nix is safe here, and convince him that she doesn't need to be married off. It worked for my great-grandmother, so why shouldn't it for me?"

"That sounds like a grand plan," Jinky said. "Though in the novels, they fall in love at the end. You may be getting more than you asked for."

I rolled my eyes. "Not going to happen. I am done with love."

"Yes, Your Majesty," Jinky said with a small smile.

AFTER JINKY WAS satisfied with me—outfitting me in a floor-length plum-colored baro't saya with narrow sleeves cinched with silver bangles, complete with delicate orange flowers in my hair—I went to the guest wing to pass along the details of my plan. But when I knocked, Heng answered the door, frowning at me as if I were interrupting his day.

"I would like to speak with Qian," I said. Then I corrected myself. "I demand to speak with Qian." I had to stop asking for permission to do things. I was a queen and needed to start acting like it, confident and commanding. I straightened my shoulders to strengthen my words. Heng looked me over, eyes narrowed.

"As you wish, Your Majesty." Heng's voice was low but flat, and he stepped aside, letting me through.

The guest rooms were some of our more practical spaces. They were often used for visiting delegates from neighboring regions, intended as a place where guests would mostly sleep and not spend a lot of waking time. There was the standard four-poster bed; a large bamboo mat with pillows on top, used for resting; and open doors leading to a balcony overlooking the garden. The sky was a flat gray, churning with the storm, and rain pattered against the glass, throwing the candlelight of the room into a cozy haze of safety. The remnants of Qian's breakfast had yet to be cleared away from the center table, but his clothes had been laid out for him, neatly pressed and hanging on the privacy screen.

But there was no sign of Qian from what I could tell, and when I was about to ask Heng where he was, the door to the en suite bathroom opened, and Qian stepped out, shirtless. He patted his face dry, then noticed me over the plush white towel. He froze for a moment, and then he smiled.

My eyes landed on his toned abs, his narrow waist, and the three jagged lines of scars running across his side. They looked like . . . claw marks. Heat immediately rose on my cheeks. I spun around, allowing him some dignity, and clasped my hands in front of me, trying not to wring them. I wasn't used to seeing half-naked princes in my immediate presence.

"Good morning, Your Majesty," Qian said, a note of amusement trailing on his words.

"Good morning," I replied stiffly.

"What brings you to me so early? If I'd known you were coming, I would have made myself decent."

"Heng let me in."

Qian let out a huff of a laugh. "His idea of a joke, I would imagine."

"I don't find it particularly funny."

"It was not at your expense, I'm sure, but mine."

I tried to swallow the lump in my throat, but it was stuck there. My heart beat so loud in my ears, I was absolutely sure Qian could hear it.

"Did it frighten you?" he asked.

"What?"

"Seeing my scars."

"No," I said. "I . . . . It wasn't that."

"Most people are frightened."

I risked a glance over my shoulder, but Qian was still shirtless. He picked a grape off his breakfast plate, and I averted my gaze once more. "I'm not most people."

"No, you're not. And you don't have to look away for my sake."

I bit my lip and willed myself to get it together before I slowly turned around. The initial peek I'd had didn't show the whole picture. I'd been so distracted by his abs, I'd almost missed all the other scars. Some smaller ones across his arms, faded with time, and some larger ones, but the claw marks on his side and shoulder were the worst. The scars were pink and defined. If I had to guess, he was lucky to have survived them.

"I have nothing to be ashamed about," he said. "They're part of me."

"What happened?" I asked.

"Monsters," he said, and my eyes widened. "I have seen up close and personal just how dangerous they can really be. I like to think of my scars as badges of honor. This one"—he pointed to the pink flesh on his side—"was from an Aoyin, this great beast with sharp claws and a long tongue. It feeds on human brains."

My jaw dropped. I'd never heard of such a thing.

"And this one"—he pointed to the slash on his shoulder, which I realized now looked like a burn—"was from a jiangshi, a reanimated corpse that sucks the yang energy out of the living." He pointed to various other scars on his body, recalling injuries he'd sustained from other creatures I'd heard of, like a dragon and a Minotaur. He remembered every mark on his body.

"You've been all over the world?"

"You thought I'd help only Jade Mountain? Wherever there are monsters, I am there, too."

"You killed them?"

"To their credit, they tried to kill me first," he said, with a roguish smile. "Silver usually does the trick, though."

"Silver?"

Qian went to the door, where a quiver of arrows was propped up against the wall. He plucked one out, showing the silver tip of the arrowhead. I remembered the rest of his men having a similar arsenal. Were they all one monster-fighting team? "I never go anywhere without them," said Qian.

"Why?"

A flash of pain darted across Qian's face, and heat rushed to mine.

"I'm sorry—" I started to say, but he shook his head and lifted a hand.

"Someone very close to me died at the hands of a monster."

It felt as if I'd drunk an entire tub full of ice water.

"Oh, I'm sorry," I said. I could tell it was a sensitive subject, and he didn't expand on it.

Qian nodded once and then put the arrow back. He cleared his throat and mercifully changed the subject. "So, to what do I owe the pleasure of seeing you this . . . rainy day?" He gestured out the window at the rainstorm and moved to his privacy screen to put on his clothes.

It took me a second to find the words. I felt unmoored. "I would like for you to join me on a retreat." I could hear him moving behind the screen, sliding the hanger off the rack, and shuffling fabric as he pulled his shirt over his head.

"A retreat? For what occasion?"

"I have a vacation home in the mountains, Mount Makiling, a place where many peace agreements were forged. I would like to use it as an opportunity to extend a measure of good faith and to see if we can come to an agreement that both of us will find acceptable." I tried to sound diplomatic, but the heat never left my cheeks. Why he made me feel this way was baffling for a number of reasons. I had to remind myself that this was Nix's older brother. It would be crossing a dozen lines of our friendship if I even so much as looked at him in any kind of way that wasn't purely platonic.

"A vacation home," he repeated. He poked his head out from behind the screen. "This is certainly not how I expected events to unfold when finding my sister."

"You would be staying as our guests, you and your men."

"And Nix?"

"I haven't asked her yet, but . . . I'm sure she'll be in attendance."

"Not that I'm in the habit of declining a much-desired vacation, but this palace isn't suitable enough for our needs?"

When he stepped out from the privacy screen, Qian was fully

dressed. His tunic shirt was slightly unbuttoned, revealing a hint of pale skin on his chest, and my eyes flicked to it against my will before I forced them back to his eyes. He noticed, of course, but didn't move to cover himself or make any mention of it. Instead, he smiled at me.

"I'd like to clear the air between us," I said. "I thought we started off on the wrong foot. If we went someplace else, we could begin again. Better this time."

Qian ran his fingers through his wet hair, combing it back from his face, but his hair stubbornly flopped down the middle once more. It was a small, endearing quality that I couldn't help but notice.

"I believe you're right," he said. "We have started off on the wrong foot." The healers had done a good job returning his nose to normal, but it still didn't diminish the fact that I'd broken it in the first place. Our meeting had been less than stellar, but now I felt like we were seeing eye to eye. That had to be a good sign.

"I think your idea sounds . . . appropriate, given the circumstances," Qian said. "It would be a step in the right direction. When would you like to depart?"

"As soon as possible. Perhaps after the storm clears. Unless you would like some time to prepare?"

Qian jutted out his lower lip and looked around the room. He hadn't brought any personal effects for an extended journey, so there wasn't much by way of packing, and I thought he was amused by that fact, too. "I think I'll be able to get ready by then."

"Good." I spun around and headed to the door. "I look forward to our journey."

"Me too, MJ."

I opened my mouth, automatically ready to ask him to call me by my full name, but thought better of it. This would be the second time he'd used my nickname, and I found that I didn't mind the way he said it. I closed my mouth, tipped my head, and took my leave.

His smile stuck with me even when I left his room, but the moment I closed the door, I was intercepted by a frantic-looking Ayo.

"Your Majesty," he said, gasping for air. He looked like he'd sprinted all the way here. "You must come at once."

"What is it? What's wrong?"

"There's been an attack."

8

I COULDN'T RUN any faster to the throne room. In actuality, it took me only a few minutes, but panic made the halls grow longer with each stride. An attack? Here? In Biringan City?

When I burst through the doors, I found Elias standing near my throne. He held himself with one arm and the other he used to cup his chin, his expression grave. He was talking with a couple—a woman with long red hair and a man with blue curls—and I let out a gasp.

I froze. My heart plummeted like an iron weight.

It was the couple from my dream.

But . . . but how?

I'd never met them before, and yet here they were. And I thought . . . I thought I'd killed them. I could remember how it felt to tear into flesh, to rip muscle and break bone. But it had been just a dream. It couldn't have been real.

Then I noticed the blue-haired man had a large gauze pad pressed against his cheek. Already blood was seeping through in a long gash as if he'd been clawed. The red-haired woman also looked badly injured. She had a cloth wrapped around her shoulder, a horrible cut tearing her from clavicle to under her arm. Tears shone in her eyes.

Elias's gaze landed on me when I came in, his mouth pressed into a hard line, then turned back to the couple.

"Please," he said to them. "Tell me again so I'm not misunderstanding. What happened exactly? Leave no detail out."

The couple held each other's hand, squeezing tightly, both of them trembling.

"Sir, I know it sounds unbelievable. But there's no mistaking what attacked us," the man said.

"A manananggal," the woman cried. "It was horrible."

"A manananggal?" Elias stared at them, eyes wide, alarmed. His wrinkles became more defined, as if he'd aged a hundred years. He was afraid.

"It looked like a woman with long black hair and claws!" The man continued in a rush. "And her mouth . . . it was full of fangs! And she had wings like a bat. She swooped down from the roof and killed one of our goats. She tore it to pieces, and we fled."

The woman nodded vigorously.

Elias shifted nervously and glanced at me again before saying, "We haven't had a manananggal attack in this region for thousands of years. Are you certain it wasn't an amalanhig or some other aswang?"

"No! There was no mistaking it! It was a manananggal!" the man said, sounding desperate to be believed. He closed his eyes and clenched his free hand into a fist; he was still shaking. "She— she didn't have the lower part of her body."

My insides went cold, like I'd been dropped in ice. I couldn't move, I couldn't think.

Was my nightmare real? Was this . . . was this my fault? How? How was any of this possible?

I think I made some kind of sound because the couple turned. When they saw me, they each immediately dropped to one knee and bowed their head. "Your Majesty," the woman said, her voice thick.

I blinked. My eyes burned at the sight of their wounds. Had I done this? Had I hurt these people?

Elias came to me, took my hand, and guided me to my throne. I think he realized I might faint, because he sat me down. The couple stood before me, somber and ashen-faced, and I couldn't take my eyes off them.

Did they recognize me? I didn't think so. They only knew me as their queen. But I knew them. I'd seen their faces last night, seen the terror in their eyes as I got close, smelled their horror, heard the fear pulsing in their hearts. I had intended to kill them. I'd *wanted* to kill them. I was going to puke.

The woman explained, "I didn't want to believe what we saw, either. My grandmother used to tell us stories about the wild ones, and it's exactly like what she said! Bloodshot eyes and everything!" The woman sounded like she was on the verge of tears. Recalling what happened seemed to be causing her distress, and the man held her.

"You have to believe us," he said, his voice ragged. "Please."

I was still too stunned to speak, but Elias didn't need me to. "Of course. We believe you. Sir Lucas!" Elias called.

I dropped my head when I heard the opening doors and the steady clip of Lucas's boots on the marble floor. I was too numb to do or say anything.

"Yes, sir?" I heard Lucas ask.

Elias instructed him to go back to the couple's home, to survey the damage and search for any clues as to the feral manananggal's whereabouts. Their conversation turned into a low drone in my ears, a steady hum, and my vision tunneled. I could still feel skin tearing, still hear the screams, still taste the blood sliding down my throat. What was happening to me?

I felt a firm hand on my shoulder, and I looked up at Elias, who stood tall at my side. Lucas had long gone.

"We'll do everything in our power to ensure this won't happen again," Elias said to the couple.

"Thank you, my lord," the man said, and then to me, "Thank you, Your Majesty."

I almost burst into tears. I just looked at them, speechless, and wanted to say something, but words failed me.

Elias stepped toward the couple, gesturing to the door. "Please, see our healers and tend to your injuries. You have the throne's full attention."

The couple left, holding each other.

When the door closed, it felt like all the air in the room had left with them.

I covered my face and shut my eyes tight, hoping I would wake up from this nightmare.

Elias let out a long sigh and said, "Do not be afraid, MJ. A wild manananggal is nothing to be alarmed about. We're lucky no one else was hurt."

"I've seen manananggals here, in Biringan, but . . . I don't know much about them. What are they exactly?" I had to know, even if it terrified me.

"There are some that live here, yes, but there are wild ones that plague remote areas. Those are terrible creatures that prowl the night, attacking couples and drinking their blood. You might be more familiar with its cousin, the vampire. But wild manananggals are far more rare, and we don't know how they come to be. Like I said to the couple earlier, we haven't had an attack in this region for thousands of years. Manananggals sever their lower halves, leaving them behind when they transform to hunt. They feed on flesh and blood, often leaving a bloody trail in their wake. They reattach themselves to their legs before sunrise, and turn human once more." Elias softened when he saw the terror on my face. "Please, MJ, don't worry. We'll get it sorted soon enough."

Growing up in the human world, of course I knew vampires, but vampires in human folklore didn't detach their lower halves and fly. A manananggal sounded way worse. Of course I was afraid. Last night hadn't been a nightmare. What if I was turning into this thing? What if it happened again? What if I killed a person instead of a goat next time?

What if I told Elias? I knew he loved me like a father, but would he still love me after this? I wanted to believe he would, but doubt kept my mouth shut. I just looked at him and tried not to cry. He patted me softly on the shoulder. He thought I was afraid.

I was, but not for the reasons he assumed.

It all seemed so impossible, but I knew it was true.

It was real.

I was a monster.

THE MOMENT I left the throne room, I went to my bedroom, closed the door behind me, crouched to the floor, and silently sobbed into my knees. I wasn't sure how long I stayed that way, but by the time I was done, some of the flowers had fallen out of my hair, my eyes felt puffy, and the skin on my cheeks was tight with dried tears.

I stood up and went to my vanity to check if I could see anything different, but my own face peered back in the mirror.

I stared at myself and tried to imagine a manananggal. That couple called her—*me*—hideous, with a mouth full of fangs and bloodshot eyes. I ran my tongue over my teeth and found none of them feeling particularly sharp, simply normal. My eyes, blue as a cornflower field, were only red from crying. This morning Jinky had twisted my hair up into a diadem of small flowers, turning me into the picture-perfect image of a queen, but on the inside, I knew what I really was: a monster.

I didn't know how long I could keep this secret. I felt fine now, but I knew there was something dark and horrible lurking inside me, waiting to come out.

I gripped the vanity table as I lowered my head and closed my eyes, trying to think.

Elias didn't know where a manananggal came from, how it was created, but how was I turning into one? What if it was a curse? What if a mambabarang had put a spell on me? I could only guess. It was hard to wrap my head around any of it—the waking nightmare, the transformation, the bloodlust. How did I sever my lower half at night? I didn't remember doing anything like that, so perhaps it was like sleepwalking. I wouldn't even know it was happening until it was too late.

Maybe I could chain myself to my bed at night so I couldn't escape. I would absolutely have to lock and bar the windows and, especially, the door. Except I could fly. Would that be enough to stop me?

I looked at my hands, inspecting them in the light. In my cuticles were trace amounts of something dark brown. I scraped it away with my nail and knew, with a sinking feeling, what it was: dried blood. And then I remembered the way my claws tore into the goat's rib cage and scooped out its heart. The human side of my mind had stopped the manananggal from hurting those people somehow, but how long would that last?

The most horrifying part was that the blood had tasted so *good*. It had satisfied some animalistic need in me to consume. I knew I'd want more and soon.

I didn't know how to stop it or whom to turn to for answers.

I had already invited Qian to Mount Makiling; I couldn't back out of that now. But if I transformed while I was there, I could be seen, or I could hurt someone. He was a famed monster hunter; of course what was happening to me would only complicate things. Would he understand, or would he try to kill me? Then again, maybe he'd encountered something like this before. Maybe he would know what to do. But could I risk it?

The last thing I wanted to do was tell anyone what was happening to me. Not even Nix. I didn't know how anyone, even my best friend, would react to me turning into a monster.

One thing was for certain: I had to find a way to stop this from happening again. Now. Before it got worse.

I lifted my head to face the mirror again. There I saw what the couple had seen. Bulging red eyes; a wide, lipless mouth; gums receding from rows of fangs; gnarled hair plastered against my skeletal face. But I blinked, and the visage was gone. It was just me.

I backed up, heart pounding, and wiped the tears from my cheeks.

I would not let this be a death sentence. I was going to find out what was going on, and I was going to stop it.

THE ONLY PLACE I could think of to find any information on manananggals was the palace library. It was so massive, it was practically an institution. It had one of the largest collections of books, official papers, and treaties on this side of the world, let alone Biringan City, as well as all historic, scientific, and ecological records. Academics from BANA often came here to complete dissertations or find articles for research.

The size of the library rivaled the ballroom, with which it shared a wall. Grand oak shelves stood like monuments under circular stained-glass windows, cutting the stormy daylight into color. An encanto had hundreds of years to live, and still I didn't think it was possible for anyone to read all the books that were housed here. One would need a ladder to reach the very top shelves by the ceiling, high as a cathedral's. But everything was quiet, and the echoes of my heels clacking on the marble floor seemed to stretch for miles. I got the sense that I was the only person here. Good. I didn't want anyone to ask what I was doing.

Toward the rear of the library was the natural sciences wing. Inside, hundreds of animals of Biringan that had been stuffed and mounted leered at me from pedestals and walls. I tried not to look at them because they gave me the creeps. Everything here smelled musty and old. I didn't want to linger any longer than I had to, so I found the book as quickly as I could.

The tome was on a high shelf. It was large and heavy, and a thin layer of dust coated the cover. I gently blew on it and wiped the spine with my thumb, clearing the title: *Monsters of the Hidden World*. The author was a renowned naturalist I'd learned about at BANA. It was the first place I thought to look.

I carried the book to a nearby podium and flipped it open. It was an encyclopedia of sorts, a record of all known creatures in the fae and encanto realms across the world. It included detailed analyses of each creature, subspecies, and known population. Most of them had been rendered extinct, largely due to habitat destruction or by encanto hands. Included with the thorough descriptions were some detailed drawings of monster anatomy and eyewitness accounts. Some of the records I recognized, and I realized that some of these monsters, like fire-breathing dragons, trolls, and yetis, had breached the hidden realm and encountered humans, but the moment I flipped the page and found the manananggal, my heart dropped.

My throat tightened when I gazed upon the ink drawing.

It snarled at me from the page, a mouth full of sharp fangs, a long, snakelike tongue curling into the air, eyes bulging and hungry. Long, stringy hair, slits for nostrils, tattered shirt that had been slashed to pieces. Ten-foot-long wings, veiny and demonic, stretched wide, lifting the torso to the sky, its intestines hanging like vines from its halved body. Even though it was just a drawing, I could tell it was howling, curling its long black claws toward me, startlingly looking both hungry and in agony. I forced myself to tear my gaze away from its horrible face and read the entry.

Manananggal, also known as "The Separator"

A bloodsucking aswang of the Biringan region. By day the manananggal assumes a human form, but at night it separates its upper body from its lower half, leaving it behind, to hunt. Favored targets include pregnant women, newlyweds, and bridegrooms.

Potential weaknesses include iron, garlic, and ash.

Garlic. So that explained why I didn't want to eat the garlic rice that Jinky brought for breakfast. My stomach churned thinking about it, but I kept reading.

Population: unknown. Last known attack during the reign of King Manolito.

Little is understood about this elusive species, especially those in the wild, and numerous theories abound. Manananggals are rare, so eyewitness accounts and scientific documentation are often contradicting or unfortunately lacking. Some scholars theorize that the

mananangal is created after a bride is left at the altar, while others
believe they are born with the affliction or are the dead returned, but
the prevailing theory is that the manananggal is a result of a curse.
However, some manananggals may not even realize they are one.

That caught my attention. I leaned closer to the page, heart in my throat.

Unfortunately, the manananggal turns to ash upon its death, which
makes it difficult to study. Information about the species is conflict-
ing at best. Regardless of its origins, precautions can be taken to
ward off manananggals, including hanging garlic above all win-
dows and doors and sleeping with salt and ash under one's pillow,
but sources are few and far between to determine if any protection is
more effective than the other. The manananggal is nocturnal, leading
most scholars to believe it transforms with the setting sun. Therefore,
a suspected manananggal must be locked away with iron before sunset
to prevent them from harming themselves or anyone else.

My heartbeat roared in my ears after I read the page in its entirety three times, hoping that maybe I'd find some answer or cure. Instead, there was none. Only more questions. I looked at my own hands, imagined them turning into claws, and I squeezed them into fists.

Maybe I really was cursed.

I needed to find more information about the last manananggal sighting. The records said it was during the reign of King Manolito, so my next stop was the records room. It was where all the documents, decrees, and decisions made by the royal family were stored for historical reference, along with books detailing the biographies of all of Biringan's rulers. The second I took the throne, even my most mundane days were logged and catalogued by an archivist. The books were nested into thousands of cubbies. Recordkeeping was an important process in the history of Biringan, so it was only natural to assume that there would be documentation of a manananggal attack. It would have been important enough.

My eyes bounced over all the names on polished brass plaques before I found King Manolito's section and took his tome to a reading chair. King Manolito had ruled over Biringan for two thousand years with his daughters—Devera and Soledad.

King Manolito's tome was as thick as my hand, but there was no mention of a manananggal. I checked his daughters' records next. Princess Devera, who married into a djinn royal family, had officially incorporated algebra into encanto academia, calling it a universal language. And Princess Soledad struck up a trade agreement with Avalon that still continued today. But for the life of me, I couldn't find any information about a manananggal.

After King Manolito died, the crown passed on to his brother, King Rio.

My eyes ached, and the words on the page started to blur together. The heart of the storm raged against the window, rapping like fingers on the stained glass, throwing shadows across the page. Thunder rolled overhead and the sky darkened. It was as if the weather was mirroring my own thoughts, tumultuous and fearsome.

One thing stood out to me: If King Manolito had two daughters, princesses in their own rights, why hadn't either of them become queen? Why had the crown passed to his brother?

There was something I was missing. There had to be. And why wasn't there any sign of a manananggal encounter in these records? The book of monsters couldn't have gotten it wrong, could it? It didn't make any sense.

When I went to put away Devara's book, ready to give up, another book caught my eye. It had been shoved into the back of the shelf, originally obscured by the others. I reached in and pulled it out, finding it surprisingly light.

A name had been etched into the hard leather: Yara Liliana. Below her name was a triangle symbol and her date of birth but no date of death. Inside, the book was completely empty, but not because it was blank. The pages had been torn out, leaving nothing but ragged remnants in the spine.

I returned to the other records of King Manolito's family, flipping back and forth between pages just to be sure, looking for her name, but there was no mention of her.

That couldn't be right. Any royal, regardless of standing, should have been recorded and documented. Why else did she have a book in the first place? The archivists kept detailed records of every royal, every marriage, every failure, every success, practically every meal they ate on every day.

And yet Yara Liliana's book was the only proof she had ever existed. But then why keep it? Unless . . . unless it was left here as a reminder.

She had been erased from history. And maybe it was for a reason.

A thump outside the archive room made me jump. I looked to the closed door, waiting for it to open, but it didn't.

"Who's there?" I called out.

No answer. But a shadow passed in front of the keyhole. Someone was on the other side.

Heart racing, I closed Yara Liliana's book and shoved it back into its hiding place on the shelf before I crept to the door. A rational part of me thought that maybe an archivist had come to transcribe today's events, but another part of me thought the worst. Was someone here to hurt me?

I put my hand on the doorknob and wrenched it open quickly.

Half hunched over was Amador, peering through the keyhole. Her head jerked up, and her jaw dropped in shock. She righted herself and smoothed out her blue-and-white dress, the colors of the Sigbin Court.

"Can I help you?" I asked. I couldn't help the sharpness of my tone. Amador was one of the very last people I wanted to see right now.

"I—" She halted, as if thinking. "I'm looking for Lucas," she said quickly.

My hand squeezed the doorknob. "Of course you are. Why would you think he's here?"

Amador lowered her shoulders, stretching her neck to look as poised as possible. "I heard a noise. I thought it was him."

I could tell she was lying. I could almost smell it on her. "Well, he's not here," I said through gritted teeth. "Anything else I can do for you, Grand Duchess?"

Amador's lips curled into a sneer. "No. I'll be going now." She lifted her nose to me and spun around, disappearing down the row of books, her heels clacking annoyingly as she left.

I let go of the doorknob as my anger ebbed away, but when I did, I noticed the doorknob was dented in, with the distinct shape of my fingers in the brass.

9

I HAD ELIAS arrange for a convoy to escort Qian, Nix, the rest of Jade Mountain, and myself to Mount Makiling, which provided a much-needed distraction. I had one last thing to do before we left to ensure I didn't hurt anyone while we were away, and no one could know about it.

I changed into a simple linen skirt and a soft cotton blouse and tied my hair up in a ponytail. When I glanced at myself in the mirror, I looked more like I did when I was growing up in the human world, and that was the perfect disguise from looking like a queen. For the finishing touch, I grabbed a cloak and pulled the hood over my head.

I left the palace as hastily as I could, avoiding anyone by hiding in small alcoves or behind large planters until the coast was clear. The heavy rain held most people's heads down, focusing on not slipping and keeping the mud out of their shoes, so I was able to sneak out of the palace unseen. Sneaking around the grounds, just like how Lucas, Nix, and I had when we solved my father's murder, used to give me a slight rush. Doing it alone now felt . . . wrong somehow.

The Royal Dock, despite the rain, was bustling with activity. Most of the ships waited for the storm to pass before they set sail again, so sailors sat under palm-woven lean-tos, playing cards, drinking from brown jugs, or napping until they got orders from their captains. Fortunately, no one looked my way as I headed toward one ship in particular, the *Paradise*. I didn't know a lot about boats, but it was a big one, with three masts and a sirena carved into the wooden bow. Its sails had been hoisted, and it bobbed in the churning waters.

A long-haired man with an equally long sword sat near the wooden plank leading to the main deck, shielding himself from the rain with a wide-brimmed salakot perched low on his head. He looked up at me from picking some dirt out from under his fingernails with a toothpick. At least, I thought it was dirt.

The man practically snarled at me when I approached, his face twisting a long, pale scar on his cheek. He snorted and then spit a great green loogie at my feet, stopping me in my tracks. He snorted and put the toothpick in his mouth.

"What's your business?" he asked. He didn't recognize me.

"I need to speak with Romulo."

"What for?" He snorted again and swallowed whatever was in his throat. Gross.

Trying not to gag, I said, "That's between me and Romulo."

Romulo was a smuggler, one of Lucas's contacts. While Lucas was in charge of protecting the crown, he had to know of the black-market dealings, and when it came to dangerous and forbidden books, Romulo was his go-to source of information. For a hefty price. Lucas had hired him to find *The Mysterious Properties of*

Magical Herbs, a reference for making all kinds of poisons. If anyone was going to have any information, Romulo was my best bet.

Romulo's man, though, didn't seem convinced. He scanned me up and down, still sneering. "He's busy."

"I can wait," I said, and folded my arms over my chest, hoping it came off as confident.

"Be my guest."

So that's exactly what I did. I sat on top of a few weathered wooden crates, pulling my cloak tightly around me to block out the rain, and waited for what felt like hours, even though it was probably only twenty minutes. I was starting to get used to the smells of brine and fish guts when I heard a voice coming from the ship, getting closer. It was Romulo.

"As always, it's a pleasure doing business, Sir Lucas."

My heart skipped, and I lowered my head, shielding my face with my hood when I heard his name.

What was Lucas doing here? If he saw me, it could ruin everything. He'd start asking questions—questions I was absolutely not ready to answer. Plus, he'd blow my cover. I couldn't let him notice me. I did my best to blend in with the other sailors lying about on the docks, even started swaying a little like I'd imbibed a few too many drinks at the pub, but my heart was beating furiously as I pricked my ears to listen.

Lucas's heavy footsteps pounded on the wooden planks leading to the dock. He stepped into a puddle in front of me and turned, the stitching with the looping *L* on his boot unmistakable. His tone was professional when he said to Romulo, "I trust I have your discretion."

"Of course, good sir. My discretion is as good as your gold."

Lucas paused, probably giving Romulo a nod before he turned and walked down the dock. He didn't break stride when he passed me, and I lifted my eyes to watch him go. He pulled the hood of his cloak up over his head and left his secret meeting with the smuggler like nothing was out of the ordinary. Of course, who was I to talk? I was going to be doing the exact same thing, but why was Lucas talking to Romulo now? What business did he have that needed such discretion?

"This one's been waiting for you, boss," the man with the toothpick said, and it snapped my gaze away from Lucas.

Romulo stood on the gangplank, looking exactly as I remembered him: brown skin, bald head, long, scraggly brown beard, and tattoos covering both of his arms. He wore a sleeveless jerkin and pants, and in one hand, he held a small canvas pouch. "And you are?"

I lowered my hood and stood, and at the sight of me, his expression blanched.

"You all right, boss?" the toothpick man asked.

Romulo didn't answer. He just waved me on board.

The captain's quarters on the ship were cramped, serving as both his room and office. His bed, raised on pulleys, hung above our heads over a large table, where a series of maps and a lumpy sizable sack sat, open and ready for business. Romulo stuffed the bag into his pocket, and it jangled, no doubt full of coins. It smelled like tobacco in here, and I did my best not to wrinkle my nose.

"What can I do for Her Royal Majesty?" Romulo asked, rolling up the maps and organizing his table.

"I was hoping you could help me."

"Help from a simple merchant such as myself?" That was putting it nicely.

"I need a few items that I'd like to be kept . . . quiet."

Romulo seemed amused. "Such as?"

"Do you have any kind of . . . manacles? Shackles?"

"Shackles?" The way Romulo stared at me, I knew it was an odd request. What kind of a queen ordered shackles? "None of my business to know why. Luckily for you, I've got some shackles on board. You know captains have needs for such things, though I rarely like to use them."

"Are they made of iron?"

Romulo narrowed his eyes at me. "Of course. Made by the finest dwende ironworkers of Tikbalang, enchanted to fit any wrist."

"I will take a few," I said, though I shuddered to think what they'd been used for. But if the book said that the manananggal was vulnerable to iron, it could be enough to keep me contained if—*when*—I became one again.

Romulo whistled through his teeth, summoning one of his men, who fetched the shackles for me.

"Anything else I can do for you?" Romulo asked.

"Yes, actually. I was hoping you could find information. About a princess of Biringan, Yara Liliana."

Surprisingly, Romulo seemed confused. Rarely did he not know something. "Who?"

"She was one of my ancestors. I need to know more about her."

"Well, I've never heard of her."

"It seems no one has. I discovered some discrepancies in the royal records, and I want to know why hers are missing."

"Not sure how much I'll be able to find if even the royal archive doesn't have anything."

"That's why I came to you. If there is information about her out there, I knew you'd be the one to find it."

Stroking his ego seemed to do the trick because a self-assured smile replaced his confusion. "Correct, Majesty. I know of a few places to start where I can loosen some tongues. Of course, you remember my services are not free."

"I know," I said. "You're not going to hurt anyone, are you?"

"Of course not!" Romulo scoffed. "Finding your lost ancestor shouldn't require too much blood to be spilled. If I haven't heard of her, I doubt other people have, so my usual—uh—*techniques* would probably be unsuitable. Shouldn't take more than a few days."

I wasn't sure I had a few days, but I had to believe he could get what I needed. "Okay, good."

My eyes went to the rolled-up maps and the bulge of coins in his pocket before I said, "What were you and Lucas talking about?"

"Afraid that's client confidentiality, Majesty," he said, smiling. "The same courtesy, of course, would be extended to you. But it will cost you. Which I'm sure won't be a problem for one such as yourself."

It was true. I didn't care about the money. And while the desire to know what business Lucas had here was almost too hard to ignore, I couldn't push my luck with Romulo's good graces. I needed his help, and I didn't want to squander it now.

"Thank you, Romulo. I know you won't disappoint," I said.

WHEN I RETURNED, the caravan was waiting for me outside the palace gates, along with my bags, which Jinky had packed for me. The iron shackles weighed heavily in a rucksack slung over my shoulder. I'd stuffed my bag with spare clothes and anything else I could think of to bring with me.

Qian and his retinue had already chosen their horses and were preparing for the afternoon's ride through the mountains with small provisions and weather gear. The mountains were known for their sudden rainfall and passing storms.

The sky above the palace had cleared up significantly. Droplets still clung to the white sampaguita blossoms and sparkled in the sunlight like diamonds. The air smelled alive, and everything looked impossibly green. It was as if the weather itself had realized we needed a break. I took it as a good sign as I walked toward the back of the caravan line.

Nix stood halfway inside a covered calesa and waved when I approached. It was a relief to see her smile. Qian's men, on the other hand, stared at me as I passed, no doubt thinking I looked far from royal because I was still wet from the rainstorm. Qian was the only one who smiled.

"Hello, Your Majesty," he said, and I nodded to him. I felt his eyes on me when I reached Nix.

"You're okay riding in the calesa?" I asked her.

"Yeah," Nix said. "Elias mentioned you requested they get your horse ready."

I adjusted the rucksack on my shoulder. "I want to show

everyone that I'm not some pushover who needs to be driven everywhere."

Nix's eyes narrowed when she took in my face. "Are you sure you're okay to ride?"

She knew something was wrong. For a moment, I wondered if maybe I should tell her about what was happening to me. She'd been my friend for long enough now that I knew I could trust her, but at the same time, I didn't want to frighten her. Before I could open my mouth, I noticed Elias and Lucas walking toward me, with Lucas leading a horse by the reins. My heart at first leapt upon seeing him, on instinct at this point, before it plummeted to my toes. Lucas being here could only mean one thing.

"You're coming with us?" I asked him.

Elias answered instead. "Lucas is your datu. You may feel that you're safe in a remote home in the mountains, but you still need protection."

Lucas's gaze captured mine momentarily before I forced myself to look away. What was he planning with Romulo? It ached not knowing. "Fine," I conceded.

Elias sensed the tension in the air and glanced at Lucas, too. He knew all about our breakup, but it didn't seem like Elias was at all worried about that interfering with Lucas's duties.

Meanwhile, Lucas excused himself with a stiff bow, leading his horse toward the front of the caravan.

I thought I'd had enough to worry about. I clenched and unclenched my fists in an attempt to calm myself down, but I heard a shrill voice cut through the air.

"Wait for me!"

To my dismay, Amador came into view from around the bend, a gaggle of servants in tow, carrying a cartful of luggage. She walked ahead of the group, head held high as she led the way. She was not dressed for a journey; instead, she wore one of the finest silk dresses I'd ever seen her in.

Is she for real? I thought, then asked, "Who invited her?"

Elias said, "I did."

"Why?"

"Members of the other courts should go, too, for diplomacy. It's a sign of respect. The bigger the trip, the more serious you seem. It proves that you really care. And you need the full support of the kingdom to have any leverage, MJ."

I let out a huff. This was just getting worse and worse. I chewed on the inside of my cheek and glared at Elias, but he only gave me a single raised eyebrow, as if to say, *Be nice.*

I took a deep, measured breath and glanced at Nix, whose cheeks had turned a bright red upon seeing Amador. The promise of a relaxing trip was crumbling down. But it was too late now. Amador was here. Not even a minute had gone by before she was already annoying me.

"Don't tell me we'll have to ride *horses* all the way there." Amador scoffed, scowling at the dirt trail that would lead the way through the mountain.

Something horrible rose up my throat, a vicious and biting anger that made my blood boil, but I swallowed it down and forced myself to take a breath. I would not give in to this ugliness inside me, even if it tried to claw its way out and tore me apart in doing so. Those iron shackles Romulo gave me had better work.

"You can ride in the calesa," I said. Anything to make sure she was as far away from me as possible. "Or you can be dragged behind it. Your call."

Amador's eyes darted to Nix, still standing in the doorway of the covered calesa. Of course she would want to be in a comfortable carriage for such a long trip. I shouldn't have subjected Nix to that kind of torture, being with Amador for a whole day, but surprisingly, Nix didn't put up a fight.

Nix blinked, the color deepening on her cheeks, as she and Amador stared at each other. Finally, Nix mumbled, "She can ride with me if she wants. Or whatever." She ducked inside. She must be so angry with me for offering it to Amador, but I'd make it up to her somehow.

Amador let out a haughty *huh* and inspected me with a pinched expression. "That will be acceptable, I suppose."

She instructed her valets to arrange a mountain's worth of luggage into the back of the calesa, and I was relieved to walk away from her.

Nearby, I found Lucas adjusting the stirrups on my saddle for me. He didn't look at me while he worked, but I got the sense that he was forcing himself not to do so. His gaze was flat, like he wasn't seeing anything at all.

"I can do it," I told him.

"I know you can." His hands kept moving the straps through the golden loops.

"So let me."

"I'm making sure it's secure." His jaw muscles were as tight as his shoulders.

"It's secure."

"I'm just doing my job."

"I will tell you when I need help," I said coldly.

Finally, Lucas's gold-flecked eyes met mine briefly before he held up his hands in surrender. "Yes, Your Majesty."

A part of me wanted him to fight with me, to argue for a little while longer. I ached for a reason to talk with him, even if it hurt, and instead, he had given up so easily. Somehow that hurt even more.

I adjusted my stirrups while Lucas tended to his own, and we worked back-to-back in silence, readying ourselves for the journey. I could feel him behind me the whole time, and his presence burned like a bonfire. I was drawn to his heat, always aware of where he was and how close he stood to me. I had hoped this trip would be a way I could be rid of him, but of course I couldn't escape Lucas. He was my head of security, after all—my loyal datu, above all else.

I noticed he cinched his weapons into holsters on the horse's saddle, and my breath hitched. I knew it was a precaution, to protect me. But would he kill a monster even if the monster was his queen?

He noticed where my attention was, and our eyes met once more before I hauled myself onto my horse and took off without him.

We were nothing more than a sovereign and a knight. What we'd had couldn't interfere with our respective duties. There was too much at stake now. Nix relied on me; my kingdom relied on me.

At the front, Qian was waiting for me, hunched casually atop his gelding, his arms crossed lazily on his saddle horn. "I didn't expect you would ride with us," he said.

"Then I'm full of surprises." I meant to sound flippant, but my words didn't have any heat behind them. I realized it was because I actually meant it. Having been raised in the human world, I wasn't going to act like any other queen he had ever encountered.

Seemingly impressed, Qian smiled, and together, we led the way down the trail. Lucas and General Heng rode behind us, and the rest followed after, with Nix and Amador taking up the rear.

It was going to be a long day's ride, and the whole time, I could feel Lucas's eyes on me. I never looked back.

10

THE GREAT HOUSE was nestled near the summit of Mount Makiling, tucked away inside the verdant green jungle of the Paulanan Mountains. The path there was narrow and overgrown, curtained in vines and orchids, and the wildlife didn't seem frightened by us moving through the trees. Macaques and great colorful cuckoos watched us from branches overhead, curious about where we were going. Bugs buzzed and frogs croaked from invisible spots in the dense jungle, which made the mountain feel alive as we made our way two by two.

After a few hours, when we turned down one of the narrow ledges spiraling its way up the mountainside, we got our first glimpse of the manor. It jutted out from the treetops, like a large salakot, on the highest peak. A waterfall cascaded below it, curtaining the summit in a white mist that billowed in the wind, making it appear as if the manor were floating on a cloud.

I imagined that my father and ancestors had made this same journey many times before me and had seen the manor from this very spot, too, and I felt more connected to them than I ever had.

We still had a way to go, and the path took us deeper into the jungle. My butt ached from the constant bump and bustle of my horse, and I readjusted myself for what felt like the hundredth time. Qian, on the other hand, didn't look bothered at all, even though we'd been riding for the same amount of time. If he was sore, he didn't show it, but I doubted he was. He was a royal, born and bred, so he was no doubt used to riding for long hours by now. Being a hunter, he was probably accustomed to long treks into the forest, searching for his monsters.

He must have noticed I was looking at him, because his gaze slid toward me, and I turned away, pretending I hadn't been. I hadn't meant to stare, but Jinky was right—he was easy to look at.

"How are you faring, Your Majesty?" he asked.

No way would I tell him that my butt ached so much, I doubted I'd be able to walk straight after this. I lifted my chin and said, "It's no big deal."

The corner of Qian's lip quirked up just before Heng rode to meet us, pulling back slightly on the reins to match our speed.

"No sign of trouble, my liege," he said.

"Of course not," Qian said. "I told you there was nothing to worry about."

"What are you looking for?" I asked.

Heng's stare was as cold as a blade. "I am always alert." He didn't answer my question. To Qian, he said, "I will remain vigilant until we are safely at our destination."

He left, returning to the rear of the caravan to make his rounds.

"What's his deal?" I asked Qian.

"Heng is always on the lookout for anything that might want to attack us. You know what they say about these mountains. He's wary of the stories, even if they are commoners' folktales. Can't be caught unawares."

I furrowed my brow. "Folktales?"

"You don't know?" Qian looked genuinely surprised. "I would have thought that, since this is your land, you'd have heard the stories. They're so pervasive, they've even reached our land."

A prickle of embarrassment made my nose itch. "Forgive my ignorance."

Another voice spoke up. It was Lucas. "They say that Mount Makiling is haunted." Lucas had ridden up behind us, casually swaying with the stride of his horse, and he glanced at the abundant green all around us.

I almost forgot my rancor, my curiosity winning over. "How can a mountain be haunted?"

"They say a spirit named Maria Makiling, the lady of the mountain, lives in the jungle. She protects the land, imbues it with abundance, and makes unlucky men disappear."

Qian smiled at him. "Exactly right! I didn't think you were one for superstitions, Sir Lucas."

"I grew up in these mountains, heard the legends, too. People in nearby villages claim to see the lady wandering the forests, dressed all in white, gathering fruits to bring back to her hidden cave. They say she's beautiful, with flowing dark hair and skin like golden honey. Though any man who tries to approach her is never seen again. Perhaps it's a story to keep people away from the royal house, but I'm not sure. If it's not a ghost, then history haunts this land."

"That's poetry," Qian said, a layer of teasing in his tone.

"How come no one told me about this?" I asked Lucas.

Qian answered, his tone bordering on condescending. "Perhaps because it's not true."

"You believe in mythical monsters," I said. "You hunt them, don't you? What's the difference?"

"Monsters are real. Ghosts are not."

"I wouldn't be so certain, Prince Qian," Lucas said. "History and legend are connected in ways even encantos don't understand. Anything can live up in these mountains. Especially beings that don't want to be found."

"I never took you for one to believe in ghosts," I said.

Lucas shrugged. "I like to keep an open mind about the unknown."

Qian huffed a laugh, doubtful. "I'm more worried about the creatures of the material plane."

"Why does she take men, though? The lady of the mountain?" I asked Lucas. I wanted to know more about her.

Lucas shrugged again. "Some say she falls in love with them and steals them back to her house to be wed. Others say it's because she's a spurned lover jealous of other people's happiness."

A pang of sympathy resonated in my aching muscles. I lifted my chin. "Maybe she makes men disappear after they've done something to anger her," I said.

Lucas's gaze pierced mine. I wished he would look at me longer, but when he turned away, I felt like I could breathe again.

"Yes," he said. "I could imagine so."

IN THE MIDAFTERNOON, we arrived at the front gates of the grounds. A stout encanto wearing a butler's sash stood at attention, flanked on both sides by rows of housekeepers and servants, dutifully waiting for our arrival. The man, a light-skinned encanto with a thin mouth, a thinner mustache, and a bald head, bowed when we approached. His precise movements and the small round spectacles that perched on the end of his nose gave him the appearance of a bird of prey.

"My queen, Mahalina Jazreel," he said. "I am Edgardo Ignacia, your butler. Welcome to the great house."

"Thank you," I said. "I'm sorry I couldn't come sooner to meet you."

"Not at all, Your Majesty. It's my pleasure to keep your home well looked after. And we welcome any and all guests of Her Royal Highness," he said, addressing the rest of the party.

Qian had dismounted from his horse, which was already being led away by an attendant. He smiled and took in the house with bright eyes.

"I could get used to this view," he said, turning to face me.

I felt a blush creep up my cheeks, but he was right. The manor was breathtaking. It was reminiscent of a tree house, but that description would be doing it a disservice. It was easily the size of my old school in San Diego. The palm trees had grown in such a way that they wove together like a basket forming the main structure, merging with natural stone in the cliffs and allowing for fresh flowers and vines to crawl up to the grass roof that loomed tall like the mountains around us. Large glass windows and balconies stretched around three stories, no doubt meant to capture the beauty of the outdoors, where hammocks were already strung up and shaded with parasols.

"Wow," I said to Edgardo. "This is perfect. You've kept my family's manor in fantastic condition."

"You have not seen everything yet, Your Majesty," Edgardo said, tipping his head in acknowledgment and stepping aside to let me walk into the house.

He was right. I'd spoken too soon. The main foyer had high ceilings and a mahogany floor, and I felt like I'd walked into a dream. Real palm trees grew out of small indoor gardens like pillars all around us, and colorful birds swooped from one branch to another, calling out to one another. Natural archways lined the entrance, leading to the wings of the house. The air smelled like rain, vines crawled up and down the limestone walls, and a burbling fountain stood in the middle of the hall. The structure of the fountain itself was seemingly made out of mist, too. The statue in its center depicted a strikingly beautiful woman with flowing hair and a heart-shaped face, her palms up and her eyes raised toward the ceiling as if she were catching the water that fell around her.

"The lady of the mountain," Edgardo said. "She watches over us here."

"She's real?" I asked.

"She is the mountain," he said. "And the mountain is as real as you and me. We believe all things in the material universe have a spirit. The old ways are strong here."

Out of the corner of my eye, I saw Lucas give Qian a sidelong glance, but Qian simply put his hand on his sword and did a slow circle around the entrance hall.

"My staff and I have fully prepared for your every want and need," Edgardo continued. "There are one hundred twenty-five acres of jungle and lakes for every outdoor activity you can possibly imagine. The residence has sixty rooms, including a library, a morning room, a billiards room, a breakfast room, a dining room, a fully stocked wine cellar, sporting pitches, and an indoor hot spring. You will be without want here."

My jaw hung loose for a long moment as I took everything in. All this was mine?

Nix nudged me in the side, noticing that I'd gotten caught up in the luxury of it all, and I closed my mouth. Right. I had to act like this wasn't a novelty. I could barely think about where to start.

"It's magnificent," I said. Edgardo smiled, knowing it was true.

Amador was busy directing staff to carry her luggage. "Where is my room?" she asked impatiently.

"Allow my staff to show you," Edgardo said. A couple hand-maids appeared and whisked Amador and her wardrobe away. Lucas followed obediently.

"Forgive my short notice," I said. "I didn't expect to have such an entourage. But Prince Qian and his men are my guests. Please see to it that they're comfortable. He's mentioned he went hunting with his father as a pastime. Is that something that can be arranged?"

"Hunting? I've never had such a request, but . . . I don't see why we can't make an exception."

"An exception?"

"Your Highness, forgive me. We are cautious with the wildlife here. Every living thing on Mount Makiling is under the lady's protection, and we don't want to upset her."

"Of course, you're right." I'd have to find some other way to occupy Qian's time, get him to relax and be more friendly.

EDGARDO INTRODUCED ME to the handmaids in charge of my suite, three encanto girls who were a little older than me. The one in charge and the eldest was Clarissa.

Clarissa wore her blond hair in a braid running down the length of her back. She barely spoke while she led us through the great house, taking Nix and me to our rooms. The great house was in actuality several houses connected to one another by covered walkways, sheltered on either side by the lush rattans and curling vines. No wonder royals before me came here for rest and relaxation. I was starting to feel better already. Around seemingly every corner was a new thing to take my breath away. It was as if the building had grown out of the jungle itself. Hundreds—maybe thousands—of butterflies hung from the rafters in a reading room; in another room, a waterfall flowed down from a hole in the ceiling to create an indoor pool; another room was completely made of salt, lit only by sunlight that filtered through the thin places carved out of the rock in intricate, swirling designs.

Everything was so amazing, I almost forgot what we'd come here to do. Nix, too, seemed enraptured by the house; all the worry that had creased her brow these past few days had disappeared.

"Do you like it?" I asked Nix.

She looked at me, her eyes huge. "Like it? Can we live here forever?"

I couldn't help but laugh. "How was your ride with Amador?"

Nix craned her neck to look around the corner at the dining room, already being prepped for dinner. "It was great."

"Really? I half expected you to throw yourself out of the calesa rather than be stuck with her all day."

Nix blinked rapidly and fumbled over her words. "Right! She was motion-sick most of the ride, so she didn't talk too much. She barely acknowledged my existence, so I'll take what I can get. It's the little victories, right?" She smiled a little too tightly.

"Your room, Princess Nix," Clarissa said, gesturing to a door at the end of one of the covered walkways.

"Thank you!" Nix said, and dashed for the door. "I'm totally beat. I think I'm going to skip dinner and go to bed early if that's okay. Maybe being around Amador took more out of me than I realized."

"You don't have to ask me for permission," I said. "You can do whatever you want here."

Nix nodded. "You should get some rest, too."

I desperately wished I could. My eyes felt puffy, and all I wanted was to close them and bury myself under a pile of blankets, but I just smiled and said, "I've got some things to do first. See you later."

Clarissa continued leading me deeper into the house, but I felt Nix's eyes still on me as I followed. When I heard her door close, I let out a breath of relief. I hoped she didn't sense my nerves.

Maybe the energy I was giving off seemed more like exhaustion than anxiety. I just had to get through tonight.

My room was on the top floor, the farthest away from everyone else's, which was yet another relief. Everything in my chamber was mostly wood, from the floor to the ceiling, and it was furnished with rattan chairs and a large four-poster bed draped with a mosquito net. A huge tree trunk grew straight through the middle of the room and into the ceiling, exactly the kind of tree house I had dreamt about having when I was a kid. Moving around so much with my mom meant that was impossible, but being in one now made my heart leap with joy.

My things had already been delivered to the master suite, stacked neatly near a wardrobe and privacy screen. The balcony in my room overlooked the hot spring, and beyond that, I had a spectacular view of the waterfall and the surrounding rainforest. Separating us from the rest of the mountain was a fluffy white cloud that moved like waves. In the distance, I could see the ocean. It felt like a world away.

"Thank you, Clarissa," I said to her as she waited patiently by the door.

She bowed. "Shall I collect you for dinner, Your Majesty?"

"No," I said, trying to smile. "I'll see myself down. I want this trip to be as casual as possible. No schedules, no formality."

"Yes, Your Majesty."

"I'm serious about the formality thing. I'm never formal with my ladies-in-waiting. You can start calling me MJ." Clarissa winced, and I added, "Unless that makes you uncomfortable."

"It may be a hard habit to break, Your Majesty. If you are interested in health and restorative programs, I can arrange for a number of massages and skin routines to ensure you have the most relaxing and pleasurable time here. Or I can request a spiritual healing and a guided meditation, if that is what you need."

I perked up. "A spiritual healing?"

"Yes, but . . . these healers aren't exactly . . ." She trailed off, trying to find the right words. "They're called manghuhulas—spiritual healers whose practices aren't always understood. Some deal in spirit magic, exorcisms, even necromancy, but some have been known to be curse breakers."

My eyes widened. Would that help me? Maybe they would know how to fix me, but would I want to risk letting a stranger know about what was happening? But Clarissa must have mistaken my silence for disapproval.

"Please forgive me," she said. "They are distantly related to mambabarangs. I understand the crown has exiled their kind ever since your father's assassination, but—"

"No! It's okay!" I said, easing her with an outstretched hand. "I truly don't mind. I didn't know such a job existed. So, yes! Please! That would be amazing. A meeting with a manghuhula sounds like I could right some wrongs on that front as well."

Clarissa's smile twitched, but she seemed relieved that I wasn't mad. "Okay, I'll see to it."

"Thank you." I ached all over. While I had the meeting with the manghuhula to look forward to, the talks with Qian still loomed like a shadow over my mind, but I knew that if I didn't get ready for tonight, I might regret it later. "I'm a little tired, though, Clarissa. So I think I, too, will go to sleep early. I would request not to be disturbed at all while the door is closed, please. And don't worry about waking me up tomorrow. I'll manage on my own."

"Very good, Your Majes—MJ."

I smiled as Clarissa closed the door behind her.

Once she was gone, I checked the door. Since this was the master suite, it was outfitted with an intricate locking system that was supposed to stop outside attackers from getting in. But what about something trying to get out?

I traced my fingers on the magically enhanced latch, feeling its power humming like a live wire, and I locked the door.

I did the same to the French doors leading to the balcony. But what if my screams carried across the grounds? Was any of this good enough?

I opened my rucksack and took out a pair of the iron shackles I had tucked away in there. Two iron cuffs were connected by a short iron chain. Romulo had told me they were magical, that the chain would elongate to fit around whatever it needed to in order to anchor the person in place. Not only that, but they locked with a secret word. All I had to do was say "magkandado," and they would stay fastened around my wrists until sunrise.

I wrapped the chain between the two cuffs around the tree in the middle of my room, and like Romulo had said, the chain magically grew long enough to accommodate it. I just had to make sure that none of the servants saw any of this tomorrow morning. Too many questions—let alone the rumors—would only make things more complicated for me. Until the manghuhula arrived, I had to do everything I could to protect people from me.

There was a knock on the door, and I instinctively hid the manacles behind my back. I'd told Clarissa not to disturb me, but it could have been Edgardo or one of the other staff members who hadn't been informed yet.

Heart pounding, I stuffed the shackles under a blanket, then went to the door and opened it. The last person I had expected was standing there, smiling at me.

"Qian!" I said. "Wha . . . what are you doing here?"

Qian glanced around, eyebrows raised. "Is this too presumptuous of me to knock on your door?" When he looked at me again, he had a boyish glint in his eye that was remarkably charming.

"No, I just . . . It's a nice surprise."

"I promise, I am not here with unsavory intentions. I wanted to bring you something, as a token of appreciation."

In his hand was a bouquet of gorgeous plumeria flowers, as blue as sapphires.

"They reminded me of your eyes," he said, holding it out to me.

My face felt hot when I stared at the flowers and then at Qian. He had thought of me, even when we had been apart, and that was more flattering than I had realized.

I took the flowers from him, but he plucked one from the middle and took it back. "This one, though," he said, holding it up to his nose, "is for me."

My brain had gone fuzzy, and it was hard for me to find any words. I couldn't even think to say thank you. He turned and walked back down the hall, leaving me standing in the doorway, but glanced over his shoulder once to smile at me, flower still in his hand.

My heart skipped into my throat, and I closed the door quickly, locking it once more.

Did this mean . . . ? Did Qian like me?

The last time anyone had brought me flowers was Lucas. He'd picked a whole bouquet of them just for me, and then we had kissed. The memory of that night still sent a rush down my spine.

And now Qian had done the same—hand-delivering flowers for no other reason than to see me. Was this real, or was this some sort of political maneuver to get me to send Nix back to Jade Mountain? Why would he like me? Why would *anyone* like me? I was a monster.

I was so tired, it hurt to think about it. In fact, I was having a hard time thinking about anything at all, aware only of the citrusy scent of the plumeria.

I put the flowers to my nose and went to the window overlooking the grounds. Outside, I spotted two people standing at the tree line separating the grounds from the jungle. They were hard to make out since the shadows were growing darker, but I knew they were Lucas and Amador. They were talking to each other, too far away for me to hear, but I could tell they were arguing. Lucas paced back and forth, running his hands through his hair, while Amador gestured at him, her posture tense.

After a moment, Lucas dropped his hands to his sides and took her hand. He held it tight in his own and said something to her that made her take a deep breath. He kept holding on to her hand, gazing at her with such tenderness, and I remembered how he'd looked at me like that.

Watching them made something sour and bitter rise in my

throat. Jealousy dug its ugly claws into me, and my heart lurched. I wanted him to look at *me* that way. I remembered how safe I'd felt when he did, how strong I'd been knowing that he was there with me. And now it was over.

I knew I needed to let it go. I had to get over it. I hated myself for feeling this way, and it was slowly eating me alive. But I couldn't stop the longing in my heart for something I couldn't have.

I put the flowers to my nose again and inhaled, closing my eyes. Qian's gift consumed my thoughts, and by the time I opened my eyes again, Lucas and Amador were gone. They'd disappeared behind the house, but the sludge inside my gut seemed to spread. Like oil, it coated my stomach, making me sick.

When I turned back to face my room, the world tipped under me. I stumbled to catch my balance, but I was too dizzy. Nausea rolled over me like a sea wave, and the flowers slipped from my hand and fell to my feet.

"What . . . ? No . . ."

The room spun like I was on a Tilt-A-Whirl. I turned around to the window again to see that the sun was starting to set, casting the room in an orange glow. I hadn't noticed it earlier; I was too focused on Lucas and Amador. Long shadows stretched out toward me, and darkness filled my vision. I shook my head. I could feel it. The darkness spread inside me.

I was changing, and I couldn't stop it. I was running out of time. I needed to get the iron . . .

I stumbled for the manacles, but my knees gave out, and I hit the floor. My blood roared in my ears, drowning everything out, and I tasted bile.

The manacles lay inches away from me. I grabbed for them but missed with clumsy fingers.

I barely managed to slide the manacles over my wrists, though I couldn't clasp them. I didn't have control of my hands anymore; they'd gone numb.

"Magkandado," I gasped, desperate, but I knew it wouldn't work. The manacles weren't secure. They wouldn't lock. "Magkandado," I said again, even as darkness gripped me in its claws and dragged me under.

11

THE NEXT MORNING, I woke on the floor of my room.

Bright sunlight poured in from the windows, beaming down on top of me like a spotlight, and I thought I was still dreaming. It was so warm and safe. But when I finally opened my eyes, the first thing I saw were the manacles lying beside me, unlocked. Last night crept back into my mind. I didn't get them on in time; I had changed. And I had escaped.

I dragged myself up and looked around.

My room was a mess. The bed was stripped of all its sheets, the pillows clawed to shreds, and feathers littered the floor. The privacy screen lay on its side; my wardrobe was scattered all over the room. A fist-sized hole had been punched into the vanity mirror.

I didn't remember doing any of this.

The balcony doors were still open, letting in a gentle breeze.

Last night came back to me in bits and pieces like a dream— the feeling of flying, the smell of fear, the taste of . . . I looked at my hands. They were covered in blood, sticky and dark and cold.

I scrambled to my feet and went to the bathroom to wash my

hands, but there I saw the missing sheets from the bed had been stuffed into the tub, completely covered in blood. The floor, too, was smeared in it, but it looked like I had tried to clean it up in a semiconscious state. There was so much blood. Too much.

"Please tell me I didn't hurt someone," I whispered.

When I glanced at myself in the mirror, I half expected to see that monstrous face, but it was only me. Pale, exhausted. A scared girl.

I turned on the faucet to soak the sheets with cold water, but it only made them worse. I scrubbed at the sheets with soap, trying to get out the stains, but they weren't worth saving. The harder I scrubbed, the worse it got. The water became a horrible shade of pink, and the air smelled like iron. I sat on the edge of the tub and stared at the mess I'd made.

I knew I had killed something and eaten it. I could feel it in me—a satiated hunger that didn't feel like it belonged to me. It belonged to something else. And it would be hungry again.

I tried not to cry. It was getting worse. *I* was getting worse.

I left the sheets in the tub and scrubbed the blood off my hands before I went and tidied my room. What clothes I hadn't torn to shreds last night in a blind rage I put back into my luggage, and the rest I threw in the tub with the ruined sheets. Everything was going to have to go. Most of the clothes Jinky had packed for me were rags now. What was left were some of my T-shirts from the human world that I wore to sleep, a few Maria Clara dresses, and a couple pairs of jean shorts. It wasn't the wardrobe of a queen, but it would have to be enough.

I chose a T-shirt-and-shorts combination and tied my hair up into a ponytail as I rushed out the door. When I did, voices were coming from down the hall. I'd heard them before they saw me.

"—a winged monster, that's what he said!"

"A stable boy? How do we know he's not lying?"

"He sounded convincing enough!"

They were a pair of laundry maids, both of them carrying stacks of clean sheets and walking toward me.

My stomach dropped when I realized they were headed to my room. I put on a tight smile and stood in front of my door. "Good morning!"

The laundry maids jumped when I greeted them. They clammed up, quickly curtsying. Their eyes went round, and their faces paled. "Your Majesty! We didn't recognize you."

"Sorry!" I said, a little breathless. "I didn't mean to startle you."

"Not at all, Your Majesty," the maid with her pink hair tied into a long braid said.

"Is there something we can do for you?" the maid with large, innocent eyes asked.

"Um," I said, trying to think. "Sorry. I couldn't help but overhear. Who saw a monster?"

The laundry maids looked at each other, shocked, but the one with the long braid said, "A stable boy. He said he'd seen a monster with claws flying around last night."

My heart hitched, but I tried not to show it. I folded my arms over my chest and tilted my head to the side. "What kind of monster? What did it do?"

"He says it was a manananggal, but that's unlikely. He said it killed one of the horses. Came out of the night sky, screeching like a banshee, and picked up the horse by the neck and carried it into the jungle."

The other maid nodded, still pale.

"Did it hurt anyone or anything else?" I asked.

"No, Your Majesty," the doe-eyed maid said. "Just the horse."

Something like relief worked its way through me. I felt awful that I'd killed something, let alone a horse, but at least I hadn't hurt a person. That would explain why there was so much blood in my room.

"Oh," I said. "That sounds terrifying."

The maids nodded.

The pink-haired maid continued. "At first no one believed him. Edgardo thought the stable boy was careless and let the horse run loose, making up an excuse so he wouldn't get in trouble, but the guards found some parts of it in the jungle this morning . . ." She took a deep breath, a blush appearing on her cheeks. "I apologize. I am speaking too much. I do not mean to alarm you, Your Majesty. It's likely a great bird of prey."

"You should have nothing to fear," the doe-eyed one said.

A look must have crossed my face despite my best efforts to remain calm. When I'd broken out during the night, I had eaten most of a horse without waking up. Was the monster growing stronger? I tried my best to smile. "I'm just thankful the stable boy wasn't hurt."

"Indeed, Your Majesty," the pink-haired maid said.

I tried to steady my pounding heart and gestured to the sheets in their arms. "Are you bringing those to my room?" I asked.

The doe-eyed one held out her stack. "Yes. Clarissa told us you didn't want to be disturbed, but we were coming to turn down your bed."

"You don't have to do that," I said.

The girl looked confused. "You don't want fresh sheets?"

They couldn't see the state of my room. I had to keep them out. "Is that okay?" I asked.

They both stared at me, cheeks flushed, but neither of them could muster up the ability to speak. I don't think they had ever been asked by a royal for their permission to do—or, rather, not do—something.

I explained, "I'd like to do my own laundry, if that's not too much trouble. I don't want to take your job from you, but . . . doing my own laundry makes me feel independent again . . . You know, like before I was queen." I wanted to say "like normal," but nothing about any of this was normal, and I decided against it.

The maids glanced at each other, but neither of them seemed bothered when I explained it that way.

"Of course, Your Majesty. As you wish."

I was probably breaking a dozen house rules, but I didn't care. I thanked them when they handed me the sheets and left, heading toward the other rooms. I watched them go, my throat tight, before I went back into my room to hide the evidence.

THE AIR IN the house had changed. Either I was imagining it, or there was a nervous electricity to it. Every servant I passed seemed to be talking about the same thing: a monster. But their conversations quickly shifted once they noticed me.

I kept my head low, trying to stay unnoticed, but it was difficult. Everyone knew me, and I couldn't hide, no matter how hard I tried. People greeted me as I walked the halls of the great house, and I did my best to greet them in return, but the whole time, I was fearful that someone would scream, point at me, and call me out for what I truly was. But no one did. No one suspected that their queen was secretly turning into a monster at night and terrorizing the land. Who would ever think such a thing?

When I reached the main foyer, I heard shouts coming from the lawn, but they weren't alarming. They almost sounded . . . fun. I followed the sounds of boys yelling and cheering.

In the courtyard, Qian and his men were in the middle of an intense game of sipa, which was kind of like if soccer and volleyball fell in love and had a baby: Two teams of four kicked a ball back and forth across a net, trying to get the ball to hit the ground on the other side.

They shouted to one another, leaping and kicking the ball over the net like martial artists. It was almost hypnotic watching them flying through the air. Qian drew my eye first, especially with how he smiled and clapped every time they scored a point. He'd noticed me when I arrived but hadn't stopped playing.

Nix, Amador, and Lucas sat near a table where breakfast had been served. I was so late, I'd missed most of it. From her seat, Nix heard me coming and looked up from a plate of sliced mango. Nix's dark eyes brightened when she noticed me, and she smiled.

For once, she looked well-rested. This trip was at least doing her some favors, and I was grateful she could have a break. I, on the other hand, felt absolutely miserable. My stomach churned when I thought about eating anything.

"MJ!" Nix said. "You're awake!"

"Yeah," I said, trying to smile.

My eyes drifted to Lucas and Amador, who was lounging on one of the rattan deck chairs, her blue-black hair pooling across her shoulders. She wore a bikini and a large sun hat with equally large sunglasses, really bringing the concept of *vacation* to the vacation home. She didn't acknowledge me, even though she knew I was there.

Lucas was standing behind her, his arms folded tightly across his chest. I couldn't help but notice that he was dressed casually, too, in a loose tunic and linen pants, but his dagger was seemingly permanently attached to his hip. Even though we were on a retreat, he didn't seem relaxed. I wondered if he'd also heard talk about the monster and was taking extra precautions. His gaze was firmly fixed on the sipa match, his brow furrowed.

Something pricked my heart when I saw him, but I took a deep breath and went to Nix.

"Did you sleep okay?" Nix asked, setting down her plate.

"Yeah! Really good," I said, and Nix's eyes narrowed slightly. I swiftly changed the subject. "Sorry I missed breakfast. I'm glad you all didn't wait for me."

"Of course, we want the queen to get as much beauty rest as possible," Amador said from her spot on the deck chair. The insult was more than obvious—even Lucas scowled, but he didn't stick up for me, either, and somehow that hurt even more.

I bit my tongue and turned my attention back to the table of food, piling a plate for myself with what was left over, even though I wasn't hungry. The garlic rice set the hair on the back of my neck on end, so I avoided it.

"I'm glad to see Qian is enjoying himself," I said to Nix. "Hopefully that puts him in a good mood to talk about you staying with us."

Nix wasn't buying the topic change. She inspected me with a critical eye that I forced myself to ignore. If I pretended like everything was fine, then maybe it would be.

"Are you okay?" she whispered.

"I'm good!" When Nix gave me a doubtful frown, I added, "I'm just feeling a little under the weather, that's all."

Nix was the absolute last person I should have said that to. She pinched her lips, and concern drew her brows together. "What's going on with you?"

"Nothing!"

She snatched the plate of food out of my hand and set it back on the table, then grabbed me by the wrist and dragged me into the house. I was too tired to protest, and she led me into the salt room, closing the door behind us for privacy.

"What's wrong?" she whispered. "Tell me."

I wanted to tell her it was nothing, that I could handle it, but it was no use. I couldn't keep this up forever. She would know I was lying, no matter how many times I told her I wasn't.

I let out a strangled sigh and sat down on one of the carved salt chairs, then immediately leapt up with a yelp. The parts of my skin that had touched the salt felt like they were on fire.

Nix let out a strangled cry and rushed to me, grabbing my arm and turning it toward her. "It's burned!" My skin was sizzling like I'd placed it on a hot iron, but with each passing second, the pain faded, and so did the welt. "How did . . ." She stared at my injuries for a second and then at me.

I should have known. Salt is used to ward off manananggals. The urge to cry pricked my nose.

I didn't know where to start. The last thing I wanted was for her to run screaming away from me or not believe me. I wasn't sure which would be worse.

But this was Nix. I had to trust her.

"I haven't been honest with you," I said, finally meeting her gaze. "Something's happening to me, and I don't know why."

Nix's expression morphed from frustration to confusion. She tugged my other arm toward her, and I instinctively flinched back, afraid that something bad might happen. "MJ," she pleaded. Her grip was confident and unafraid, and she brought her hands down the lengths of my arms and wrapped her fingers around my wrists. She traced my pulse, and the concern in her brow deepened.

"Your heart rate is elevated, blood pressure up, increased levels of stress hormones in your cerebral cortex . . . You're afraid."

I clenched my jaw and let her take my vitals, but I was so afraid to tell her, my hands shook. She clasped them both in her hands and leveled her eyes with mine. "MJ, what is going on with you?"

"For the past few days . . ." I started, but stopped myself, like

I was walking up to a cliff where I knew, once I jumped, I could never change my mind. I licked my lips and found comfort in her face. "For the past few nights, rather, I've been . . . changing."

"Changing?"

"Yes, I'm not me. I'm something else. And I can't stop it. They feel like nightmares, but they're real. Every night, I turn into a monster."

The word hung in the air between us for a heartbeat, but Nix didn't laugh like I expected her to. She must have felt my pulse pounding beneath my skin. "What kind of monster?" she asked.

"A manananggal."

Nix's eyes widened, and her eyebrows shot up. Her fingers twitched like she was about to let me go, but she didn't. "How?"

"I don't know." I told her about the first night it happened, how I thought it was just a nightmare, and then the second night when I attacked a couple. That I'd killed and eaten a goat instead. I told her everything, and as I spoke, her eyes only got wider. By the time I was done, I wanted to curl into a ball and hide my face. "I can't control it."

Nix stared at me for a long time and let out a shaky breath. "I healed that couple," she said, dazed. "I . . . I'd never seen anything like what happened to them."

"I feel awful. No one else can know." My throat tightened, and it felt like I was drowning. Tears started to burn my eyes, and all my fears came rushing back like a tidal wave. "Please don't tell anyone."

Nix dropped my hands and clasped my shoulders. "I won't! Of course not! I won't tell anyone, MJ, I swear!"

My head dropped, and Nix wrapped her arms around me. She held me close, squeezing me tight, and I hugged her back. Relief quelled the sludge inside me for a brief moment. It felt good finally telling someone what was happening.

After a second, she pulled away and looked deep into my eyes. "How can I help you?" she asked. "What can I do?"

"I don't know."

"It's been happening every night?"

"So far. I don't know how or why, but it's only getting worse. This morning, I woke up with more blood on my hands again. At night, I separate from my lower half and grow wings and claws, and last night, I ate a horse. I overheard the laundry maids talking about it this morning. But I don't remember any of it."

"I heard about that, too . . . So you were going to attack people? Like that couple the other night?"

"I wanted to. I mean, the manananggal wanted to . . . I tried to stop myself, I think. But I'm not sure how much longer I can hold it off."

"You didn't tell Elias?"

"No, I didn't know how. The couple that saw me when I first changed didn't recognize me. Neither did the stable hand last night. It's like I'm possessed. I'm repulsed by garlic and, I guess, salt." I looked around at the room made entirely of it and shuddered. Was this the new normal for me?

Nix, however, was in problem-solving mode. Her gaze drifted across the room, no doubt thinking about everything I'd just told her. "But what is the source of it? Do you think it's another hex from a mambabarang?"

"I read a book in the library that said it could be a curse. Whatever it is, I just want it to stop."

Nix's eyelids fluttered as she took a moment to process. "That's good, at least. We can rule stuff out."

"Have you ever heard of anything like this?" I asked, hopeful.

She shook her head and met my eyes. "No."

"Figured," I said, and wiped stray tears that had fallen onto my cheeks.

"Hey," said Nix, wiping away even more with her thumb. "That doesn't mean we're giving up."

Something that felt a lot like hope sparked in my chest. "You're not afraid of me?"

Nix screwed up her face. "Are you nuts? Why would I be afraid of you? You're my best friend!"

That made me want to sob right on the spot. Somehow, I'd thought she'd never want to speak to me again. A fearful little voice in my head had convinced me that I wasn't worthy of her love anymore because of what I was becoming, and yet here she stood. It was everything I could have asked for.

She shook me gently. "We can figure out a way. I'm sure there's something we can do. There's a pattern, so you'll probably change again tonight, right?"

My stomach dropped at the idea. "Probably. I have these iron cuffs that might keep me from escaping, but I didn't get them on in time last night."

"That's why you need my help," Nix said. "I'll stay with you tonight."

"Nix, no! What if I hurt you?"

"I don't care. You need my help. If you don't remember what happens, I have to see it for myself. There may be more clues we're missing. I'm not letting you go through this alone."

"But I wanted to hurt that couple! I would have if I hadn't stopped myself!"

"Well, lucky for me, I can get my hands on some garlic and salt to protect myself, since you seem to be vulnerable to them, and I'll make sure you're chained up!"

It sounded like a terrible idea. What if I broke out? What if garlic and salt weren't enough?

"It's too dangerous, Nix," I said, shaking my head. "If I'd known before what I was turning into, I never would have invited anyone here. I would have banished myself, locked myself in a dungeon, and thrown away the key."

Nix frowned at me. "Did you think I'd abandon my friend?"

"Ask me again later when you see what I turn into."

Nix stared at me, perhaps imagining what it would look like when I transformed, but her resolve set her jaw. "You should see all the bodily fluids that I have to deal with as a healer. Nothing can surprise me."

Her confidence actually calmed me down somewhat. I felt better knowing that she was on my side now, and I wouldn't have to spend the remainder of the trip hiding this secret from her, but I was still dreading tonight.

"Obviously you can't tell your brother," I said. "Qian, Amador, not even Lucas can know what's happening. If Qian finds out I'm a monster . . ." I choked on the word.

"Secret's safe with me," she said, crossing her finger over her chest. "But first, you need to stop calling yourself a monster." Before I could protest, she held up her hand. "Second, we need to get all that blood out of your sheets. Fortunately for you, I know just the thing."

NIX'S HEALING POWERS proved quite effective when cleaning up blood. She waved her hand above the tub, and the blood on the sheets and staining the water disappeared like it'd never been there. "It's all part of being a healer," she said. "It's one of the first things I learned as an apprentice. The key to good medicine is cleanliness."

The sheets looked good as new, even if they were still soaking wet, and my worry disappeared like the blood. With Nix's help, I could at least keep the evidence of my secret under control.

When that was taken care of, Nix helped me clean the rest of my room, which was not something her healing powers could help with. She held up my ruined clothing and clicked her tongue over the state of my wardrobe while I told her everything that I'd discovered in the records room, including how there was a missing Princess Yara Liliana who had been erased from history.

"So a manananggal is seen around the same time a princess goes missing?" Nix asked. "Smells fishy to me."

"You don't think she could have been the manananggal, do you?" I asked. I'd been thinking about it, too, but never before could I bounce the idea off anyone else.

"It makes sense why they would want to pretend like she never existed. It would look bad if the ruler of Biringan was hunting people at night." That much was evident.

"I have to know what happened to her. I hired Romulo to find more information about her for me."

"Romulo? The pirate guy we met?"

"Yeah. It's one of the only clues I have to follow." It was easy to succumb to despair and wallow in self-pity, but I had to do my best to believe that I could fix things.

Nix crumpled up one of my Maria Clara dresses that had been torn in two and said, "It is pretty weird. Though do you really think Romulo can find anything?"

"If he can't, no one can."

Nix hummed, put her hands on her hips, and looked at the pile of clothes that I'd ruined. "Girl, we have got to get you a new wardrobe."

"That's kind of the last thing on my mind right now," I said. "Plus, with trying to convince your brother not to drag you back to Jade Mountain, my clothes are the least of my problems."

"You still need to keep up appearances. You're a queen."

"I can't be a queen if I'm a flesh-eating monster."

Nix harrumphed, lost in thought. Idly, she went to the broken mirror and traced her fingers over the cracks in the glass and then looked at the flowers I had dropped on the floor, the blue petals wilted and faded now, I hoped she wouldn't ask about them. I didn't know what she would feel if she knew they were from Qian. I wasn't sure how *I* felt about it, either. Thankfully, she didn't seem interested in them. I could see behind her eyes that her mind was already working.

"You said you start transforming during the night, right?" she asked.

"As far as I know. The book I read about manananggals didn't have many answers."

"Then we find our own." She ran her tongue against her cheek, her hands on her hips.

I knew that look. "What are you thinking?" I asked.

"What if I put you to sleep? Like, a deep sleep?"

I raised an eyebrow. "Like . . . a coma?"

"Kind of. I know of some herbs that can help with insomnia. I read about them in *The Mysterious Properties of Magical Herbs* by Lady Elowina. What if I make you a potion that will knock you out? It might be strong enough to knock out the manananggal, too."

Images of Snow White and Sleeping Beauty came to mind. Sleeping like the dead. If it was strong enough, maybe . . . If the manananggal was asleep, it could mean I wouldn't have to worry about hurting anyone. "Nix," I said, heart leaping. "You are brilliant."

Nix's smile was infectious.

Together, we headed out of the main house and toward the jungle. Nix mentioned that some of the herbs could be found in the mountains. Even though they were harmless on their own, they were a powerful sleeping potion when combined. But the fact that the recipe came from the book written by the mambabarang that had tried to kill me was less than comforting.

"You sure this isn't too dangerous?" I asked.

"Ninety percent sure," she said, picking up a wicker basket from a stack near the kitchens. "Okay, eighty-five. I'll make an antidote just in case."

I would take those odds. I was so exhausted, getting knocked over the head with a club sounded just as tempting. I trusted Nix, though. With her on my side, tonight wouldn't be so bad.

We didn't see anyone while we walked on the lawn, skirting the outer edges of the jungle, until we came upon a group of people near the front gate. There, Edgardo was speaking with some of the gardeners and other groundskeepers.

"I want all of you to be on high alert," Edgardo said. "A curfew will be in place at sunset so as to avoid any more encounters with the creature. The last thing we want is an incident that could endanger anyone." When he noticed me approaching, his eyes went wide, and he bowed at the waist. "Apologies, Your Majesty. I wanted to speak to you in person. We have rumors of a monster lurking near the grounds."

"I heard," I said. The gardeners and groundskeepers looked uneasy, and I didn't blame them. They bowed and curtsied to me as well, but the fear never left their eyes. If I didn't know what was happening, either, I would have been scared, too. "Please listen to Edgardo," I told them. "For your own safety, until we can get the matter resolved, stay indoors at night. For now, I don't think you have anything to worry about, though, not until darkness falls."

I glanced at Nix, and she nodded reassuringly.

Edgardo looked at me quizzically but decided not to press. He dismissed the groundskeepers and turned to me and Nix. "Might I ask where you are headed today?"

"We are simply appreciating the outdoors," Nix said. "It's too beautiful here to stay inside."

Edgardo seemed to take pride in that. "Ah yes. Well, be sure to be careful around the property. The mountain holds plenty of secrets, magical and mundane in nature. Might I recommend the hot spring or the waterfall? Your friend Amador was readying to take a ride."

He held out his arm and gestured toward Amador, who was sitting proudly atop her horse with a stable boy leading it by the reins. I was about to tell Edgardo that she wasn't my friend, but I held my tongue. "Thank you, Edgardo. If you'd be so kind, please tell the rest of the staff of the curfew. Everyone's safety is of the utmost importance until we can get everything under control."

"Of course, Your Majesty." Edgardo snapped his heels together and bowed, then walked away. But before we could slip away into the jungle, Amador and the stable boy arrived. Amador dismissed the stable boy and adjusted her kid gloves.

"Having a good time?" I asked, mustering a smile.

"It's not awful," she said. Her eyes lingered on Nix briefly before she looked at me. "Did you hear of the monster?"

"Oh, I figured it was right in front of me." I thought I was being exceptionally clever, but a bitterness on my tongue made the moment less sweet. I knew I was being catty, but it felt good to lash out for a bit. Amador's frown was worth it at first. Then my satisfaction ebbed away, and the bitterness stayed in my mouth.

Amador made a snooty little snort and said, "Since you're queen, you should handle the issue."

I folded my arms across my chest. "I'm working on it."

"I heard Qian and his men talking. They want to set traps, I think."

"That's not necessary," I said.

"No?" Amador tilted her head. She looked again at Nix, who averted her gaze.

"We're dealing with it," I said.

Amador's brow furrowed. "Are you, now? Though, if you ask me, I'm not sure what you can do, seeing as you still haven't learned to control your power."

Nix spoke up, surprising even me. "Come on, Amador. Ease off."

Amador glared at Nix. "She's supposed to lead us. How can we have faith in her skills if she can't even negotiate with a neighboring kingdom?"

I was tired, admittedly cranky, and not in the mood for dealing with Amador, so I held my arm out, shielding Nix. "You have no idea what I'm going through," I said to Amador. "You can sit up there and judge all you want, but it won't change anything."

Amador sneered. "I am a very good judge of character."

"If using your power is so easy, why haven't I seen you do it? Why don't you catch the monster?"

Amador's sneer dropped.

In my time in Biringan City, I'd seen many encantos use their magic freely and without care, especially for everyday uses like boiling water or making a bed with a snap of their fingers. For the life of me, I couldn't remember if I'd ever seen Amador use hers. If I were more cynical, I would have believed that she used her magic to make herself more beautiful. But Amador's hands tightened around the reins. I'd apparently struck a nerve. Her eyes darted around, maybe searching for anyone who might overhear.

"I don't need to prove anything to you," she said. Her eyes shone, and for the briefest moment, I felt as if I'd overstepped. It was so easy being mean to Amador because she was always mean to me, but for once, it somehow didn't seem fair anymore. I was about to say something when Amador changed the subject.

"By the way, Qian is looking for you," she said. Any sign of her embarrassment had vanished.

"What for?"

"Do I look like a messenger?" With that, Amador kicked her horse and took off down the path.

I scowled after her when Nix spoke up. "Just ignore her," she said. "We've got plants to find."

FINDING THE INGREDIENTS was the easy part; actually harvesting them was the hard part. Most of them were various flower petals and blooming vines, but they were often located high in the trees, forcing me and Nix to climb to reach them. My hands and arms were so sore and scraped up, I had to hope that this would all be worth it. Nix seemed far more optimistic than me, and I would be forever grateful.

It took a while, but by the time Nix and I had gathered all the herbs, stacked high in the wicker basket, we still had a few hours left before sundown, so there was plenty of time for Nix to prepare the potion for tonight.

Just before we made it back to the house, a yell pierced through the air.

"What was that?" I asked, eyes wide.

Nix flinched and stared at me, and we took off at a full sprint through the gate and onto the lawn. But when I bolted around the corner, blood running cold, I found Qian, General Heng, and Lucas grouped with the others from Jade Mountain in the yard at ease, under the shade of a palm tree. Farther away on the grass, a man in a green uniform stood near a pile of clay discs.

"What's going on?" I asked. And what was Lucas doing with them?

Nix stared at the group, looking grim. "Nothing good, I imagine."

We walked over just as Qian stepped in front of the others and hefted a bow in one hand, pulling an arrow with another. He was dressed for a day of sport, in breeches and a long shirt with the sleeves rolled up to allow for leather bracers to protect his forearms. He raised the bow and yelled, "Pull!"

The servant in the green uniform raised his arms, and a gust of wind lifted one of the clay discs up into the air so high, the disc turned into a speck.

Qian tracked the disc, following its movements through the sky. The game master moved the clay disc erratically, making it doubly hard, but Qian's eyes were narrow, focused. He let loose. The arrow whizzed through the air, smashing the disc into bits from five hundred feet away. He was an incredible shot.

His men cheered when Qian lowered the bow, grinning with victory. Lucas stood by in silence, his arms folded firmly over his chest, his expression unreadable.

Nix leaned in close to me. "That's Qian's power. He can't miss."

My heart beat rapidly against my rib cage, and I swallowed down the nerves bubbling up my throat.

Lucas was the first to notice us. The muscles in his jaw clenched before he looked away. My lungs almost forgot to take in air. Was Lucas going to join them in hunting me?

Grinning, Qian returned to the group, striding with earned confidence, and approached Lucas. "Go on, Sir Lucas!" Qian said, thrusting the bow toward him. "Give it a try."

Lucas held up his hand, palm out. "I'm good."

"What, never done it before?"

Lucas shook his head. "I'm not in the business of hunting."

"A moral stance, is it?"

Lucas squinted into the bright sky like he was checking for signs of a winged monster. "I prefer different opponents. Preferably ones who can fight back."

Qian looked amused. "A monster isn't a worthy adversary?"

"I didn't say that."

"Well, if you want to protect your queen, you should get some practice in. That monster could swoop down and take a bite." By then, Qian had noticed me, and his smile widened. "And a prettier creature graces us with her presence."

I stepped out onto the lawn while Qian's men broke off to drink fresh water and eat snacks. Lucas's eyes lingered on me for the briefest moment before he cleared his throat and secured his arms behind his back. He bowed to me, as was customary, and didn't say or do anything more. Qian, ignoring the formalities, came to me.

"You were looking for me?" I asked, attempting to sound casual. I couldn't help but stare at the quiver full of arrows at his hip and imagine what it would feel like to be shot with one. "Amador mentioned you wanted to speak."

"We heard rumors of a monster," he said. "Some sort of flesh-eating, bloodsucking creature." His eyes went to the herbs in Nix's basket, and his brow furrowed. "Were you two in the jungle?"

"Only for a little bit. We think the monster is nocturnal," said Nix.

Qian wiped sweat from his forehead with the back of his hand and said, "Can't be too careful. The both of you should stay close."

"We know," I said. "A curfew sounds like an excellent idea while we investigate further. Wouldn't want anyone to be harmed."

"Of course, everyone's safety is the top priority. Second, though, is preparedness. Do you like it?" He showed me the bow, mistaking my staring at it for interest. "It's my favorite."

"It's a beautiful weapon," I said. It was a carved wood, burned black, polished to a glossy shine. It looked deadly, even at rest.

"Would you like to try a shot?"

"Um . . ." My eyes flicked toward Lucas, who looked impassive. I couldn't tell what he was thinking. Heat welled up inside me for some reason. I wasn't sure I wanted to, but I nodded. "Sure."

Qian smiled, and my heart skipped as I saw genuine warmth there. He was excited to share. "Have you ever used one before?"

I shook my head and stepped up to the spot on the lawn where Qian had shot from. I expected him to hand the bow over, but instead, he placed it in my hand, and then he moved around me, pressing himself up against my back while he threaded an arrow from his hand into mine. His touch sent a thrill down my spine. I leaned into the sturdiness of him as he situated me into position, locking my fingers for me around the bowstring. Then he dragged his hands up my arms, and his breath was hot on my ear. "Now think of the bow like an extension of yourself. Don't look at the arrow. Simply feel."

I tried to maintain my composure, but his being so close felt like an electric current was surging through my skin. My gaze flicked toward Lucas, whose eyes were firmly on the ground, his jaw clenched so tightly, I wondered if he might crack a tooth. A slithering feeling of satisfaction snaked its way through my gut. I'd had to watch him and Amador for so long, so how did it feel now?

The bow was heavier than I imagined, and the leather wrap was still warm from where Qian had held it. His face hovered over my shoulder, his chest pressed up against my back. Surprisingly enough, I didn't mind how close Qian was. It was like he'd enveloped me in his arms, shielding me from the world. He helped me pull back the string, and the bow flexed obediently. He called for the game master to fire a clay disc. "Pull!"

The disc shot into the sky, but I didn't let loose.

"Easy," Qian whispered in my ear, helping me track the projectile. "Just watch. Focus on the target."

The disc hovered high over our heads, and for a moment, I imagined the disc had bat wings, bloody claws, and no legs. A manananggal. Me.

Qian mistook my momentary panic for nerves.

"Steady now," Qian said. His hands grasped my forearms gently and lined the sight up with the clay disc as it bobbed in the air. "Don't hesitate. Let your mind go blank. Once you've got it in your sights, let loose."

I released the bowstring, and the arrow shot out, whistling like a bullet. The arrow hit the disc straight on, splitting it in half. Too easily could I imagine the arrow piercing through flesh. I even felt the pain, heard the inhuman scream wrench from my own throat, and I lowered the bow. I was numbly aware that Qian's party was applauding me, and it took me a moment to gather myself before I turned to them and gave a cute curtsy. Qian's eyes were bright while he clapped and beamed.

"Excellent shot," he said. "The monster won't stand a chance against you."

"I would hope not." I gave him my best smile as I returned his bow to him, but inside I felt like screaming.

I excused myself, but Qian called my name.

"Be careful, MJ," he said. "Dangers may be lurking around every corner."

"I can take care of myself," I said.

"I am sure you can," Qian said. "I look forward to our talks later."

My stomach clenched. It was already so late. "Tomorrow, after you've had your fun."

Qian smiled at me, but Lucas's eyes remained on the ground, even when I walked past him to rejoin Nix and head back to the great house.

I didn't want to think about the idea that if Qian or any of the others knew that I was the monster, they wouldn't hesitate to shoot.

12

BEFORE SUNSET, NIX had finished the potion. By the time she gave it to me, I had already locked the manacles into place, securing myself to the tree trunk in the middle of my room. I wasn't going to make the same mistake this time. In case the sleeping potion didn't work, I didn't want to risk hurting Nix.

I'd moved the bed closer so I would be able to lie down while still chained properly to the tree trunk. It was messy, but it would have to do. I tugged on the manacles again and again, double-checking that I was secure, but the only way to know if it worked would be to find out tomorrow. My nerves were a jumbled mess in my stomach, like I'd eaten a colony of ants, a combination of anticipation for what was going to come and the uncertainty of Nix's sleeping potion.

"Are you ready?" Nix asked, handing the glass to me. The liquid inside was a murky brown, looking and smelling like swamp water, but I couldn't be squeamish. I needed to do this.

The last thing I remembered was putting the potion to my lips.

MY DREAMS THAT night were nothing but a world full of red: bloody claws, a river of entrails, and burning hunger. Ravenous, desperate, pleading. It was all emotion, flashing like a shutter on a camera, broken by my own vicious need to be free.

When I woke up, I saw red. But it was only the morning light. It washed over me, dragging me from sleep. After a moment, I jerked, and the chains rattled when I did. I was still secured to the tree trunk and lying on my bed. The iron cuffs around my wrists had left a red ring on my skin that was still hot to the touch, but I was human again.

I looked around the room. No blood and no entrails, but no Nix.

My heart pounded. "Nix?" My throat was raw and hurt. It was like I'd slept with my mouth open and my tongue had turned into sandpaper, but I knew better. My saliva tasted like pennies. I had transformed last night; that was for sure.

But where was Nix?

"Nix!" I called again, louder.

There was a sound coming from behind my bathroom door, and it opened. Nix appeared, her face pale, but relief washed over her features. "You're back," she said.

"Did it happen?" I asked.

"Yeah," she said, her voice small.

"The potion, then—did it work?"

She shook her head. Slowly, she came into the room and

looked around. "That was . . . a lot. But you didn't escape. That's what matters."

Tears stung my eyes, and I tried to blink them away. "Nix, I'm so sorry."

"Don't apologize! I wanted to see it for myself. Now I know what we're dealing with."

I spoke the word to unlock my manacles, and they snapped open. When I was free, I rubbed my wrists, appreciating the coolness of my fingers against the heat of the burn.

Nix sat on the edge of my bed and handed me a glass of water. I drank it greedily. I was so thirsty, but thankfully not for blood.

"What did I do?" I asked, wiping my mouth with the back of my wrist.

"What's the last thing you remember?"

"The potion, and . . . nothing. What happened?"

"Well, the second you drank the potion, you got this look on your face . . . like super calm. I asked you if everything was okay, and you answered, saying everything was fine. I almost believed you, too. And you asked why you were wearing chains and if I could take them off, and that's when I knew something wasn't right. I said I'd go and get you something to drink, and when I came back, you were . . ." A flurry of emotions passed over Nix's face, and she composed herself as best she could. "I came back, and your legs were standing upright at the foot of your bed." She pointed as if they were still there. "And your upper half was . . ."

She looked like she didn't want to say, but I pleaded with her. "Please, Nix. Did I try to attack you?"

"No, your upper half was still chained up. Your arms were cuffed to the tree. When you heard me come in, you started thrashing around, but you couldn't break free. I almost dropped the glass of water when you looked at me; I barely recognized you. You kept screaming that you were starving, begging me over and over again to let you go. Obviously I didn't."

It was easy to imagine it. My leathery bat wings, my sharp claws and teeth, my blood-red eyes. I thought about how scared Nix must have been when she saw me. My gaze snagged on the gouges in the wood of the tree trunk where the cuffs had scraped against the bark. But it had held. I hadn't hurt anyone last night. I rubbed at the raw skin on my wrists again, and Nix surprised me by pulling me into a hug and squeezing me so tight, I gasped.

"Whatever is causing this, we'll figure it out," she said. "I promise."

"The iron worked, at least," I said. "It was strong enough to hold me."

"That's a good sign. Now we just have to figure out how we can stop it altogether. I'm sorry the potion was a failure."

"It wasn't a failure. We just know now that the monster is a lot stronger than I thought. We can try again tonight."

"I might kill you if I make a stronger potion." Nix pulled away and smiled. At least the color was starting to return to her face. I felt awful for scaring her. I wasn't sure where I'd be without her. She was so brave, especially now that she saw me for what I really was. I was ashamed, but she didn't seem bothered in the slightest. In fact, behind the worry in her eyes, there was a sparkle. This was a new mystery to solve.

We both got dressed and went to breakfast, which was served in the pavilion. Everyone except Lucas was already there. They were all laughing and chatting, seemingly without a care in the world. Food was plentiful, and the mood was light. Mercifully, with me under control, there had been no more sightings of the monster lurking the grounds.

I sat with Nix, pretending like I didn't exist while the others continued their conversation.

Every sunset, I would become a monster. And I had no idea how to stop it.

"I hope it hasn't been scared off," General Heng said, leaning over the table to pluck a grape from a bowl, then popping it into his mouth. *It.* I had full clarity on what they were talking about.

"It's a monster; it isn't scared," said Qian, smiling confidently and glancing around at all of us at the table. "It'll be back." If he was disappointed he didn't get to hunt a monster, he didn't show it.

I was even more tired than before. I hadn't had a wink of sleep, and my eyes felt like they were full of sand. The conversation around the table turned into a drone, and I stared at my full plate of food that nauseated me, wondering what else I could do, barely listening as General Heng said they'd faced a similar monster last year.

Heng had the entire table's attention, including Amador's, while he told the story about Qian's heroics. Qian, meanwhile, leaned back in his chair, a small, amused smile on his face as if he was thinking fondly back on that time.

"So there he was, one arrow left, bleeding profusely from where the Aoyin tore into him, and the creature stared him down for the final kill."

Nix shifted uncomfortably next to me, but I kept my attention on the plate, trying to freeze my face into an expression of impassivity, almost boredom. I didn't want to let them in on the fact that my insides were corkscrewing with nerves at the talk of monsters.

"What happened next?" Amador asked. She seemed highly interested in the story, practically on the edge of her seat.

"I killed it, of course," Qian said, grinning. "Shot it straight through the heart."

THE SECOND I stepped into the jungle, I felt like I could breathe again. After breakfast, I'd excused myself to go for a walk. Alone. The cacophony of birdsong and the smell of blossoming hibiscus overwhelmed my senses, drowning everything else out and letting me forget for a brief moment that I was a queen and a monster.

There was plenty of time until sundown, and I needed a few hours to myself. I had terrified Nix, even though she had denied it. I felt miserable; I was on the verge of tears with each passing second. It was hard to think about anything else when my body was reminding me that I was losing myself further every night. I sensed, deep down, that the manananggal was gaining strength. I hadn't been in control of my body last night, and I had a sinking feeling that the manananggal wanted it that way. How much longer until it took over for good?

Bugs and birds, buzzing and cawing from invisible places in the jungle, surrounded me while I walked along a dirt path. I imagined this path was used by animals making their way through the underbrush, and I trusted they knew where they were going, so I followed. I remembered Edgardo's warning about the various magical trappings in the surrounding area, but I was too exhausted to care. And I wasn't frightened of any dangerous animals that might be lurking in the underbrush. If anything, they should be frightened of me.

I came upon a small stream of crystal clear water, glittering in the dappled sunlight, and decided to follow it up the mountain, toward its source. I spent a while hiking uphill and was drenched in sweat and covered in bug bites by the time I heard the sound of rushing water, louder than before.

I crested a ridge and came upon a waterfall pouring down the mountainside from so high that I couldn't see the top. Behind the curtain of water was a cave that opened into the mountain, where even more water rushed out. It kind of reminded me of the springs back home, but here, the air itself pulsed with magic. I could feel it tickling my skin, making the hair on the back of my neck stand on end. But this didn't feel like dangerous magic. Instead, it felt like the kind in the human world, like a perfect summer afternoon with my mom, drinking lemonade on the steps of the library. Time had seemed to stop then—when the light was low but the crickets had come out, as though the world itself was holding its breath. It was one of those magical moments that stuck with me whenever I thought about paradise.

Curious, I stepped into the cave, and immediately, the air got cooler but no less humid. It was almost like I really had walked into a beast's mouth. Despite the darkness, I never had to strain my eyes to see. I followed the creek flowing down the tunnel, and the longer I walked, the more I noticed that the rocks around me glowed with a soft pink light. The air in here was thicker, too, like the magic was more condensed. It had a softly sweet and floral scent, like honey and roses.

This was no ordinary cave. At the end, it opened up into a large cavern the size of my room at the great house, with a natural spring in the middle. Stalactites jutted down from the ceiling, and glittering droplets of water fell on the stalagmites below. The spring burbled, and steam came off the surface. When I put my hand in the water, it was hot but not uncomfortable.

As I dragged my hand in the water, the churning, frenetic, anxious thoughts in my mind immediately softened, like massaging a knot out of a muscle, and I let out a sigh of relief. Similar to taking a sip of hot wine, warmth spread in my stomach, and my eyes drifted closed.

Distantly, I was aware that this was not a normal feeling, that this was probably caused by some kind of magic, but for once, I felt so at ease. I was thankful for the reprieve, even though I knew it was artificial. I didn't care. There wasn't anything to be afraid of.

I was . . . content. Happy, even. So comfortable that I didn't realize I was pulling off my clothes and wading into the spring. I was operating without thinking, just like when I turned into a manananggal. But it wasn't scary at all.

I dipped below the surface, soaking my hair, and came up for air again, breathing deeply, finally relaxing. Steam surrounded me while I floated on my back. No one would find me here, and maybe it was better this way. Maybe I could float forever.

The sound of a boot on hard rock behind me made me whip around.

"Lucas," I barely managed to say without choking on his name. Instinctually, I dipped lower in the water so he could only see my head.

Lucas stared at me, eyes wide, and when he looked at the clothes piled on the cave floor in front of him, he had the decency to spin around to face the wall. Even though the cave light was pink, I could see the blush on his neck.

"MJ. What are you doing here?" he asked, his back still to me.

I swam to the edge of the pool and pulled myself out, even though I yearned to go back underwater, ignore him, and let him wonder. "I was just . . . I needed to clear my head and took a walk. What are you doing here?"

"I was, uh . . . doing the same." He was the type of person to find solace in taking a swim. I didn't blame him, especially with everything that was going on lately.

I pulled my clothes back on and wrung my hair out.

This was an almost exact replay of our encounter months ago, though our roles had been reversed. I'd found him bathing in the waterfall near the gardens and accused him of being behind the murders at the palace. I remembered how frustrated I'd been with him, how I was so suspicious of his actions. But he proved his innocence, and after then, we'd teamed up. I'd thought about our conversation at the waterfall a lot since then—just how wrong we'd both been about each other. I'd changed so much since I met him, and he'd changed, too. I thought we could really be something together.

"You're good," I said to him. He chanced a look over his shoulder and turned back around, though the color never left his cheeks.

Here we stood, like strangers, separated by all the things we couldn't say to each other.

"I'll go," we both said at the same time, and I knew I was blushing as hard as he was, purely based on the fact that my face felt like the surface of the sun.

It was worth noting that neither of us moved, as if we were waiting for the other to do something first.

"I'm sorry to interrupt you. I didn't know anyone would be here," he said finally. "I didn't mean to . . ."

"I get it. I didn't think anyone would find me . . . How'd you know about this place?"

"Stumbled upon it on the first day. A little secret spot. It's the one place I can get some privacy."

"What is this?" I gestured to the glowing stones and the shimmering water. "It's magical, right?"

"I think it's some sort of wishing well."

"Like, if I throw a coin in it, a wish will come true?"

"No, more like the things you want reveal themselves to you when you're here. It brings out your heart's desire. But it's only a theory. I just know when I'm here, I feel more at ease, and that's hard to come by these days."

So that explained why he had been missing at breakfast. I knew what he meant. Maybe there really was something magical in the air, because it felt like I had too many sips of wine, and I was already imagining myself curled up against a pile of rocks and taking a nap. I had to shake my head a little to clear it.

You want him . . . The voice in my head was my own, but it came from someplace deep inside, unknown to even myself. If I didn't know any better, I would have thought it had come from the cave.

Lucas was watching me with a kind of softness that made my insides turn to melted chocolate. That was normal whenever Lucas was around, but there was something about the way I felt that didn't seem quite natural. It was like my body was a pot of simmering water, and an invisible hand had turned up the heat, sending it into a full boil.

To break the tension, I said, "Edgardo warned us about magical traps around the house. Do you think this could be one?"

"I don't think it's dangerous. It feeds into the hot springs and all the rivers."

"That doesn't mean it's not dangerous."

"My power is sensing when there's danger. I don't feel it here."

"So this is where you've been disappearing to since we got here?" I didn't mean to sound accusatory, but it came out that way.

"Sometimes. Being in that house makes me feel like I'm suffocating."

I had seen him and Amador outside that evening, the way he held her hand, and *he* felt like he was suffocating? I almost laughed. "Not having a nice trip with Amador?"

Lucas's eyes softened. He took in a breath like he wanted to say something, but he didn't. The small voice in my head encouraged me to act on my deepest desire to reach out and touch his face. I fought against that impulse and clenched my fists. Lucas, too, clenched his.

"At least you and Qian seem to be becoming friends," I said.

"Is that what you think?"

I raised an eyebrow, confused. "You were with him at archery practice. You share similar interests."

"He has his qualities, good and bad."

"Don't we all?"

"I suppose," Lucas said, a hint of amusement crinkling the corners of his dark eyes. "But we don't exactly see eye to eye when it comes to certain things."

"Like the monster?"

He nodded. "Though I know it isn't something we should ignore. It's dangerous."

"No," I said, heart sinking. "I suppose we shouldn't."

Telling Lucas about what was happening to me was out of the question.

"I don't like Qian, though," Lucas said.

"Why?"

Lucas was having a hard time articulating it. "The way he looks at you, it sets all my nerves on end." He shook his head, like he was clearing his own thoughts, and asked, "Are you and Qian courting?"

"What? No! I'm trying to figure out how to help Nix." Then I remembered the flowers he'd brought for me. Did Lucas know? Had he seen Qian picking the flowers earlier? Had Lucas overheard Qian saying something? My chest tightened when Lucas stepped toward me, and I instinctively stepped back. I didn't want him to get too close. What if he saw that there was something wrong with me? What if he saw what I was turning into?

Even if he weren't with Amador, how could he possibly love me now?

"I don't think I can court anyone else," I said. Something like relief washed across Lucas's face, but accusation came across mine. "Why would you care? You're marrying Amador."

Lucas huffed loudly through his nose. "It doesn't stop the way I feel."

Any anger that came naturally when I was with him had been muted. My desperation won out. I had to know. "Then how do you feel? Tell me. For once."

Maybe the cave was affecting him, too, because his eyes were bright, vibrant, as if he'd downed an entire bottle of wine.

"When he was touching you, when you were learning to shoot that bow . . ." Lucas was so close now, I could feel his breath on my cheek. "I had this raging fire inside me. Because *I* wanted to be the one to touch you like that."

My stomach somersaulted, and heat rushed to my face. He'd echoed my own thoughts back to me. I'd thought those same words seeing him and Amador together. He was jealous of Qian. I remembered the way Lucas had looked, like he was going to be sick, and how I'd assumed it was because he didn't want to be near me. And here I thought I was the jealous one.

"I didn't know you cared," I said. I desperately wanted to reach out and touch him, but I fought myself, keeping my fists at my sides.

"I care about you so much, sometimes I think I'm losing my mind."

I care about you, too, I wanted to scream. Instead, I asked, "So, then, what are we to each other?"

"Every day when I wake up," he whispered, eyes roaming over

my face, "every moment before I go to sleep, you're in my thoughts. You're all I can think about. You haunt me."

It was getting harder to breathe. The magic of this cave was getting to my head. "It felt like you were ignoring me. Like I was invisible."

"Invisible?" He practically gasped, and his eyes went wide. "MJ, you're the only person I can look at."

Something like joy took root in my heart. "Lucas . . ." I whispered. The truth was right on the tip of my tongue, waiting to be let loose. I still loved him. My mind told me to stop, but my heart told me to tell him how I felt. "I . . . I can't stop thinking about you, either."

His gaze, half-lidded, dropped to my lips, and I could tell he wanted to kiss me. It was like nothing had changed between us, like nothing at all was standing in our way. No betrothals, no politics. We were alone, and we were together. Finally.

This time, it was my turn to show him how I felt. I leaned in, and my lips caught on his, kissing him like I always wanted. My eyes slipped closed, and all I felt was the softness of his mouth. He smelled amazing—of clean steel, a sharpness that sang. He parted his lips, and our kiss deepened, like he was releasing all the pent-up energy he'd been harnessing these past few days. We practically became one as his hands drew up my arms, caressing my skin with rough fingertips, and it sent rolling waves of pleasure rippling down my spine. Those hands were rough because they were meant to protect—to protect me—never to harm. They were rough and calloused so I would never be in danger.

His mouth tipped mine up, and it made me gasp when his

tongue slipped between my lips. And yet he was so gentle as he cradled the side of my face with one hand and held me upright with the other.

It felt so good, I was drunk off his kiss.

"MJ," he gasped against my mouth.

"Yes?" I asked, dazed.

"I . . ." He was at a loss for words. He never finished that sentence. All he could do was kiss me, and I understood. This was what he wanted. This was all he wished for. This was what I did, too.

With my arms between us, I traced my fingertips against his shirt, feeling the buttons that cinched it closed, and he seemed to have the same idea. His hands fumbled with the buttons of his shirt, and then he pulled it over his head in one fluid motion. His tan skin, bare and soft in the glowing pink light, was firm, and all I wanted to do was touch him, finding the warmth of his heart, beating under my hands.

He held the back of my head, fingers raking through my wet hair, and pulled me in. I pressed my palms against his chest and kissed him with a hunger I didn't know I had. It wasn't the normal kind of hunger; it was a deep lust that made my whole body ache. I completely forgot how angry I was with him, even though the echoes of his lie still thrummed in some distant thoughts. Heat rose inside me, flaring at first like a struck match until it felt like a bonfire was burning all my thoughts and insecurities away. All I could think about was Lucas.

He guided us to a slab of rocks near the spring, and we sank down together, lips locked. I knotted my fingers in his soft curls and my head swam as he traced his hands down my sides and dug his fingers into my skin like he was making sure I wasn't a dream. It felt like one. We were floating on waves of passion, our desire pouring out of us like a waterfall. I felt unstoppable, like I could do anything when he was with me, but at the same time, I knew if I wasn't careful, I could drown.

Lucas's breath quickened the longer we kissed, and I could feel his heartbeat hammering beneath my fingers. Up close, I admired how his long eyelashes rested on the soft skin under his closed eyes, the gentle points of his ears that poked through his hair, the straightness of his brow and how it furrowed slightly each time he kissed me, like touching me wasn't enough for him.

His eyes opened slightly, too, and he noticed me watching. His mouth curled up into a knowing smile.

But then I remembered I couldn't have him. This heart belonged to another. He was engaged to Amador.

Thump, thump, thump went his heart. I could feel it. I could *hear* it. The bonfire inside me blazed like a wildfire.

Outside this cave, I couldn't have him. And if I couldn't have him . . .

Tear his heart out of his chest!

The voice in my head sounded feral. Hungry. Ravenous.

My nails sank deeper into his flesh. The pink light from the rocks started to run red as my vision tunneled, my fingernails lengthened, and my teeth sharpened.

It's happening, I thought, in a panic.

Horrified, I shoved against Lucas's chest so hard, he stumbled back and fell to the cave floor in a heap, bewildered and wide-eyed.

Before he could see, I got to my feet and spun around, hiding my face in my hands.

"MJ? I'm—I'm sorry, this was too much . . ." He didn't sound hurt. My nails hadn't done any damage. I heard him get back to his feet, but I couldn't risk him seeing me. My hands trembled as the fire inside me sputtered out. My teeth dulled, and my finger-nails returned to their usual shape. I had almost turned into the manananggal. I had almost hurt him. I was so close, I could have killed him.

"Are you okay?" he asked.

"What—what time is it?" I asked, my voice so small. Had I lost track of the sun? Was it already nighttime?

It took Lucas a moment to answer, no doubt wondering why that was relevant. "I don't know. It might be getting late."

My heart thumped painfully in my chest. I'd totally forgotten the time. I should have been more careful. I'd let the magic of the cave get to me, my desire not entirely my own. I was dangerous. I was a monster. With the setting sun, he would see. He would know. "You have to go."

There was a twinge of hurt in his voice. "MJ, I—"

"Please," I said.

I heard him move behind me, and the shuffling of his shirt when he picked it up and pulled it on again. The human part of me wanted to tell him what was happening, that I truly wanted to be with him, and then he could at least know why I was acting this way. But I was terrified. I didn't want him to see how ugly I really was. How horrible I was deep down. Guilt gnawed on my insides, its teeth as sharp as the ones I'd almost used on him. It was better this way; he had to believe that.

I heard Lucas moving toward the mouth of the cave. I risked a glance over my shoulder and caught his gaze. He'd hesitated for a moment, and my heart sank when I saw that his dark eyes burned with longing, and it almost broke me in half.

And then he was gone.

13

BY THE TIME I woke up the following morning, I was still safely chained to the tree. I hadn't hurt anyone, Nix assured me. She'd stayed all night, listening to my screams.

I was starting to think my affliction wasn't centered just on my falling asleep or the setting sun. I had almost hurt Lucas in the cave, and neither of those things had been happening. That meant that with each passing day, the monster was getting stronger.

With Lucas, I had been at my weakest. Perhaps the manananggal could sense that—take advantage of it, even. But I still didn't have any answers as to why this was happening in the first place. If I could transform at any time, it meant that being around others was getting more dangerous. And I felt like I couldn't do anything to stop it. At the same time, hiding in the house wasn't an option, especially not when Qian was starting to show an interest in me. I had to keep pretending like everything was normal until we figured out what to do next.

But I couldn't stop thinking about Lucas. Yesterday had been a mistake on so many levels; I knew that. Still, the ghost of Lucas's lips remained on mine. His kisses unraveled me and made me question everything, and I could hardly think about anything else, even when I got dressed and headed to breakfast. But Clarissa was waiting for me in the hall.

"Your Majesty," she said, with a curtsy. Then she curtsied at Nix, adding, "Princess." She turned to me and said, "Your healer has arrived."

"My healer?" I asked, eyebrows drawn, and then I remembered. "The manghuhula!"

I wasn't hungry anyway. I told Clarissa to inform everyone at breakfast not to wait for us, and I hurried to meet the manghuhula. Nix was more than eager to join me.

Together, Nix and I rushed toward the sitting room, where Clarissa said the manghuhula would be waiting for us, and Nix could hardly stop talking. She did that when she was nervous or excited, but this time, I think she was more nervous. "I heard mang-huhulas dabble in necromancy and talking to spirits. That they were banished from the kingdom because they brought someone back from the dead. Do you think the manghuhula is dangerous?"

"One way to find out," I said. "And I'm not going to miss an opportunity like this because of some rumors." I was sick and tired of turning into a monster every night. If the manghuhula was my only hope, I couldn't be scared.

When we came into the sitting room, a person was waiting for us, but they weren't the person I was expecting. When I'd heard the manghuhula was similar to the mambabarang, I imagined they would be some kind of witch, a wizened old lady with scraggly white hair and a cackling laugh. Instead, the healer was a heavyset male encanto with shining blond hair and warm, dark brown eyes.

He looked like a thirtysomething-year-old human, except for the points of his ears. He was dressed in a white barong, held a small bag at his waist, and smiled when we entered, bowing.

"Your Majesty," he said. "It's an honor to meet you."

"You're the manghuhula?" I asked.

"Yes, I am Isagani of Mount Hamiguitan, but everyone just calls me Gani."

Gani came over and shook my hand. Somehow, that comforted me. "Everyone calls me MJ," I said.

"MJ," he repeated. When he shook Nix's hand next, he asked her, "You are a healer, I presume?"

"Yeah, but nothing like what you do. Just in training. I'll help in any way I can."

He smiled. "Absolutely. I need to know everything before we properly get started. Shall we move to the infirmary for the examination?" My heart thumped nervously, and he must have sensed that, because he added, "Nothing invasive, I promise."

THE INFIRMARY WAS a necessary room in the great house. With royals vacationing here for decades, it was imperative that they could get any medical attention they needed at all times. When I came inside, it reminded me of an apothecary, with dried herbs hanging from the ceiling and even more potted plants growing near the windows. In the middle of the room was an examination table surrounded by wall-to-wall shelves full of glass jars neatly labeled for every ailment.

Gani had me sit down on the examination table, and I waited

while he went around the room, gathering supplies from drawers. Nix helped him, serving as a kind of assistant in locating what he needed.

"I've been told you're looking for a spiritual cleansing. Is that correct?" Gani asked.

"Yes," I said.

"Have you been haunted by anything in particular?"

I glanced at Nix, who looked back at me, wide-eyed. Should I tell him? I wasn't so sure. I just wanted him to fix whatever was wrong with me. "Got a lot going on right now," I said.

"Being a queen is no easy task, I'm sure," he said with a smile.

Gani took the powdered herbs and put them into a glass jar filled with a clear liquid, and the second the herbs touched the liquid, they burst into flames and turned the liquid into ichor. The smoke trailing on the surface smelled impossibly like joy—that was the only way I could describe it.

His eyes were soft, though, when he handed it to me. "Drink this."

"What is it?"

"Without boring you with healers' jargon—"

"But I love healers' jargon!" Nix interrupted him.

He laughed and said, "I'll let you look at my notes if you so wish, Princess Nix, but for MJ's sake, it's a kind of light elixir. It will help us see if there are energy blocks and where they're located, like holding up a flashlight to your hand and seeing your fingers glow red."

It kind of made sense, and I made no objections as I drank the elixir. It tasted like candy when it went down.

Gani had me lie back on the examination table, fully clothed, and I got comfortable with a pillow under my head. Then Gani hovered his hands over my body like he was scanning me. My body wasn't glowing, which I half expected, so I figured it was something only he could see. Nix watched, totally enraptured by his technique.

"You mentioned a flashlight," I said. "You spent time in the human world?"

"I did. My kind isn't particularly welcome in some parts of the encanto world, but it is getting better, as you can tell. I enjoyed the human world, though. I made many friends."

"People told me that you're necromancers, that you deal with spirits."

"That's part of the job. But death is just as much a part of the natural world as life."

"What about curses?" Nix asked, agape. "I've heard you can do that, too."

"Nix," I warned. "Don't be rude."

"I'm only asking!"

Gani didn't seem bothered. "There are curses to inflict on one's enemies, but it is a mirrored arrow. What shoots forward must also shoot back. We must be careful when it comes to that sort of magic. Otherwise, we risk everything. But that is why we are so educated. People often fear what they do not understand." He hovered his hands over my body, my chest, and my head, his brow knit with focus but his eyes never ceasing to be kind. "Because to lift curses, one must know how curses work."

A look crossed his face, one that flitted away just as quickly, but I caught it all the same. "What is it?" I asked.

Relenting with a sigh, Gani tipped his head and said, "Your condition is . . . unique. I haven't encountered someone like you before."

I wasn't sure if that was a good or bad thing. I was leaning more toward bad.

"There is magic at play, though; that is for certain," he said, lowering his hands. "Tell me, have you been able to use your power at all recently?"

"I haven't tried in a while. I've been struggling to master it."

"Can we try now?"

"Sure." I sat up, and Gani handed me a copper coin.

"Please, if you will, try to turn the copper into silver. I will sense if there is any kind of interference. It should be a relatively simple transmutation."

I glanced at Nix, who nodded in support and said, "You can do it!"

While Gani hovered his hands over me, I focused on the coin in my palm. I concentrated, tried to push everything else out of my mind just like I'd been trained to do, but the copper remained unchanged in my hand.

"Do you know what's wrong?" I asked him, and handed the coin back.

He regarded me for a moment and turned to Nix. "Apologies, Princess Nix. If you'd be so kind as to give us some privacy."

"Oh!" Nix said, eyes wide. "Of course. Excuse me."

She gave me an encouraging thumbs-up before she slinked out of the infirmary and closed the door. Gani tucked the coin into his pocket and pulled up a stool to take a seat near me.

"Is something wrong?" I asked. "Do you know what's happening?"

"It's not in my nature to lie, especially to my clients. So when I tell you I don't know, I don't want to frighten you. Your condition is unlike anything I've seen before. If you're open to the idea, I'd like to do a tarot card reading. To get a greater understanding of your situation—perhaps gain some insight about the whole picture, if you will. Even see what's to come."

The fact that he didn't answer my question outright set my nerves on edge, but I took a calming breath. "Tarot cards can predict the future?"

"A possible future. Nothing is set in stone. Think of it like forks in a road. Tarot can shine a light and reveal details about the paths ahead."

I nodded, choosing to ignore the anxiety swirling in me, and Gani took a velvet bag out of his traveling case. He peeled the velvet off the deck and extended it to me, not touching the cards as he did so. Gingerly, I took the cards and fanned them out. I'd never used tarot cards before, and I didn't know what any of them meant, but I admired the artwork on each one. I could tell that they were from printed woodblocks, embossed with gold, some with images of encantos, others with mythical animals.

"Shuffle the deck as much as you'd like," Gani said. He unfolded the velvet bag, revealing that it was actually a large square velvet tablecloth, and spread it on the counter next to us. "The cards need to learn about you, get a sense of who you are. Take your time."

I did as I was told, and when I was ready, I stood across from Gani. He had me draw the top card.

"This represents your past," he said, pointing to the card facing up between us. "The Queen of Wands is all about passion and determination. But since it's reversed, upside down for you, perhaps there's an element of low confidence or jealousy."

My cheeks got hot. The card was more accurate than I had anticipated. I couldn't help but notice the queen in the card looked startlingly like me. Same dark hair, same blue eyes, same olive skin.

When I drew another card, Gani said, "This represents your present. The Two of Swords is about difficult choices, indecision, perhaps being pulled in different directions."

The woman in the card was blindfolded, swords crossed in front of her chest. Again, she looked just like me. The hair on my arms stood on end. I drew another card. My future.

"The Tower," he said. "A terribly misunderstood card."

"How come?"

"The Tower represents change, upheaval, disaster. But when used in this context, it can also mean a change for the better, a positive redirection that perhaps you aren't ready for, an unexpected shift. It can also mean the end of things, good or bad. Change can be frightening sometimes."

I stared at the card. It depicted a castle tower surrounded by roses, and a mountain range divided the night sky in the background. The tower was on fire, crumbling; people were throwing themselves out of windows, screaming on the way down. At the very top of the tower was a woman, her hands extended to the full moon, pleading for help. I didn't know how such imagery could be considered good in any capacity.

"It looks just like my palace," I said, a little breathless. I almost didn't want to believe what I was seeing.

"Does it?" Gani asked, his eyes moving from the card back to me.

"The same gemstones and pearlescent spires and everything."

"You see what the cards want you to see," Gani said. "Try not to worry. Let's do something different." He had me take up the cards again, shuffling them once more. "I want you to choose another card. One that speaks to you the most. Let's see what you have."

I placed the top card down on the table. The Tower.

"Let's try again," Gani said, his smile a little tight. "Try to clear your mind."

I did and reshuffled the deck. I pulled another card.

The Tower. Again and again, I drew the same card, even when it was in the middle of the deck. No matter what, I always pulled The Tower.

I looked at Gani. Despite his smile, his face had lost some color.

When I went to pick up the card again, Gani whipped a corner of the velvet over it, covering it completely. Neither of us said anything for a moment.

"What does that mean?" I asked.

"Nothing to fear, Your Majesty."

I thought he never wanted to lie to me. Gani made a point not to touch them when he gathered the deck up in the square of velvet once more. Did this mean I was doomed?

"Can you still help me?" I asked.

Gani's smile returned, though all the warmth had gone from his eyes. "It was a pleasure to meet you, Your Majesty."

I didn't know what else to do, so I stepped away from the table and turned to go. My knees were weak, and my head swam with confusion. What had just happened? What would I do?

Before I left, I turned back just in time to see Gani throw the entire deck, velvet and all, into the trash can, light a match, and set it on fire.

14

WHEN I LEFT the infirmary, I was too tired to put on a brave face. I had no idea what any of this meant. Was I destined for catastrophe? Would I be the one to cause all of it? The Tower card looked so similar to my palace—was it actually predicting the future? I braced myself against one of the walls in the house—I didn't know which one. I hardly knew where I was; my head was still spinning. I had to catch my breath. I was barely staying on my feet.

Gani couldn't help me. The tarot cards had shown me fire and destruction and despair. He'd said the cards could be interpreted in several ways, but I wasn't sure there was any outlook other than total disaster. With a sinking pit in my stomach, I knew I really was doomed.

"MJ?"

Qian stood at the far end of the hall, looking every bit like Prince Charming. His bow was strung across his back, and his quiver was at his hip. He stared at me curiously, growing more concerned the longer he did. His brow furrowed as he approached, and I smiled, but I knew it looked forced. When he stopped in front of me, I caught his familiar scent of bergamot.

"Are you all right?" he asked. He stretched his hand out to me, but he stopped himself just short of touching my arm. "Did something happen?"

"I'm okay." I pressed my hand to my forehead and took a breath. Being out of the infirmary was helping, but so was Qian's presence.

"You look like you've seen a ghost. Are you sure?"

"I appreciate the concern," I said. "I think I just need some air."

"Let's walk together," he said, gesturing with a dip of his head toward the outside.

Since I was still reeling, the best I could do was nod. Qian fell into step at my side, watching me. Maybe he was worried I was going to faint; I certainly felt like it.

"I hope you don't have somewhere to be," I said, trying to lighten the mood.

"I was going to practice, but I've actually been wanting to spend more time with you. I missed you at breakfast. It'll be my pleasure." His eyes shone, and he smiled.

My cheeks warmed, and I smiled back, for real this time. "Thank you. I'd like that."

Side by side, we walked out of the great house and onto the grounds. The day was bright and promising, and I tipped my head back to soak up the sunlight, closing my eyes against the bright sky, and took a deep breath. Doing so made me feel like I was coming back to life. Qian must have sensed that I was feeling better, too, because he said, "There, that's more like it. You're looking more like yourself again."

"A grisly sight before, I bet."

"Not at all. While it makes for quite a romantic scene, I'd prefer it if maidens didn't faint in my arms."

"I'm a maiden?"

"When in the presence of monsters, we all have our roles to play."

My heart lurched, and I was at a loss for words. Qian didn't seem to notice, though. "I think the creature only comes out at night," I said, "so you don't have to worry about me. We still have a few hours until sunset."

"Whatever is haunting these grounds, we need to be careful. I've sent my men all over, setting traps and the like to stop it before it hurts anything else." He looked me over again, taking in my face. "I certainly hope word about the monster isn't upsetting you."

"No!" I said, a little too quickly.

"It's okay to be afraid. I admit, though, the reason I'm escorting you now is to make sure that you're looked after."

"I'm not as helpless as you think," I said.

"No, but if anything were to happen to you, I don't think I could live with myself."

I blushed at that. The only other person who cared about my well-being so vehemently was Lucas. "Where's Nix? Are you giving her the same treatment?"

"I last saw her in the library, perfectly safe indoors."

I thought about joining her there, telling her all about what had happened with Gani, but I found that I liked being with Qian, too. This was the perfect time to get him to come to an understanding about all this. If I couldn't save myself, there was still a chance to give Nix her freedom.

"It's been nice, having all of us here. Seeing members of Jade Mountain and my court bonding is all I could have asked for. Have you considered more about letting Nix stay in Biringan City?" I asked as we followed a dirt path through the jungle.

"I'm hesitant to let her go. I heard rumors about a monster attacking a couple in your city before we left. I thought you said that Biringan had no monsters."

"We don't . . ."

"Then you may not know your kingdom as well as you think."

I clamped my mouth shut. He was more right than I wanted to believe. "You take your duty very seriously, don't you? Hunting monsters."

Qian regarded me for a long moment; then he took a deep, measured breath. "My younger brother was killed by one—a jiangshi. The same one that gave me this scar." He pointed to his shoulder, and my blood ran cold. "Of course I take it seriously."

I remembered the day I came to his room and saw all the scars on his body. His pain ran deeper than that. I remembered he'd said the jiangshi was a reanimated corpse that sucked the qi—the life force—out of humans.

"How did it . . ." I began to say, but then I trailed off, wondering if I should ask. I realized we'd become closer, but could he trust me enough with the story? He looked at me as if he, too, was gauging how he wanted to respond. I swallowed thickly and tried not to look away, because Qian's gaze on me was steady and, for what seemed like the first time, trusting. Finally, Qian gave in.

"I was ten years old. Even though it happened so long ago, I remember the day so clearly . . ." he said, his gaze distant, piercing through the dense jungle. Then he smiled. "My brother Xiaolong loved cats and sweets and, most of all, playing games. He was always the one who could make anything fun, even during a long day of our father's ceremonies. He was often getting into trouble because of it, but no one could hold it against him for too long. Everyone adored him. We would play games for hours together—games he made up or games that we had lying around the palace. His favorite was Go. It's a game of strategy, incredibly complex and difficult to master. But I think that's why he liked it so much. It's all about endless potential. You never play the same match twice. He would want to play every day, even when we weren't near a board. So instead of stones, we used different-colored adzuki beans that we stole from the kitchens so we could play anywhere. He would always beat me, too." He laughed brightly, and it made me smile, too, even though I knew how this story was going to end.

"One night, we were up late playing Go well past our bedtime. There was a scratching noise at the door, and we thought it was one of our pet cats, so Xiaolong got up to let it in while I reset the board. But after a while, he didn't come back.

"I went to check on him, half expecting him to leap out as a prank, but what I saw instead . . ." Qian let out a huff of breath like he'd been punched in the gut, and he looked pained at the memory, but he continued despite it. "I found him in the hallway with what I thought was a mandarin—one of Father's officials in a long robe and tall brimmed hat. He was holding Xiaolong by the face. I called out to them, but Xiaolong didn't move. His body twitched like he was having some kind of fit, and the mandarin, well, he wasn't a mandarin at all. The jiangshi dropped Xiaolong and turned to me, not turning its head but its whole body. It was as stiff as a board, its skin a deep shade of green, arms stretched forward as if searching for something to hold. A paper talisman was attached to the middle of its forehead, and its pale white eyes were fixated on me.

"Jiangshi can't walk or run—this one *hopped*, knees and legs locked, arms outstretched to me, gaining more speed. I'd never seen anything like it before. I didn't know what else to do. So I did the only thing I could . . . I ran.

"I ran back into the game room. It tried to grab me, just scraping my shoulder, and it burned like fire. I tripped over the Go board, knocking down all the pieces when I hit the floor. I couldn't get up fast enough. The jiangshi was almost on me, but before it pounced, it stopped. I didn't understand why it didn't attack me. All I wanted to do was get away, but I couldn't move, I couldn't scream. I just watched it as its gaze darted around the floor, at all the beans, and that's when I realized it was counting them. I only learned later that the jiangshi have an innate desire to count. They can't do anything else until they're done. I'd unknowingly set a trap. It gave me enough time to get away and get help.

"It turned out that a vengeful priest had raised the corpse to try to assassinate my father. Xiaolong was just in the way. If he'd stayed with me, if I'd been the one to go to the door . . . Xiaolong would still be alive."

When Qian stopped talking, he took a deep breath and nodded, as if he'd finally gotten it all off his shoulders and into the open. I could tell the memory hurt. The guilt he carried was heavier than any crown.

"I'm sorry," I said. "That's horrible."

"At least Xiaolong didn't suffer. He didn't have time to know what was happening when the jiangshi consumed all his qi . . . But I made a promise from that day forth that I'd never let anything like that happen again, especially not to anyone in my family. And I promised *myself* that I would never run away, never again." He showed me his right hand, gesturing to a jade ring on his thumb. "This is my archer's ring. It's a hunter's mark."

"It's beautiful," I said.

Qian tipped his head and smiled. "Thank you."

I couldn't think of anything else to say, but it seemed like Qian didn't mind the silence, so we quietly continued our walk through the jungle. His gaze remained distant, like he was caught in a memory, but he held his head high. To have lived through something like that sounded traumatic and terrible, and it made sense why he would be so protective of his family after surviving such a thing. I understood completely why he wanted to keep Nix close.

"I bet your brother would be really proud of you," I said.

Qian smiled sadly. "I think so, too. Though I haven't been able to bring myself to play another game of Go since then, and I imagine he would be upset about that. It just doesn't feel the same without him. Though I think with the right company, I could play again." His eyes locked on mine. The implication made my stomach flutter.

"Who, me? I've never played Go before," I said. "I'd probably be so bad at it, I'd be doing Xiaolong's memory a disservice."

"I doubt that. Everyone starts somewhere. But if you're so set on diminishing your abilities, I can think of a number of other activities I'd like to do with you . . ." His words were silky smooth. He flashed me a rakish grin, like he knew exactly what was happening and was pleased with himself about it.

My brain couldn't quite process it, and the way Qian was watching me made me all the more flustered. For once, the horrible, hungry voice in my head was quiet. Unlike when I was with Lucas, it didn't lash out. It occurred to me only now how alone Qian and I were, and my heart skipped a little at the thought of it. I wasn't afraid of Qian, not in the slightest. Being with him was normal and felt suspiciously like we were on a date.

We could share a kiss here, and no one would know about it.

The idea sent a thrill through me. But he was still Nix's brother, and he was off-limits. I couldn't believe I could think such a thing. Besides, I couldn't be as open and honest with him as he was with me. I couldn't tell him my deepest, darkest secret. He hunted monsters, and I was turning into one. It didn't matter that I was starting to like him or that he might like me; we couldn't be together.

But he smiled at me with an easiness and warmth that made it hard for me to look at anything else. I wanted to ask him what he was thinking, but a part of me was afraid to know. Could there really be more happening between us, or was I just imagining things?

"Why were you so troubled earlier?" Qian asked. "Do you want to talk about it?"

"Not particularly. It's . . . a lot."

"I could tell."

I sighed deeply and mustered the courage to be a little more forthcoming. "I had my fortune told. Tarot cards. And I didn't like what I saw."

"Your fortune?" Qian raised his eyebrows and jutted out his lower lip, as if he had expected me to say something different. "You believe that?"

"We live in a world full of magic. Is fortune-telling that far-fetched?"

Qian wrinkled his nose. "Fair point, but perhaps I'm more unwilling to let a deck of cards tell me what's to come. Life is too complex. And I'd much rather live in the moment than worry about what might happen. Wouldn't you?" He smiled again, and it made me feel better.

"I like that a lot, actually," I said. "I guess I'm just looking for answers wherever I can get them."

"Life's all about little surprises." He plucked a flower from a nearby tree and presented it to me. It was an orchid, its white-and-pink petals looking like candy. He placed the flower behind my ear, and the tips of his fingers brushed my skin, sending a shiver down my spine. "Did the cards by chance tell you that I would do that?"

"They did not," I said, trying to maintain my composure, but a smile crept its way onto my lips. "I'd love to see what other surprises you have in store."

Qian's smile spread wider, and something sparked in his eyes that made my stomach swoop. I hadn't meant to say it like that . . . or had I? Talking with Qian had become so natural. I looked at him—*really* looked at him—and it was then that I realized how good I felt when he looked back at me. *Saw* me. I felt wanted, and it surprised me just how much I'd missed that feeling.

But when bright sunlight cut across our faces, our gazes on each other broke.

We had unknowingly come upon a low stone wall surrounding a large clearing in the hillside. Hundreds of stone slabs jutted out of the soft grass, the older ones covered in moss and vines the farther into the clearing they went.

"It's a graveyard," I said, taken aback by the scene at first, but then I recognized the insignias on some of the grave markers. "It's the final resting place of some of my ancestors."

"It's certainly a beautiful place to be laid to rest," Qian said, eyes on the jungle surrounding us. Everything was lush and green and full of life. It wasn't creepy, like I would have otherwise expected.

At the very center of the graveyard was a stone mausoleum. It was one of the oldest buildings in the graveyard. It looked like it had been consumed by the jungle itself. But the symbol above the door made me pause.

I recognized it, even if it was worn down by the elements and faded.

It was a triangle. Just like on the cover of the missing Princess Yara Liliana's archive.

"What is it?" Qian asked. He'd noticed I was staring. "Is everything okay?"

I wasn't quite sure. My body hummed with familiarity. Something tugged behind my sternum, drawing me forward. I approached the closed door and pressed my hand to the stone, wiping away the dirt and moss that had gathered there. But then I realized it wasn't just a triangle. It was a delta.

Recognition resonated deep inside me, down to the marrow of my bones. In math and science, delta was the symbol for change.

"I have to check something," I said.

Qian didn't stop me as I pushed open the door, crossed the threshold, and entered the mausoleum.

The first thing I noticed was the smell. The air was distinctly thick and musty, like laundry left in the machine too long, and it took a second for my eyes to adjust to the dim light. It pooled through holes in the mausoleum's roof, casting pillars of light down from above and throwing the rest of the room into shadow.

Qian followed me, moving quietly, perhaps reverently, because in the very center of the room was a stone sarcophagus. Lying atop the lid was a stone carving of a woman, her hands resting on her stomach, holding a crown. Her face was carved with such precision, her delicate features so lifelike that I almost wondered if she would sit up and talk to me.

"Looking for something in particular?" Qian asked.

"Does she look familiar to you?" I asked, still staring at the woman's face.

"I don't think so. Do you know her?"

"From somewhere . . ." Then it hit me. I'd seen her face when we first arrived. "That's the lady of the mountain."

Qian's eyes widened when he realized I was right. She looked exactly like the statue from the fountain in the great house. "It's probably a coincidence."

I wasn't so sure about that.

The tomb had been long forgotten. No one had visited this place in centuries. Cracks in the sarcophagus had spread like spiderwebs along its base; one created a hole big enough I could see inside. A name had been carved in the stone.

Yara Liliana.

It was the missing princess. I'd found her after all. I almost couldn't believe it. Gani had mentioned that the future wasn't set in stone, but I couldn't help but wonder if I was supposed to be here right now. As if . . . *I* was meant to find her.

The hair on the back of my neck stood on end when a breeze cut through the mausoleum. I rubbed my arms, stamping out the chill, and my eyes set on the statue's face. She looked barely older than me. *What happened to her?* I wondered. *What was she doing here?*

Something wasn't right. None of this made sense. Why hadn't the historians recorded her death? Why was she hidden away in the mountains? Why had they erased her from the history books? Why was she buried in the middle of the jungle, never to be spoken of again? I had to see for myself.

I put my hands on the lid of the sarcophagus. "Help me," I told Qian.

"I didn't take you for a grave robber."

"Just help me, please."

Qian didn't protest again. Together, he and I shifted the lid ever so slightly, letting the sunlight pour into the casket.

But it was empty.

There was no body. No bones. Nothing at all to suggest anything had been placed inside.

Yara Liliana wasn't here.

I almost didn't hear the sound coming from behind me; I was too focused on the empty sarcophagus. Qian did, though. He grabbed me tightly around the arm and yanked me off my feet.

My back hit the floor of the mausoleum, and I let out a yelp, but Qian clamped his hand over my mouth and put his own fingers to his lips, quieting me.

In a panic, I tried to shove him off, but the fear in his eyes made me freeze, and that's when I heard it, too—the heavy whoosh of wings pumping through the air, massive and rhythmic.

Qian lifted his hand off my mouth, and I hardly dared to breathe. We were so close to each other—he was shielding me with his body; our hearts were practically touching. He leaned over me, turning his head ever so slightly to see out the open door.

Every bone in my body was trembling. I couldn't even think. Instead, I focused on the lines of Qian's face, the edge of his jaw, the thump of his pulse in his neck, the curve of his ear. He didn't seem to be breathing, either.

Whatever had made that noise, it sounded like it was moving away from us, the flap of its wings growing fainter.

Then the ground shook, and the both of us tensed up. Something huge had landed just outside the mausoleum, but I couldn't see what it was. I didn't think Qian could, either. His gaze was hard, fixed on the open door, ready to strike. The creature squawked and chattered like a bird, and then there came a sound like branches breaking, followed by a horrible squelching noise. That was when I realized it wasn't branches breaking—it was bones and flesh. The sound turned my stomach.

There was another rush of flapping wings, this time far away, and a shadow cut across the door when something took to the sky. Was there more than one?

But all had gone quiet outside. Qian and I waited with bated breath, listening, but I couldn't hear anything except for my own heartbeat pounding in my ears.

Was it gone?

Qian looked at me, grim determination setting into his features. He mouthed, "Stay here."

I shook my head, but he lifted himself off me and went to the door, crouching low. He slipped his bow off his back and peered around the corner into the graveyard and then darted out into the open, leaving me in the mausoleum. He was quiet as a hunter.

A mixture of panic and frustration swirled inside me. I didn't know what to do, but I didn't want to hide here and leave Qian all alone. I scrambled to my feet and looked out into the graveyard. It was empty, with no sign of Qian or whatever that thing was. Was it safe to go out?

"Qian?" I whispered once, and then again, a little louder, "Qian." No answer.

I didn't like this. Light on my toes, I left the mausoleum and crept across the grass. Nothing moved among the headstones, and I couldn't find any trace of Qian. I moved around the building, keeping an eye on the sky, and stumbled upon a collection of large branches nestled up against the back of the mausoleum. At first, I thought it was the result of a fallen tree, but the closer I looked, the more I realized how precisely the branches had been placed.

It was a nest.

Inside it were a few eggs, each as large as a basketball, and nestled among them was a decapitated horse's head. It stared at me with lifeless white eyes, its blood coating the nest's branches. I stumbled back and clamped my hand over my mouth to stop from screaming. We needed to get out of here right now.

A shadow loomed over me, and I looked up.

Sitting on top of the mausoleum roof, its wings spread wide enough to block the sun, was a giant birdlike creature, almost as big as the mausoleum itself. It had scales and feathers, and its black eyes were fixated on me.

I froze, cold with dread.

Talons the size of kitchen knives clutched the mausoleum roof, and its wings looked just as razor-like, with feathers glistening like blades. The creature opened its beak and revealed dozens of sharp teeth. It let out an earsplitting shriek, then leapt from the roof, talons pointing at me.

I screamed and threw out my hands.

An arrow sliced through the air from my right, hitting the bird in the eye. It let out a screech and crumpled to the ground at my feet. It was dead in an instant.

"MJ!" Qian ran out from his cover behind a headstone and rushed to my side.

I grabbed on to him, clinging for dear life as he wrapped his arm around me and held me tight. I buried my face in his shirt. "I thought I was going to die!"

"Are you all right?" he asked. He held me at arm's length and looked me over, brushing my hair out of my face, worry hardening his eyes. He'd saved me. He was a real hero.

"I'm okay," I said. My heart felt like it was going to explode out of my chest, but seeing Qian, I knew I was safe. "What was that thing?"

We both looked at the bird. It was like something out of my nightmares.

"I don't know," Qian said. "Whatever it is, it's dead. It won't hurt anyone anymore."

15

I HARDLY NOTICED where I was walking, only realizing I'd made it back to the great house in a haze of near delirium.

Edgardo was the first to meet us on the lawn, no doubt noticing the state we were in, and asked what had happened. Qian told him everything—about the bird, about how it almost got me.

"I thought it had left," I said, still shocked. "It took off and sounded far away."

Edgardo's eyes widened, and he shook his head, stunned. "You could have been killed. That was a wakwak," he said. "They're carnivorous birds in the mountains. They have the ability to throw the sound of their wingbeats, creating the illusion that they're farther away than they actually are, which makes them exceptional hunters. In actuality, the fainter the sound, the closer they are. You're lucky you weren't seriously injured, Your Majesty."

"Qian saved me," I said.

That's when Lucas, Amador, and Heng came over to see what the commotion was about. My throat tightened when Lucas met my gaze. Someone took my hand, and I jumped, but then I realized it was Nix. She'd come to check on me.

"Are you okay?" she asked.

I nodded, but I slipped my hand out of hers and backed away. I just wanted to be alone.

"The wakwak must have been the thing that killed the horse the other night," Qian said. "We found evidence of it left behind. I did what anyone else would have done." He turned to Heng and said, "We found a nest as well, with eggs. Go and destroy it before any of its offspring hurts anyone else."

"Yes, sir," Heng said, and together, he and several of his men went back the way we came, weapons at the ready.

I couldn't meet Lucas's gaze, even though it burned through me.

"Could there be more of those things?" Amador asked, fearful.

"It's very possible," said Edgardo.

Qian hefted his bow. "Then we have work to do. Sir Lucas," Qian prompted, "would you like to join us?"

Lucas glanced at Amador and then at me. He swallowed thickly before he nodded. A duty to protect.

Before he left, Qian took my hand. "Don't worry, MJ. You're safe now." He gave my fingers a small squeeze before he and Lucas disappeared into the jungle. I couldn't watch them go.

I marched as quickly as I could inside. Nix followed close behind.

"Do you want to talk about what happened with Gani?" Nix whispered. She leaned in so no one else would hear, but I shook my head and kept walking.

"I just want to lie down," I said. "I'm going back to my room."

Alone, I walked as if floating, because I was so tired and frustrated and confused, and I just wanted to be somewhere far away from everyone. But everything went away the moment I came to my door. Sitting on the floor in front of it was a book with a note taped to it.

Special delivery, from your good friend Romulo.

I snatched it up off the floor and burst into my room, eager to read what he'd found. My heart hammered in my ears as I flipped through the pages. Every one had delicate, neat handwriting. It was then that I realized what it was.

"A diary?"

I went to my bed, shoved aside the manacles, and sat down to read.

Miguel left me.

I went to see him tonight, and he told me he didn't love me anymore. He said that he had fallen in love with someone else. I begged him to tell me why, asked if I had done something wrong, asked him if I had angered him somehow, but his mind has been made up. He is marrying Lucia.

My heart might as well be torn from my chest. I am alone. I cannot get out of bed. I cannot eat. I am pitiful. I cannot take care of myself, let alone take care of my people.

This was Yara's diary.

How could Romulo have gotten his hands on such a thing? It must have been incredibly difficult to find, and no doubt expensive, too. I couldn't stop reading. Her words seemed similar to how I'd been feeling. They resonated deep in my bones.

Something terrible is happening to me. A change has overcome my body.

I went to see the royal physician. She is a venerated mambabarang, with decades of expertise. She would know what is afflicting me.

She said that my heart has been damaged. No potion she's brewed, no talisman, can cure me. She says that my affliction is too powerful for any medicine. I must marry another to mend what's been broken.

Only a vow of true love is strong enough to break this curse.

A curse. My heart thumped as I turned the page.

Suitors from across the land have come to see me, but my transformation is quickening. I am afraid to let any of them see the monster I've become. The men visit me behind a curtain, ask to kiss my hand, but I will not let them. They cannot know that my hand has turned into claws. They will fear me the moment they know the truth.

One suitor, a prince from Avalon, attempted to pull the curtain back to see my face. He said he wanted to take in my beauty for himself, but I nearly clawed his eyes from his head out of fear. He's now already engaged to someone else, after telling me how much he loved me only days ago.

No one will have me. I am alone.

I am running out of time. How can anyone love me enough to marry me?

I flipped the page, fearing I already knew what was going to happen.

I am more monster now than I am human. What few hours I have as myself I spend recording my days here in this journal. It reminds me of what I have, for when I become the monster, I no longer remember my own name. I cannot remember what it's like to feel sand beneath my toes, the salt water on my legs, the taste of fresh fruit, or the warmth of sunshine on my skin. Such things sicken me. I hide indoors, fearing that anyone who sees me will know the hideousness that lurks within. Fewer suitors arrive on my doorstep. Rumors have started to spread. All know that a monster lurks in the palace.

The mambabarang says that with the waxing moon, the monster grows more powerful. When it is full, I will be a monster forever.

At night, my body separates. My upper half grows wings, and I soar through the kingdom, attacking anyone I find. A bounty has been put out on my head, but no one knows my true nature. I have killed. I truly am a monster. My own father fears me; my sisters abhor me. If I were to fall by a brave datu's blade, I would know it was for the best.

I've sent myself away to live in the great house in the mountains. There, I will be sure not to hurt anyone. I will live in solitude for the rest of my days. I am resigned to my fate. Deep in my soul, I know that this is the last day I will have a human body, human hands to write, a human mind. Who would hate me so much to curse me so? My own family has disowned me. I fear I am already dead to them. I pray that no one will ever suffer like I have. No one deserves such a fate.

I have one last hope. One last chance to save myself. My power is my only salvation.

The last page was covered in hundreds of handwritten triangles. Delta signs. They were the same as the symbol on the empty tomb.

Change, change, change.

What did it mean? What did any of it mean? She was just like me. She was the manananggal all those years ago, and she had been right—the historians had made sure no one spoke her name ever again. She was worse than dead. Only one thing was for certain . . .

"Full moon," I said, staring at the orange glow of the setting sun. "I only have five days left."

16

MY EARS WERE still ringing even when I left my room the following morning. I needed air. I had woken up feeling more terrible than ever. My wrists stung from where the shackles had burned me. The marks weren't fading like they used to, so I had to cover them with a long-sleeved T-shirt.

Time was running out. If Yara's destiny was what awaited me, I was going to turn into a manananggal in four days. Permanently.

I rushed from my room and stood in the sunlight, gasping for air that felt too thin here in the mountains, and yet it felt like it was closing in around me, trapping me. I barely noticed that anyone was awake until I heard the familiar din of the men from Jade Mountain, murmuring excitedly to themselves in the shade of nearby palm trees. Breakfast was served.

I cracked my eyes open to spot Qian among them, who by now had noticed I'd arrived. He was one of the last people I wanted to see, and I stuffed down my panic, quickly gathering myself to hide my racing heart.

"Just in time, Your Majesty," Qian called over. "How are you feeling?"

Nix stood near him, arms folded tightly across her chest. She waited with a frown for me to answer. Obviously, she knew something was wrong.

"I'm okay, thank you," I said. Nix's frown deepened.

"With the wakwak disposed of, I think it's only fitting we celebrate with a game," Qian said. "Talking about Xiaolong with you stirred something inside me. I was hoping you'd like to join us."

At her brother's name, Nix's eyebrows rose. She might not have expected Qian to share his story with me. I wasn't sure how to feel about that. "More hunting?" I guessed.

The corner of Qian's mouth lifted. "Not quite. Today, we're doing a scavenger hunt."

"Ooh!" Amador's voice chimed loudly across the lawn, and I turned to see her fluttering over, dressed like a bird of paradise in her rainbow-colored sundress with flowers in her hair. Lucas, I noted, trailed behind her looking somewhat annoyed. His eyes met mine briefly before he occupied them on the horizon. Guilt about our secret kiss in the cave churned in my gut, but I swallowed thickly and bit my tongue.

"May we join you?" Amador asked.

"Fantastic, Duchess," Qian said. "Make it a friendly match between kingdoms. Good sportsmanship and all. How about we split into teams of two, and whichever kingdom finds the prize first wins?"

"Sounds fun!" Amador said, glancing my way. "Will Her Majesty be joining us, too?"

My first instinct was not to play. I was worrying so much about becoming a manananggal, I could hardly think about anything else.

But if I didn't play, it wouldn't help Nix stay in Biringan City. I needed to keep playing host, make it seem like I was a good queen, that I had everything under control. Qian needed to be assured that Nix was safe in our kingdom, that she didn't need to go back to Jade Mountain. So, for the sake of diplomacy, I nodded. At least it would be a temporary distraction from the chaos swarming in my head.

"I'm staying here," Lucas said.

That seemed to take Amador by surprise, because she whipped around. "Why?"

"I don't want to play," he said. "I've got work to do."

I realized that if Romulo had dropped off the book to my room, maybe he had come through with whatever Lucas needed from him, too.

"Come on, Sir Lucas," Qian goaded. "You can afford to take some time off."

Lucas narrowed his eyes so slightly, it almost went unnoticed. "I've made up my mind. Excuse me." He left without a glance back.

If Qian was disappointed, he didn't show it. "That leaves Her Highness and the grand duchess," Qian said.

"What about Nix?" I asked.

"Nix is with Jade Mountain," said Qian. "Or is that going to be a problem?"

I bit my tongue. "She can join whichever team she likes."

But Nix stepped away from the group. "I'm not playing, either," she said. "I'm busy, too. I'm going back to study in the infirmary." She gave me an apologetic look before she, too, left.

"The teams are unfair," Amador said, her voice bordering on whining. "Jade Mountain has the advantage."

"I think having the queen herself on your team is more than enough to even the odds," Qian said, giving me a charming smile.

I didn't have the energy to tell if he was flirting with me or not.

"What are we looking for, exactly?" I asked. My thoughts were cloudy, and the only thing I could think about was getting away from here.

"Rumor has it that there's a pink azalea that grows in these jungles, a rare flower that feeds off the magical springs and smells like your one true love. Find one and bring it back here before nightfall to win . . . a kiss."

His eyes danced when he said it.

True love . . . Yara's words came back to me. A vow of true love could break the curse. But was it enough? Lucas had kissed me in the cave, and I was still cursed. Had that kiss not been a vow? Or did he really not love me enough for it to work?

"So if we lose, we have to kiss you?" Amador said with a sneer.

"If you win, we get to kiss you, too."

If I had been less sleep-deprived and distracted, I might have said no, but I nodded before I could stop myself. I didn't care about a kiss. Yara's words still haunted me.

Qian's smile widened.

He gave the signal, and the teams of two split off into the surrounding jungle, whooping and yelling like foxes on a hunt. I stomped off without waiting for Amador, determined to get as far away from her as possible. I didn't care about winning the game. I just wanted to go . . . anywhere.

But Amador hurried after me, determined to keep up.

We broke into the jungle in a random direction, and the

moment I did, my thoughts settled like a concrete block in my mind. I was running out of time, and I might not be able to appreciate the world around me. Yara had talked about never feeling the sand under her toes or the waves on her legs. I might never be able to walk on my own two legs again in a few days.

I couldn't appreciate the beauty of the jungle anymore. I knew it was all green and lush and vibrant, but my mood had turned my world into gray. I stumbled upon a small path, instinctually followed it, and then turned abruptly off it, throwing us deeper into the trees. No matter how far I walked, I couldn't stop thinking about Yara. I couldn't stop thinking that what had happened to her would happen to me.

Lucas had mentioned the lady of the mountain was a ghost. Was that what Yara had become? Was she stuck in this realm, haunting it, like the stories said? Spirits couldn't move on if they had unfinished business, so was she angry that she'd been forgotten by history? Was she trying to ask for help, or was she warning me? It still felt like I was missing something—some clue—but I didn't know what.

All that was around us were green vines and even greener ferns. As we walked deeper into the jungle, I tried to make sure that whenever I pushed aside a branch, it would snap back and hit Amador. She'd huff and groan, and I could feel her eyes burning a hole in the back of my head.

"Are you sure you know where you're going?" Amador asked, the sound of her crashing through the underbrush coming from behind me.

"No," I said. "I'm intentionally trying to get us lost."

"Well, great job!"

I bit my tongue to stop myself from snapping back, but something moved out of the corner of my eye. Long black hair, whipping through the breaks in the trees. At first, I almost thought it was my imagination. But I froze, goose bumps rising on my arms.

"Did you see that?" I asked.

"What?" Amador followed my line of sight, but whatever it was had disappeared. She scrunched up her nose, annoyed. "Whatever. Let's turn around," she said. "I'm tired of being bug food."

I rubbed my arms, trying to soothe myself, but it was so creepy. I knew I hadn't been getting a lot of sleep, and I must have been imagining things.

But then I saw it again. Farther away this time but moving just as fast. Long hair, smooth like silk. A woman. She vanished into the trees. It could only be one person.

The lady of the mountain. Yara Liliana.

I ran after her, Amador trailing behind me. She called my name, but I ignored her. I charged through the underbrush, breathing hard. If there was a way I could speak with Yara, I had to try. I had to know what happened to her.

To my right, I saw her again. I even heard her laugh, light and melodic. She had to be real.

I changed direction and hurried after her, and Yara's name stuck in my throat. I couldn't lose her.

Amador caught up to me, but I didn't think she could see Yara. "What are you doing? What did you see?"

I didn't answer. I didn't want to be wrong. I didn't want to feel like I was losing my mind any more than I already was.

I kept running, then spotted her again. Her arm was wrapped around a tree, her hand tracing down the bark as if she was circling it. I rushed to the other side of the tree, expecting to see her, but there was nothing but a patch of moss.

Yara was gone.

Amador crashed through the jungle, gasping and groaning. "What's gotten into you?"

I didn't answer. My chest felt too tight, and my eyes stung. I was chasing a ghost, and no matter how hard I tried, I'd never be able to reach her.

Suddenly, Amador gasped, and it made me jump. She pointed to our right, where I, too, saw a flash of pink behind all that green. "There!" she said.

I charged into the underbrush, and sure enough, there was an entire bush of the pink azaleas. Amador burst through the foliage next to me, leaves stuck in her hair, and a wild and hungry gleam in her eye. She was competitive, that was for sure.

Had Yara led us here? I looked around, but she was still nowhere to be seen.

Amador picked up one of the flowers and put it to her nose. I caught its smell, too—the faintest whiff of steel, the sharp tang as familiar as his palm on my cheek. It smelled just like Lucas, but in the next instant, the scent was replaced by notes of bergamot. That couldn't be right, could it? How could a single flower smell like two different people?

"It's perfect," Amador sighed. "Roses and mint."

Was that what Lucas smelled like to her? I was about to ask, but something on the forest floor stole my focus. At first, I thought it was just a root, but the line was too straight to be natural. And then I saw another. Then another, and another. All crisscrossing in perpendicular lines. Amador stepped toward them.

"Wait—" I reached out to grab her, but it was already too late.

Something snapped, and the forest floor moved. They weren't roots but ropes. It was one of the traps Qian's men had set up.

A net whipped up around us and took our feet from under us, dragging us into the air.

17

AMADOR CRASHED INTO me as the net yanked us into the air, tangling us up and dangling us twenty feet above the jungle floor. We swung back and forth in the trap with no way of getting down.

Amador thrashed next to me, and her elbow knocked into my head. I couldn't hit her out of revenge. My arms were wedged behind my back, and one of my legs was crunched up underneath me.

"Help!" Amador screamed, her shrill voice echoing through the jungle. "HELP!"

"No one can hear us. We're too far from the house."

"Someone has to come! They have to know we're trapped!"

"Are you done screaming?"

"I am not staying trapped here with you! What if there are more wakwaks out there?" She squirmed, and her elbow hit me in the head again. I was tempted to bite her, but what good would that do?

Amador kept screaming for help until her voice gave out. I didn't know how long we'd been stuck here, but I'd already started losing feeling in my fingers. All I could see was the jungle floor.

I had no idea what time it was or how long we had until the sun would set. I tried my best not to panic, but dread was starting to creep its way into me after Amador's voice cracked for the fiftieth time, and still no one came looking for us.

"It's no use," Amador cried. Her voice was rough, and I heard desperation there. All I could see was the side of her face that was scrunched up against the net. "I can't believe I'm stuck with you."

"It's not my definition of a party, either." If I really had seen Yara Liliana, I doubted a ghost could be of much help anyway.

We fell into silence, listening to the sounds of the jungle returning. Birds and bugs flew around us, no doubt checking out what had happened but doing ultimately nothing to help our situation. All we could do was wait for someone to notice we'd gone missing.

"Can't you use your power to get us out of here?" Amador asked.

I ground my teeth together and tried to move my arms, but it was useless. I couldn't use my magic anyway, even if my hands were free. Amador seemed to get that, too, because she groaned and rolled her eyes.

"You do it, then," I snapped.

Amador clicked her tongue and didn't say anything. "Nix will notice we're not back, and she'll help us."

Nix probably had her nose buried in a book by now. "When it starts getting dark, sure, but then it'll be too late."

"Why? Is the monster going to come get us? Are we going to be bait laid out on a silver platter?" Her fear made her voice pitch into a shriek.

"Nothing's going to eat you," I said. "We just have to get down."

"Why do you sound so sure?"

"Because I just . . . know."

"Well, I don't want to die here with you!"

"You're not going to die. Just shut up for a moment so I can think."

Amador had the sense to stop talking, at least. But I couldn't think about anything that would help. All that went through my head was the slow passage of the sun across the sky. If we didn't get out of here, Amador really could be in trouble. Even though I hated her, I didn't want anything bad to happen to her. I wouldn't be able to stop myself from hurting her if I turned.

The net swung gently back and forth, making me slightly sick, and I could tell Amador was getting uncomfortable, too, because she kept shifting around. At least she was quiet now.

"Lucas will come for me," she said. "I know he will."

A twinge of anger made my eye twitch. I tried to take a calming breath, but I knew it came out more like a hiss.

"What's wrong with you?" Amador said. "Lucas will save you, too. You're the queen, after all."

I hated how she talked about him. I hated that she could say his name like she owned him, because she did. They were a matched pair, and I was an outsider. I knew it wasn't helpful, but I imagined how good it would feel to lash out and hurt her like she had hurt me.

It would feel so good . . . that voice in my head said. *How easy her flesh could tear. How her bones could break under your hand. Make that pretty face of hers bleed.*

"No, no!" I said, and shook my head.

I could feel Amador get very still. "What's *really* wrong with you?" she asked.

"Nothing," I said, clenching my teeth. I would not let the manananggal consume my own thoughts. Yara had said she was losing part of herself every day, that she was becoming more of a monster after every transformation. We had to get out of here, or I really might hurt Amador.

You could shut her up forever. She would beg for her life. And you could take it from her. Like she's taken so much from you.

"Shut up, shut up, shut up," I growled.

I knew Amador was watching me, but not giving in to the voice was taking everything I had.

"MJ?" Her voice was small. I was scaring her.

Good. Let her be frightened of you. Let her wish she'd never crossed you. Make her regret every little thing she's ever done to you. She's happy and in love, and you're not. It isn't fair. Maybe it's not fair that she's still breathing.

I clenched my eyes shut and forced the voice to go away. My thoughts did not define me. I wouldn't let them. I was still in control. I was not going to let the manananggal win.

I took another breath, this time letting it out slowly. Neither I nor Amador said anything for a moment, and I appreciated the calm so I could gather myself once more. We had to think of a way to get out of here.

"You were talking to yourself . . ." Amador said.

Panic rose up, threatening to overwhelm me. I wanted to run as far away as I could, but of course I couldn't.

"What's going on?" Amador genuinely sounded concerned.

"Nothing."

"It doesn't sound like nothing. It sounded like . . . something . . . horrible."

"It's none of your business."

"Seeing as we're trapped here together and you're acting like you're possessed, it kind of is my business. I'm not stupid."

What choice did I have? Would it be a better idea to tell her that the queen of Biringan was losing her mind and talking to herself with a monstrous voice? Or would it be better to tell the truth? She was my archnemesis, the very last person I ever wanted to know about this. I would rather have died first than let her find out, but if I didn't warn her, she might not be careful around me. She might get hurt because I couldn't control myself.

"I killed that horse. Not the wakwak." My words felt like they were strangling me.

"What?"

"I'm a monster. I'm turning into a manananggal."

After a moment, Amador scoffed, but I could hear the edge in her words despite her sarcasm. "Ha ha, stop scaring me."

"If you don't want to see for yourself, we have to figure out a way to get down. Now."

Her bemused smile fell. All I could do was close my eyes. I hated the way she stared at me, like she was trying to see the truth.

"You're serious?"

I didn't answer, but I opened my eyes.

I waited for her to hold this fact over my head, dangle it like a juicy piece of blackmail that I knew she would be desperate enough to wield against me. I was trapped with my worst enemy.

The corners of Amador's mouth scooped down, and she scoffed. "You're not," Amador said, but I could tell she believed me, even if she didn't want to.

"I am," I said, glaring at her.

"No, no way. That's not possible—"

"You heard about the feral manananggal attack in the city? It was me. I didn't know what was happening then, and it's only getting worse."

"And were you planning on telling me before I went marching off into the woods with you?"

My face got hot with anger. "It's not like I asked for this," I said. "I don't know what's happening to me, and frankly, you're the last person I want to know about it."

"Who else knows?"

"Why does that matter?"

"Who else?" she asked again. There was something in her tone, though, that didn't have the edge I had expected.

"Nix."

"That's it?"

"Go ahead, make fun of the girl with one friend. Does it feel good?"

But Amador only huffed, and she rolled her eyes.

"The faster we get out of here," I said, "the faster I can get back to my room and lock myself up so no one gets hurt."

Amador fell silent, staring at the jungle with a stony expression equal to mine.

"I know it's hard for you to empathize. You're the one with the perfect life, the perfect fiancé, the future. So you win, I guess."

At the word *fiancé*, Amador's eyes darted to me. A paleness fell across her face, and she lifted her chin. "You don't know me at all."

"You haven't exactly been the most fun person I've met since I've come here."

Amador looked a little guilty, but the snootiness didn't leave her face. "How do you stop turning into a monster?"

"Why do you care? Once it's permanent, you'll never have to see me again."

"Shut up!" Amador snapped. "I want to help you!"

"Why? You have done nothing but make my life miserable ever since I met you."

I could feel her anger radiating toward me, and it felt good to finally call her out.

"I have until the full moon. And then it'll be permanent. Before that, someone has to make a vow of true love, probably marry me, and the curse will be broken. But you've stolen the only person I've cared about." Of course, I didn't need to say his name. We both knew where we stood on that front.

Amador's eyes were round as she looked at me. "Lucas?"

"Yeah," I said. Admitting it felt good, like a weight had been lifted off my shoulders. It didn't change anything, but it felt nice to say it. "That's who you could smell in the flower, right? Rose and mint?" I scoffed. "Not like you care. You can't help but parade him around in front of me. So my options are becoming limited, thanks to y—"

"It's not my choice. My mother is making me marry Lucas," she blurted out, interrupting me.

I almost didn't understand her. I paused. "What does that have to—"

"I'm gay."

"You're . . . what?"

"Gay. A lesbian. I like women, all right?" It sounded like the words were caught in her throat, and it took everything to get them out.

It was like I'd been hit by a truck. Never before would I have thought that Amador—the spoiled duchess who flaunted her betrothal to Lucas in my face, who took every chance to hang off his arm when I was near, who made every interaction with her an act of torture—wasn't who I thought she was.

And then I realized, maybe all the hate between us had never been about me at all.

Amador's face had turned bright red. She didn't look at me as she spoke. Her eyes, shiny and forlorn, were turned to the floor.

"I'm not judging you for being a lesbian, if that's what you're afraid of," I said.

"It's not that. It's . . . You don't understand anything about me. Okay? Court politics are brutal. As the grand duchess and my family's only child, I have to find security and keep our family's political standing. My father . . . he's not absent. He's hiding. He made bad investments, and our entire future hinges on me now to pay back his debtors. It's all on me . . . When I was a child, my mom always told me that I would marry a handsome man some-day, a man who could protect me, give me children of my own, give me a title. But I'd known even then that I was different . . . I told my mother that I liked girls. She laughed at me like I was joking, and said I didn't. And I wanted to believe her. Because otherwise, that meant I was different.

"I thought something was wrong with me, so I felt like I had to prove to the world that I was in love with Lucas. I tried to convince everyone that we were in love, because maybe then I could convince *myself* that we were in love. But nothing changed. I still liked girls. Me being happy doesn't matter. My parents only want to think about their position in court, and they'll use me to get what they want."

"Does Lucas know?" I asked.

Amador swallowed thickly and nodded. "He was one of the first people I came out to. He was one of the *only* people I've ever told." She glared at me. "I guess now you, too."

"So he's still marrying you?"

"He's protecting me," she said. "He would never hurt me. He's keeping my secret. He promised never to tell anyone. And I owe him everything. He even talked to some smugglers about sneaking me out of the country so we wouldn't have to marry, but there is a magical clause in our oath of devotion that keeps me bound to him. My mother made us sign it, and I didn't know about the clause at the time. We signed it right when we got engaged. I found out the day we came here."

Amador was signing away her freedom just as much as Lucas was signing away his. It all started to make sense. This whole time, I'd thought Lucas used me, lied to me, dumped me . . . But now I understood. He couldn't be with me, not for selfish reasons but out of duty to his oldest friend. He wasn't who I had thought he was. He was noble and kind, and he was going to sacrifice his own happiness to protect someone else.

Was this why he had been talking with Romulo? To get Amador out of Biringan City?

When I'd asked Lucas that night we met Qian why he was marrying Amador, why he'd lied to me, and he said he couldn't tell me, it was because he'd made a promise to her. And I'd hated him for it.

My heart lodged itself in my throat. It explained so much, especially all those times we kissed. His desire to be with me was so powerful, but he wasn't a cheater. He was true and good. Again, I'd misjudged him.

"Can't you call off the engagement?" I asked.

"I can't." Tears swam in her eyes. "I wish I could, but I can't. I don't want to live like this anymore. I want to be with the person I love."

Roses and mint . . . Those were what she had smelled in the flower. Her heart really did belong to someone else. "What's stopping you?" I asked.

"You don't get it!" she snapped. "The oath of devotion is powerful magic. It binds our souls together. If either one of us breaks our promise to the other, we die. We need magic to lift it, but my family is determined to see me married. I'm powerless." The word escaped her like the wind had been pushed from her lungs, and I realized it was because she was crying. She laughed breathily. "I'm literally powerless."

"What do you mean?"

"I can create lightning, storms, or I used to be able to . . . Ever since I came to terms with the fact that I am a lesbian, I haven't been able to do so much as summon a static shock."

"And you've been taking out your insecurities on me."

"I don't need a therapy session from you!" Amador snapped.

Seeing her like this, her eye makeup smearing down her cheeks and her face getting all puffy, made her look . . . well, human.

"So, since I'm going to die here, you might as well know! There you go! Are you happy now?"

"No," I said truthfully. My heart hurt for her, and that was honestly something I never thought would have happened. "I'm sorry you're going through this."

Amador hiccuped and stayed quiet for a moment before saying, "I'm sorry you're turning into a monster . . ."

I didn't think I'd ever heard her say those words before: *I'm sorry*. An amused smile worked its way onto my lips. "Do you know this is the longest conversation we've ever had?"

Amador sniffled but didn't say anything. Maybe she, too, was thinking about all the times we'd fought. I didn't know about her, but I was tired of it.

"You're not going to die here, okay?" I said. "We have to work together if we're going to get out."

Amador let a final fat tear roll down her cheek before she nodded. "Okay. What's your plan?"

"See that rope there?" I asked. I had to use my chin to point. "That's the rope that's holding up the net. If we can cut it, we can get back to the ground."

"You mean fall."

"Do you have a better idea?"

"No."

"Can you grab it?"

Amador wiggled next to me, and I didn't complain when her elbow dug into my shoulder. "I think so."

She stretched her arm out through the net, but her fingers just barely missed.

"It's too far. We have to swing," she said.

"Together," I said.

It took us a second to coordinate, but once we started shifting together, leaning from one side to another, the entire net started to swing back and forth until, finally, Amador was able to grab on to the rope.

"Got it!" she cried.

"Awesome. I've got a knife at my hip. Can you reach it?"

I never went anywhere without Elias's gift. It was like a reminder that he was always there to watch over me. Now it really felt like he was.

I felt her fingers brush against the hilt of my knife, and she huffed and puffed, straining to grab it. "Almost," she said. "Hold on." She gave one final push, and the knife slipped out of its sheath. She let out a gasp of victory and then yelped.

"What?" I asked, panicked.

"I nearly dropped it. I've got it, though."

"Okay, good job. You're doing great."

Amador seemed taken aback that I actually gave her a compliment. She cleared her throat. "Okay, hold me steady. I'm going to cut us loose."

The rope vibrated while Amador started sawing through the net, making a scraping sound as she went. At first, it was slow going, and then gravity took over. The net broke, my stomach floated up with a horrible lurch, and we fell into a heap on the jungle floor.

Amador let out a cry, and my back slammed hard onto the ground, but we were free. I kicked the net off us and found Amador clutching her wrist. Fortunately, neither of us had landed on the knife. It lay on the ground safely away from us, so all I had were a few bumps and bruises.

"I'm okay," she said, clutching her wrist to her chest, though her eyes swam with tears. "Just a sprain."

Amador and I stayed there on the ground for a moment to catch our breaths.

"I'll keep your secret, too," I said. "I won't tell anyone."

Tearily, Amador looked at me, color rising in her cheeks, and then back up at the sky. "Tha—thank you. I'll do my best to help you however I can . . ."

"Really?"

"We can't have a monster for a queen, can we?"

18

BY THE TIME Amador and I made it back to the great house, everyone else had already returned. It had been a while, and obviously we had worried them. Qian ran up to us, breathless. "Are you all right?" he asked. "We started to wonder what happened to you."

"Here's your flower," I said, holding it out to him.

His eyes went wide. "You actually found it?"

"You didn't think we would?"

"We looked everywhere and didn't find any."

"Then I guess we're better at hunting than you are," I said.

Qian's mouth lifted up into a smile, and he laughed. "I think so. Then I owe you this."

He took my hand and kissed my knuckles. It shocked me how soft his lips were, and I almost flinched away, but I was hypnotized by his touch. I could smell him—bergamot, just like the flower.

"Your prize," he said, looking up at me under his brows.

"Thank you," I said, taking my hand back. My skin felt electric where his lips had touched it. I didn't know he could rattle me like this.

"What happened here?" he asked, moving to Amador next.

"We got caught in some kind of net," Amador said.

Qian's eyes widened again. "A net? Ah!" He cursed. "We must have missed one. It was supposed to catch the monster. But it seems it caught the maidens instead."

"Well, the flowers were right by the trap," I said, lifting my chin. "Clearly you weren't paying enough attention when you laid it."

"Clearly not. I apologize, Grand Duchess Amador. Truly, if there's anything I can do—"

"I just need to go to the infirmary. Nothing to worry about." She looked down her nose at him. "Though I won't be so forgiving next time."

I took Amador by the elbow on her uninjured arm. "If you'll excuse us," I said to Qian, and left. I could still feel him watching me, even with my back turned, and I tried not to think about how I liked the way he had kissed my hand.

In the infirmary, we found Nix and Lucas. They were chatting, just like old times, and when we walked in, their smiles fell.

"Amador's hurt," I said.

Amador held out her wrist, and Nix looked flummoxed. Lucas went to her with concern all over his face.

"What happened?" he asked Amador, putting a calming hand on her elbow, guiding her to sit.

"We fell into one of the traps Qian set," she said.

Nix made a disturbed noise, a kind of squawk that reminded me of a chicken's. "What?! That's so irresponsible of him! Why didn't he warn you? You're lucky you didn't get more hurt!"

Amador said, "Yeah. Fortunately, I wasn't alone."

Lucas looked at me, and I felt the heat rising in my cheeks.

I wanted to tell him I knew what I knew, but I didn't want to go back on my promise to Amador, especially so soon. I would pretend I didn't know her secret for as long as she needed me to.

Even though I knew the truth about him, still he couldn't be mine. It was no matter that I was a queen; I couldn't interfere in the betrothal between members of the court. Amador's family was determined to see her marry him, and all I could do was watch from afar and know that it was because he was a good person who would not turn his back on his friend.

"I should have been there to protect you," he said to Amador.

"It's nothing to worry about at all," she said.

Nix gently took her wrist and turned it over, inspecting the injury. "Nothing to worry about? You broke bones," she said, face pale.

I heard someone come into the infirmary, and I turned around to see General Heng. He had on his usual dark uniform, his knife ready at his side. "Sir Lucas," he said.

"What?" Lucas asked. I knew he didn't mean to sound so sharp, but he was frustrated. I didn't blame him.

"Prince Qian requests your assistance."

"What for?"

"We need you to search for any more traps that we may have missed. If you would be so kind as to follow me." He didn't wait for Lucas before he left.

Lucas let out a sigh and looked at Amador. "Go," she said. "I'm in good hands." Her smile was kind, her eyes bright, and there was a softness in them that I knew was true affection—a result of years of friendship.

Reluctantly, Lucas nodded and bowed to me before he left. As he did, I caught a whiff of him, the smell of steel, like a freshly sharpened blade. It brought me back to that cave, the closeness of him, the desire pulsing through his veins, and I tried my best not to linger on it. Knowing the truth only made me want him more.

I was cursed in more ways than one. I was cursed to become a monster, and I was cursed not to be able to love him.

"What happened, exactly?" Nix asked as she started working on Amador's wrist.

Amador explained the trap, but I filled in the rest.

"You're honestly really lucky," Nix said. "It could have been so much worse."

I didn't want to think about it. Guilt was hard to shake, even if I hadn't turned into a manananggal. The idea that it *could* have been worse was bad enough.

Amador glanced at me briefly before looking away, swallowing thickly. I knew she was itching to ask me more about what was happening to me, but she kept silent while Nix worked on her hand.

None of us spoke, and the air around us felt full with all the things that went unsaid. I couldn't take it anymore.

"Amador knows that I'm a manananggal," I said.

Nix gasped. "What?"

"I'm getting worse. I was angry, stuck in that net, and I could feel the manananggal trying to take over. I didn't want to hurt Amador, so I told her." It was a reality I had to face. "The manananggal isn't just coming out at night anymore. She's getting stronger."

"Is that what Gani told you when he asked me to leave?" Nix asked.

Before I could answer, Amador interrupted. "Wait, so is that why there was a manghuhula here? Was he helping you?"

"We thought he could cure MJ," said Nix. "MJ hasn't always been like this. He thinks that magic is making her turn."

"And I'm running out of time," I said.

"What?" That was news to Nix. I hadn't told her about the diary yet, so I did now.

I told them both everything, about the diary, about the mausoleum for Yara, the empty tomb, the full moon, all of it. I had to fill Amador in on most of the details. "At the full moon, it'll be permanent. If I'm like Yara, I'll be a manananggal forever. It's what her diary said."

"We have to tell Gani right away," said Nix.

"Not sure what he can do about it," I said. "Besides, he's long gone by now."

"Then you have to tell Elias. You can't keep this a secret anymore. Maybe he can help!"

I knew he was the second-best person to talk to, but I wasn't sure what else could be done. "Maybe. But . . . what if it's too late?"

Nix pressed her lips together and looked back at Amador's wrist, tracing her hands over her skin as she worked her magic.

No one spoke again for a long time. My thoughts swirled with everything that'd been happening. With Lucas. With Qian. With Nix. And now with my destiny. Was I really doomed? I was so tired, my thoughts were difficult to contain, hardly slowing down long enough for me to take a breath.

I rubbed my eyes with the heels of my palms and forced myself to think. Too much was at stake for me to lose any sense of myself now. I had to stay strong. But it was getting harder every day.

"All done," Nix said. She and Amador locked eyes briefly before Amador stood up, rubbing her newly healed wrist.

"Thank you." She cleared her throat and added, "Thank you, *Nix.*"

"Don't mention it," she said.

The air buzzed with tension, and their gazes lingered on each other for a little too long before Amador flattened her hair, tidying any wisps that had escaped, and left. Admittedly, it was odd to see Nix helping Amador, let alone Amador actually thanking her.

When Amador was gone, Nix let out a deep breath, like she'd been holding it.

"You okay?" I asked.

"Why do you keep asking me that?" She tidied up the infirmary, setting bottles and herbs back into their shelves and drawers. "You're the one we should all be worried about!"

I tried to laugh at the misery of it all, but it sounded weak.

"I think that's the first time I've ever seen you and Amador not biting each other's heads off," Nix said.

"I know. It's a new feeling, for sure. We might be on the same team now."

The tips of Nix's ears were pink. She passed me, and I caught a whiff of mint.

"That would be lovely," she said.

19

THERE WAS A knock on my door the next morning, and I opened it to find Amador standing there with a stack of books that was nearly as tall as she was.

Nix, who had been helping me tidy up my mess of a room from last night's transformation, chimed in from behind me, "Need any help?"

"Yes, please," Amador said. I didn't think I'd ever heard her say the word *please* before in all the time I'd known her.

Amador and Nix spread out all the books on my bedroom floor, arranging them into piles based on subject. Amador only briefly glanced at the manacles I'd used last night, still lying on my bed.

I had started to change before sunset last night. I had tried to stay in my own mind, but it was one of the most difficult things I'd ever done. It was as if some magical power was constantly dragging me down into inky blackness. Even if I paced my room, did jumping jacks and yoga, read horror books, it wasn't enough. I'd blink and find myself on the floor, with no recollection of ever lying down.

Once, I woke up standing at the window, my hand already on

the latch. It was terrifying. It was like I'd interrupted myself, like I wasn't in control of my own body, and the harder I fought it, the more it wanted to take over. Nix had barely managed to get the manacles on me in time.

From the safety of the bathroom, Nix had said she heard me talking to myself, laughing, too. I didn't remember doing anything like that. The rules were changing; the manananggal wasn't coming out just with the setting sun anymore. My time being human was growing shorter as the date of the full moon drew closer.

"What is all this?" I asked Amador, staring at the books.

"Helping you, duh," she said, like it was a stupid question. "This one here is about folklore and mythology." Amador pointed to one pile that consisted mostly of illustrated stories. Nix picked up the top book and flipped through it. "This one is history, and this one is a random stack I thought might be helpful."

"Where'd you find them?" I asked.

"The library. Where else?"

"I never took you for the studious type."

"Amador is full of surprises," Nix said, and then she went pale. "Not that I would know."

Amador pretended like she hadn't said anything and helped herself to the breakfast that had been brought up for us. I glanced at both of them, sensing that there was something they weren't telling me, but I kept my thoughts to myself.

While we ate, the three of us scoured every book Amador had brought. It helped that Amador had grown up in Biringan, so she had heard all the stories of the manananggal before, but she was lacking knowledge about myths from our world. It was so normal seeing monsters in movies and reading about them in books, it was basically common knowledge.

"So, explain to me what a vampire is again," Amador said. "How are they created?"

"Becoming a vampire can happen a few different ways," Nix said. "Sometimes they're bitten and 'infected' in a sense, other times they're killed and then resurrected, and sometimes they're not turned but born that way."

"A manananggal isn't so different, I guess," Amador said. "They walk around like anyone else during the day, but at night, they hunt for their victims. Some of them don't even realize what they're doing. It's like they have two different minds in one body."

"That's what it feels like," I said. "And I only have until the full moon to figure out a way to stop turning into a manananggal."

"Like what happened to Yara?" Amador asked, and I nodded. "Well, I'd never heard of her before, especially not in class."

"I think she died," I said. "Her diary said that she was becoming less human every day. After that, she was never seen again."

"It still doesn't explain why her tomb was empty," Nix said.

I nodded. "I think she became the lady of the mountain. I . . . I think I saw her ghost."

Both Nix and Amador leaned forward. "You did?" Nix asked. "Where? When?"

"Yesterday, before Amador and I got caught in the trap."

Both their eyes got round, and they stared at each other. I think they believed me. Why would I have any reason to lie?

"But how could Yara have possibly turned into a ghost haunting the mountain?" Nix asked.

"I don't know." I didn't mean to sound so defeated, but it definitely came out that way.

Amador tugged another book from the stack toward herself. "Obviously, some kind of magic has to be at play. We just need to find out what."

We got straight to work, doing all the research we could. But trying to find any information about a cursed princess was nearly impossible. Without any proof or documentation of what happened back then, it was hard to know what we were looking for.

As the day stretched on, it became harder for me to keep my eyes open, and the urge to nap in the warm afternoon sun started to take over. I had only meant to close my eyes for a little while, and I didn't realize I'd fallen asleep with my face between the pages until I opened my eyes, momentarily blinded by the sun. I thought I was dreaming. I swore I saw Nix brushing Amador's hair behind her ear and Amador gazing into her eyes. But the next time I blinked and sat up, Nix and Amador were on opposite sides of the room. I sat up and stretched, and Nix perked up when I did. "Good! You're awake! We found something."

That woke me up even further. "Oh yeah? What?"

Nix sat down beside me and opened a book about the five elements: earth, air, fire, water, and spirit. She pointed to a page that was covered in diagrams. "This chapter is about the magical properties of the four elements of nature, and this section is about the healing powers of water. It says here that there is an incantation to make the water even more pure. What if we used one of the natural springs here to amplify the effect? Edgardo said that the springs around here have some minor healing abilities, so all we'd need to do is say the right spell and *bam*! Super mega healing water."

"Of course! Kind of like how vampires are weak to holy water!" I said, smiling. "It's the next best thing, right?"

"Maybe we can wash it away like tar—scrub the curse out of you!" Nix laughed for what I think was the first time in days.

I turned to Amador for a little support, but she kept her face buried in a book. I could see the blush on her face even from behind the cover. "What are we waiting for?" she asked. She snapped the book closed and headed for the door.

She was definitely acting strangely, but I was too excited to care.

We wasted no time in heading to the springs in the jungle. Amador had been to them all since we got here, and she remembered each and every one. She led us to a spring that was about a forty-minute walk from the manor. At least one of us had been enjoying our vacation.

It was an almost perfectly circular spring, with a giant rock outcropping that jutted overhead like a tall diving board. The water was so blue, gradually deepening in color in the middle. It reminded me of the swimming holes in Mexico called cenotes.

I could already feel the magic in the air.

Nix and Amador stayed on the shore while I waded waist-deep into the spring, fully clothed. The water was the perfect temperature; it almost felt like I wasn't in a spring at all.

Nix called out to me, "I'll try to bring out the healing properties as best I can and say the incantation. If you feel anything weird or if you think something is wrong, let us know, and we'll pull you out."

Amador nodded, and I pressed my lips into a firm, determined line. I really hoped this would work.

As I waded deeper into the water, disturbing the glass-like surface, Nix raised her arms over her head.

"Oh, water, giver of life, hear my voice." She muttered the incantation under her breath and focused her power into the spring. At first, it felt like nothing was happening, but then I noticed that the spring was starting to glow, much like lights in a swimming pool, a kind of muted yellow from below.

When I cupped the water in my hands, it still had that same glow, like I was holding a pool of sunlight in my palms.

"You're doing it, Nix," Amador said.

Nix didn't open her eyes, but her eyebrows raised as if she, too, was surprised. "Wash away the darkness, cleanse and purify and renew."

My muscles relaxed as the water temperature rose, soothing my body into a soft daze. I dropped forward and below the surface, then sank down to the sandy bottom.

Sounds dulled to a low drone, and I realized it was the blood rushing through my ears.

The bottom of the spring was bright and alive. Nix's incantation made all the aquatic life bloom. Purple and pink seaweed grew so fast, it was like I was watching a sped-up video. Underwater moss and lichen stretched out across the rocky floor, moving with the power of her magic.

I closed my eyes and focused on the heat rising in my chest. Nix's magic, too, was working its way through my body. But just as it was filling me up, it began swirling . . . going down, somehow.

Like a black hole was dragging Nix's magic out of me.

The manananggal was fighting back.

I tried to do something, focusing my own power on controlling it to my will, but like before, my talent abandoned me.

My lungs burned for air, but I didn't want to give up. I had to keep trying. I put my hands to my chest, willing Nix's power in, but whatever was inside me fought back even harder. The hole in my chest was getting bigger.

Behind my closed eyes, I could see Nix's magic darkening as the monster consumed it, like it was desperate to fill the emptiness with whatever it could get its hands on.

It was then that I realized . . . I was hungry.

The edges of my vision turned red, like my eyes were filling with blood.

You think you can get rid of me so easily?

The voice made me spin around.

There, floating in the pool right in front of me, was . . . me.

I nearly screamed. It was like staring into a mirror. Same flowing dark hair, same heart-shaped face, same smile.

But her eyes—*my* eyes—were different. They were all red. Vicious, cruel, horrible.

The manananggal. This had to be a vision. This couldn't be real.

You can't kill me. I'm you, she said. Her smile was wicked and hungry. Her teeth turned into fangs.

My chest heaved, begging to inhale. My heart raced. Panic seized me like a cold fist.

The more you try to fight me, the stronger I get.

As she spoke, more blood filled my vision. She was changing, right in front of me, and so was I. She was making me. Like with her reflection, when she moved, so did I. I didn't have any control.

Her smile split wider; her hands turned into claws. I didn't want to watch, but she made me. Her claws moved down to her hips, and her tongue lolled out of her gaping mouth. I matched her movements. Her fangs looked needle-sharp. She laughed when she began to twist her torso back and forth, back and forth, separating herself from her legs. Pain ripped through my own stomach as she did. Muscles, spine, intestines—

No, no, no! Bubbles burst out of my mouth, and I screamed. But I wasn't just screaming. I was laughing, too.

Just then, a hand plunged from the surface and grabbed my shirt, and I broke out into fresh air, sputtering and hissing. *Amador.*

I'd made it out, but all I saw was red.

I distantly heard Amador screaming and then felt a cool hand on my forehead. *Nix.*

I swiped out with my claws before everything went black.

The next second, I blinked, and I was lying on my back at the edge of the pool. I was me again, not a monster. Nix's magic must have triggered my transformation somehow, but she had stopped it.

Amador and Nix were collapsed on either side of me. Nix panted heavily, her hand still on my forehead, and stared at me with wide, wet eyes. Amador, on my other side, was gasping for breath. She'd dragged me to the shore but slipped on the mud and fell next to me. She'd ruined her dress doing it.

"Did I . . ." I looked at my hands. There wasn't any blood on them, but I couldn't be sure what was real. "Did I hurt you?"

Both Amador and Nix shook their head. "You were turning, though," Nix said. "We had to pull you out."

So it hadn't worked. My heart sank. I sat up and looked out across the spring. I needed to see if *she* was still in there, if she'd been real after all. But I knew, deep down, that it had all been in my head.

"I thought you were drowning," said Amador. "Can you imagine if the queen died because of something I did?"

"My magic," whispered Nix. She looked stunned. "It was like you were . . . consuming it. I've never felt anything like that before."

"I was hungry," I said. "Or the manananggal was." Though at this point, I was starting to wonder if we weren't one and the same.

I sat in the soft grass, my knees tucked up to my chest, while Nix and Amador went through more pages of the book, talking between themselves about the next possible solution. But the manananggal's words still rang in my ears. *You can't kill me. I'm you.*

"It was a good effort," I said, making them both turn to me. "We'll just have to try something else."

Nix's gaze danced across the surface of the water, her lower lip jutting out. Amador sighed and crossed her legs, wringing out her dress with her hands.

I scrubbed my hand down my face and tried to take a calming breath. "If Qian or anyone else from Jade Mountain sees me, I'm in serious trouble."

"It's my fault they're here," Nix said. "If I'd just stayed in my kingdom, they wouldn't have come for me."

"But then you wouldn't be in my life," I said. "And what would I do without you?"

Nix smiled sorrowfully, then said, "Maybe I should go back to Jade Mountain."

Immediately, both Amador and I rounded on her.

"Absolutely not," I said.

"You can't!" Amador cried.

Nix's lower lip trembled. "But I can't find a way to help you. I don't know what I'm doing. And with Qian here, I'm putting you at risk."

She was trying her best to help me; I'd never blame her for anything.

WHEN WE MADE it back to the grounds, I spotted Qian on the lawn, bow in hand once more. To my surprise, Lucas was with him.

Qian handed Lucas the bow, and Lucas stepped up to take a shot. They were shooting clay discs again.

I kept my head down, hoping neither of them would notice me, but as usual, Qian did. It was like he had eyes on me at all times.

"Your Majesty," he said, smiling. Then his eyes fell to my soaked clothes. "Are you all right?"

"Fine," I said. "Decided to go for a swim."

Lucas took in the state of my clothes, too, his ears turning pink briefly before he yelled for the game master to pull, and the clay disc shot up into the air.

He let loose, and the clay disc shattered into pieces. Bullseye.

"Changed your mind about hunting?" I asked.

Lucas handed Qian the bow and swiped his hair back from his forehead. "Yes, my queen." Formal as ever.

He was keeping his distance from me, even though I knew the truth. He'd put up his walls once again.

Qian hefted the bow and clapped him on the back. "Good shot, Sir Lucas." They were acting friendlier toward each other, at least. Qian handed the bow to another one of his men before he walked up to us.

He dipped his head to get a better look at Nix, whose head was lowered in defeat. "You feeling all right, little sister? You seem a little peaked."

Nix did look sick, but I imagined it was because of the enormous amount of magic she'd summoned into the spring. "I'm fine," she said. Before Qian could ask more, she turned and left, Amador rushing after her.

I should have gone, too, but my feet felt glued to the ground. Nix must have felt like she was failing me—that she was failing her kingdom as well. It was a lot of pressure to put on one person. I didn't know what to say to her that would make it all better.

Qian's gaze caught mine, and he smiled. "Would you like to see if you're a better shot than Sir Lucas?"

Lucas barely reacted to that. He took a sip from his drink, doing his best not to look at me, but I knew he was fighting his instincts. I could feel it radiating off him, the hammer of his heart-beat, and then I realized it wasn't me who could sense it, but the manananggal.

A shiver ran down my spine and I focused on Qian. The warmth in his eyes was like an anchor. He was the one person whose mind I could change. Even if I became a manananggal forever, at least

Nix could be free. But also, I found myself actually wanting to be with Qian more and more. He made me feel less afraid about everything these days, though I knew that sense of safety would be jeopardized if he ever learned what was happening to me . . . And yet, I still found comfort being in his presence. He was the eye of the storm, and the closer I was to him, the calmer I became.

"Sure," I said. "I'll take a shot."

I had to keep my distance from Lucas. For his sake. Even though it was like I was cutting a part of my body clean off by denying the pull to him, I had to let Lucas go.

I followed Qian to the spot on the lawn where one of his men had just finished his shot. He'd missed, drawing jeers and teasing from his friends, and Qian handed me the bow just like last time.

I felt Lucas's eyes on me, but I focused on the feel of the bow in my hand. Qian guided my arm into the right place. I had the distinct impression that he was only doing it now as an excuse to touch me, and for a brief moment, I was fine with that. I liked the way his body felt next to mine, his bergamot scent enveloping us.

I peered down the line of the arrow, and the game master shot the clay disc into the air. I tracked it, lining up the disc with the sight, and let the arrow fly.

Qian whooped with the others when the disc burst into pieces, but the first person I looked at was Lucas. He simply bowed his head and took his leave.

"Thank you, Prince Qian," I said. "It was fun."

"Back to formalities?" he asked. "Have I done something to upset you?"

"Just the opposite," I said.

The way he was looking at me made my insides fuzzy. I excused myself. It was starting to get dark, and I had to prepare for tonight, but I couldn't stop thinking about the way I felt in Qian's arms. I hadn't felt that safe in a long time.

As I headed indoors, an idea wormed itself into my brain.

20

I FOUND NIX in the infirmary, and she wasn't alone. Amador was with her. They were seated around a desk, their heads bowed low together as they read over a book about curses and jinxes. I almost reconsidered interrupting them; they looked to be having a peaceful moment skimming the pages together. They were still searching for ways to help me, even though I knew that the cure could only be true love. That's what the stories were about. Every fairy tale my mom told me growing up ended with true love's kiss, with the curse being broken and the couple living happily ever after. If I was going to get my happily ever after, though, I needed to ask Nix for her permission.

"Hey," I said. It was like my voice had broken a spell. Amador and Nix jumped to their feet and lurched away from each other, acting like they'd been caught in the act of something shameful. Amador's eyes flitted in Nix's direction before she dragged them to the opposite wall, staring intently at the glass jars. Nix's face had turned pink, but she looked at me solidly.

Her reaction almost distracted me from why I'd come here in the first place. "Are you okay?"

"I should be asking the same of you. What brings you here?" Nix asked.

I swallowed nervously. I wasn't sure how she would react to my idea. "Would you like to sit down?" I gestured to the chair, and Nix sat, but Amador didn't.

"Is this about your curse?" Amador asked.

"Yes," I said, meeting Nix's eyes.

Nix's face brightened. "What is it? Did you find a new clue?"

"Kind of. Yara was cursed after she got her heart broken. That's something we have in common. She said that the mambabarang had told her she needed to find her true love—marry someone to break the curse. So maybe that's what I have to do, too."

Nix looked at Amador briefly, then back at me, confusion knitting her brows together. "Okay, so does that mean you and Lucas will find a way to be together?"

"No, it can't be Lucas," I said. "It has to be someone else."

"Someone else?"

My smile twitched. Maybe in another life we could have been together, but Lucas was bound to Amador. It was too late for us. "I've come to realize that even though I'm a queen, I can't always get what I want. I have to think of my kingdom now and how I can best serve my people."

Nix's confusion turned into concern. "What do you mean?"

I took a breath. "The only way I can ensure peace between Biringan and Jade Mountain is . . . with marriage."

I saw Nix doing the calculations in her head, her eyes boring into mine. "You mean, you're going to marry Qian? You're going to marry *my brother*?"

I flinched. "That's why I wanted to ask you first—"

"MJ! You can't marry him! You don't even know him!"

"It's what Yara couldn't do; it's the only way. If I marry Qian, take a vow of true love, I can break the curse. And at the same time, you'll get to stay in Biringan, and war won't break out. Our families will be united. Our kingdoms will be allied."

Nix stood up and paced the room, dragging her hands through her hair and pulling it out of her bun in the process.

"You don't think we could be happy?" I asked. "He's noble, and protective, and heroic. You know him; you know it's not the worst idea."

"No, but you don't love him. You love Lucas."

Amador looked guilty, but she kept unusually quiet, even when Nix looked her way as if asking for backup. Nix was right. I did love Lucas. He was the only person I could truly imagine spending my life with, but he wasn't an option anymore. It didn't matter if he and Amador didn't have a romantic relationship. I had to let him go.

"Not trying to say one way or another what you should do," said Amador after a moment. "But shouldn't you consider how Qian might feel? Doesn't he deserve to be with someone he loves and who loves him?"

That was the first time I'd heard Amador care about anyone else's feelings. But she was right.

Nix said, "Qian is a protector. He knows just as well as any of us that marriage for royals is more than that. Marrying MJ would mean he gains a valuable ally with Biringan. He values family more than anything, and if he can protect them, he'll see it done." She looked at me and asked, "Have you told him?"

"No, Qian doesn't know yet. I came to you first—"

"Not Qian. Lucas."

Heat rose to my cheeks. "No."

"So, then, what if it doesn't work?" Nix flung her arms wide. "What if you marry Qian and you're still a manananggal?"

"I know it's a risk, but it's one I have to take. I'm running out of time anyway, and it's my best shot."

"That's the worst excuse I've ever heard."

"We will be sisters," I said. "Real sisters."

Nix gaped at me like I'd told her I was moving to Mars. "You're giving up on Lucas to save me?"

When she put it that way, it formed a lump in my throat. "There are a lot of reasons why marrying Qian is what's best. It could be a good match. I'm sure Elias and my mom would approve. And trade agreements would be favorable. And Jade Mountain could use the alliance—"

"Stop talking like a queen and start talking like my friend."

That made me clamp my mouth shut. She was right.

"I like Qian," I said. "He's proven that he cares about you as much as I do, and we can have common ground on that front. You'll be free."

Nix's eyes swam. I knew I'd touched a nerve, but she had to know that I was doing my best to help her, just like she was doing her best to help me.

"So I'm asking your permission," I said. "I'm going to ask Qian to marry me."

Nix looked at Amador again, but Amador couldn't offer anything else. As daughters of rulers, we all had our destinies sealed the moment we were born. It wasn't fair, but at least I had the power to protect the ones I loved. I could prevent Nix from sacrificing her freedom in exchange for mine.

Nix rushed to me and wrapped me in a hug.

When I went to the overlook, Qian was already waiting. His back was to me while he looked across the expanse of the green mountains. I took a steadying breath before he noticed me. Amador had helped do my hair into an elegant knot, and Nix had weaved in a tiara of jasmine flowers, making me up to be presentable for my proposal, but I had no idea how he would react. I wrung my hands, my stomach full of butterflies, and I approached Qian.

My fingernails felt sharper; so did my teeth. I had checked them over and over in the mirror while Amador and Nix were getting me ready, but my mind was playing a cruel trick on me. I couldn't actually see any difference, but I felt it. I didn't have much time left, but I needed to do this if I had a chance at saving everyone. But turning into the manananggal in the pool had felt more complete than before, as if I was becoming the thing I was supposed to be all along.

When I got close, Qian turned around, and he smiled when he saw me, at least for what I was on the outside—a beautiful queen.

"Good afternoon, MJ," he said. "You look lovely."

"Thank you," I said, but I didn't feel lovely. I felt wicked, but it was the sickness of the manananggal inside me that was waiting to come out. I had only three nights left before it would be permanent.

"What did you want to meet me for?" Qian asked. "The steward just said something about you wanting to see me, but he didn't specify what about."

"I have a proposition," I said.

Qian's eyebrows shot up, intrigued.

"I know you are not engaged, and you have yet to start courting anyone, but I think it would be a fine match if we were to marry. Soon."

Qian stared at me for a brief moment; then an amused smile slid across his face. "Well, now, I wasn't expecting that, I have to be honest."

My stomach hung high with nerves, and Qian must have seen the tension on my face, because he laughed. "Is this how engagements are always done in Biringan?" he asked. I noticed the playfulness in his eyes. "Royals here certainly know what they want, and they go for it."

"I would hope that you can see why we would be good together," I said.

"Oh, I do indeed."

"Is that a yes?" I hated how eager I sounded. Desperate.

"I would have at least liked to have dinner with you before we leapt to such a conclusion," Qian said.

"I can arrange that," I said. "I am hoping to bring cooperation to our engagement."

Qian stepped toward me. I kept my shoulders back and my head high. In that moment, I could picture myself standing with him, hand in hand, greeting our kingdoms together in a united front.

"Will you marry me?" I asked.

Qian's eyes flashed with excitement, and then his gaze drifted over my shoulder. I turned around, and my stomach dropped. Lucas.

He'd stopped in his tracks, unknowingly walking in at the worst possible time. My entire body went cold as he stared at us, his eyebrows raised, his mouth slightly open. Based on the hurt on his face, he'd heard everything. It was like I'd shattered his heart into a million pieces, and all he could do was watch in disbelief at what was unfolding. He had to understand. I had to be strong.

An eternity passed before anyone moved, and Lucas gathered himself, drawing his face into a neutral expression that I knew required great effort because I was doing the same.

"Pardon," Lucas said stiffly, then backed away. I watched him go, noticed the tightness in his shoulders, the drop of his head, but Qian's hand slipped into mine, and his touch made me turn back to him.

He smiled at me and kissed my knuckles like he had earlier, brushing his lips so gently across them that it sent a shiver down my spine. His eyes ensnared me, head still lowered, and he smiled.

Seeing Lucas had shaken me, but I wanted to focus on what was happening now, and Qian's hand in mine was warm and strong. I could make this work.

"Tradition in my kingdom requires me to put in a little effort to court a beautiful queen. I would like to accept over a toast."

Qian called for servants to bring out a table, chairs, food, and drink, and together we sat overlooking the jungle. The waterfall rushed nearby, sending up a mist around us, which made the strawberries and mangos that had been brought out sparkle as if they were covered in dewdrops. A bottle of champagne sat open in front of us, which Qian poured into crystalline glasses.

Qian and I sat on rattan chairs across from each other. My stomach was in knots while I watched Qian pour our drinks. I could hardly believe that I was sitting across from my fiancé. It was difficult to wrap my head around it; everything had happened so quickly.

"I had no idea, based on our first meeting, that we would end up engaged," Qian said.

"It's not every day that your future fiancée punches you in the nose."

Qian's smile was warm. "When most people want to marry me, it's not the first thing they do."

"You've had suitors before?"

"Twice. Both times were not good matches. It seemed they loved the title of empress more than they loved me."

"Doesn't that come with the territory of marrying a prince?"

"I don't have any aspirations of being emperor," he said. "I find it's too limiting. As an emperor, I can't fight for my people the way I want to. There are rules and parameters I must abide by. It's not the life I want to live. I won't take my father's throne. The title will pass on to my younger sister Mazu. I can do more good as a prince, I think."

I understood where he was coming from. He didn't have the hunger for power that some might. He wasn't ambitious or marrying me for a title.

"Though if you accept my proposal," I said, "you'll become king of Biringan."

Qian's eyes crinkled when he smiled. "Simply a formality. I do believe we would make a great pair, though."

"You would be free to spend time in Jade Mountain with your family. I would not force you to choose to live with me if you didn't want to."

"I appreciate that. And I would not ask you to move to Jade Mountain."

"Don't you think you're being a little hypocritical now? What about Nix?"

Qian turned to gaze across the valley, and I saw his face in profile. He was regal, and still, and gentle, and I could tell he had a lot on his mind. He tapped his finger thoughtfully on the back of his hand as he held his hands together. "I believe you're right," he finally said. "Nix is free to stay in an ally's domain. I'm sure she would like that."

Relief washed over me. Peace was all I'd ever wanted. "Good," I said. "I'm glad."

"Me too. And since we're moving awfully quickly through our betrothal, I didn't have proper time to find you a gift, but I want to make sure we follow protocol, to the best of my ability."

He took off his archer's ring and slipped it onto my finger. It was a little too big, but it was made of pure jade. With a little magic, it would fit perfectly.

"This ring protects the skin of my thumb when I draw my bow, just how I protect the ones I love. The symbolism is not lost on me as I give it to you now." He smiled. "On Jade Mountain, our wedding customs are a little more involved. This is the least I could do on such short notice."

"Oh!" I said, and reality sank in. We were getting married. *Married!*

"Would you prefer more flowers?" asked Qian with a tip of his head.

It took me a moment to realize he thought I was disappointed. "N-no!" I stammered. "I just . . . it's beautiful. I can't believe it; that's all."

"I hope this is an adequate display of my affection for you," he said.

I stared at the ring. The stone was warm and smooth, just like his hand. "Qian, I . . ." When I looked up at him, his eyes captured me. He watched me with bated breath, and my own lungs hitched. This was a part of being queen. I could make a life with him, strengthen our kingdoms' bonds, provide a future for everyone. And maybe someday I could even love him. "Yes."

Qian smiled and leaned in. I could smell the champagne on him, and my eyelids fluttered. His lips looked soft, and his eyes were heavy, their blueness deep. The temptation to close the gap was overwhelming.

"I very much like you," Qian murmured. "I hope you feel the same way. You have a knack for driving me crazy."

"I do?"

Qian nodded, his eyes drawing to my lips.

"I didn't know I had such an effect on you," I said.

"It's hard to look away when you walk into a room. Everyone stares." His eyes met mine again, and my pulse quickened.

"Being a queen helps."

"Not just that. I see the way Lucas looks at you."

Heat rose to my face as I thought about our meeting in the cave. "He's engaged. We're just friends."

"You don't think he loves you?" Qian asked, with a curious tilt of his head.

I thought about what to say for a long moment. "He can't."

"And you don't love him?"

"I'm his queen."

"You didn't answer the question."

I chewed on my lip and lowered my head. Qian reached out his hand and placed his palm on my cheek, tipping my face up to his. His hand was large and strong, and my spine tingled with anticipation. I found myself leaning into his touch.

"I don't want to be a consolation prize," he said, his words barely above a whisper. "I'm yours, or I'm nothing."

He was right. It wasn't fair if he thought that I was marrying him because I couldn't have Lucas. It was the truth, but it would be an awful way to start our future together. "You're mine, and I'm yours."

Qian's eyes bored into mine, and I could have fallen into them. Desire filled me up like an overflowing cup. I could stare at his face for hours, admiring the slope of his nose, the curve of his lips, the fullness of his eyelashes. His hand moved from my jaw to my hair, brushing a piece out of my face and behind my ear. It sent a shiver down my spine, and heat rushed through me.

I put my hand on his, finding that my own were trembling. We were so close, and Qian was all I could see. Then I leaned in and kissed him.

Qian's lips met mine, gently at first, and then more fervently.

His fingers curled against the back of my head. I could feel his pulse under my hands as I traced them up his neck.

It was the type of kiss that felt explosive, like fireworks. His touch sent my mind spiraling with sensation and pleasure. It was incredible. We broke apart for a moment before Qian moved in again, more forcefully this time, crashing his mouth into mine. I melted into him, into how good it felt. His breath was hot, and his tongue slipped between my lips. A gasp escaped me, and I could feel his smile against my mouth. I held on to him, pulling his body toward mine, and kissed him back.

He was my future. I could break my curse, unite our kingdoms, and maybe, finally, be happy. It was all I could ever hope for, and Qian could give it to me. He wanted to give it to me. The way he kissed me was enough to show it.

When he pulled back, his hand still knotted in my hair, his gaze cast up and down my face, drinking me in. He must have seen the flush on my cheeks and the puffiness of my lips, because he grinned.

"I look forward to an eternity kissing you," he said.

It made me feel so light, I swore I could fly away. My eyes dropped to his lips again, our eternity with each other starting now.

When we came back into the great house, hand in hand, Qian's guards erupted in cheers. Even Heng clapped and smiled. Lucas, Amador, and Nix stood with them. Nix looked relieved but guilty, and she cheered, along with Amador. Lucas, however, looked like he'd seen a ghost. All the color drained from his face. When our eyes met, he looked like I'd stabbed him, all betrayal and hurt.

That was our fate. To love each other but forever be apart. Our duty to others would always come first. I didn't realize it until my eyes started stinging, tears threatening to come, but I blinked them away.

Qian spun me around and dipped me low, kissing me in front of everyone. He grabbed my hand and held out my new ring. Everyone went wild—everyone except for Lucas. He closed his mouth, took a breath, and his gaze fell to the floor. Lucas had made his choice, and so had I.

Qian righted me back on my feet, making my world spin, and he held me steady as I wobbled.

"It's official!" Qian said, holding my hand aloft. "This calls for a celebration, don't you think?"

"What did you have in mind, Your Highness?" Heng asked.

"First, drinks!" Qian called for a steward and ordered more champagne. When he glanced at me, grinning from ear to ear, I couldn't help it. I smiled, too. Qian radiated pride and excitement, and it was infectious.

In a matter of seconds, servants appeared with glasses of golden liquid and platters of food.

Nix went to Qian first and hugged him, and then she came to me. She took my hand, the one not still holding Qian's, and she looked at me with such tenderness, my heart ached. "I am so happy for you," she said, eyes swimming. "You're my best friend."

I hugged her close, and over her shoulder, I spotted Lucas and Amador. She was talking to him, but his eyes were fixated on me. Heartbreak was written all over his face, but I needed to be strong. I didn't know what Amador was saying to him, but I realized that maybe I didn't want to.

"How should we celebrate properly? How are royal weddings celebrated in Biringan?" Qian asked.

I wasn't sure. I'd never asked about it before, honestly. I didn't think I would be getting married so soon. I floundered for an answer, but Qian thought of an idea before I did.

"Perhaps a tournament," he said, "in the queen's honor."

His men cheered at that.

"A tournament?" I asked. I couldn't help but be intrigued. "Like a joust?"

Qian laughed at that. "Sure. Why not? A joust, melee, archery, you name it. We'll have all the best knights from both kingdoms compete, the winner named your champion. Heng here will no doubt put his name in the ring."

Heng looked pleased with that and smirked as he put the glass of champagne to his lips. "As you wish, Your Highness."

Qian grinned and said to me, "What do you think?"

The entirety of Biringan could celebrate, and everyone loved tournaments, didn't they? It would definitely be a way to show off our commitment to the entire world.

"That sounds like a spectacular idea," I said.

"I'm sure Sir Lucas would love to enter his name, too, wouldn't you?" Qian said, tipping his head toward Lucas.

Solemnly, Lucas nodded. "It would be my honor."

21

IT WAS THE last night before we were to head back to Biringan City. I'd already sent a messenger ahead of us to relay news about my and Qian's engagement so Elias could make preparations. Already I could imagine my mom's reaction to finding out I was going to get married. I wished I'd had more time to prepare her for the news, but it was almost the full moon. I still needed to make sure that I wouldn't hurt anyone when I turned into the manananggal tonight.

Nix fastened the iron locks on my wrists and tugged on the chain, making sure it was secure. My lips still tingled with Qian's kisses. During the celebration all afternoon, we couldn't keep our lips off each other. His touch was electric, making my body feel like it was buzzing. But the sun was already starting to set, and my eyes were growing heavy. I'd had to excuse myself before the worst happened.

"Are you sure you're going to transform tonight?" Amador asked from her spot on the lounge.

"Why wouldn't I?"

"You and Qian kissed. True love's kiss can break curses, right?"

"According to Yara's diary, it wasn't enough. I need to be married. A vow. That's why the wedding needs to happen as soon as we return to Biringan." Butterflies fluttered in my stomach at the idea that I was going to be wed in a couple days' time. I never thought something like that would happen to me, especially not with Qian. It felt like my whole future had shifted drastically over the course of this past week.

"It will definitely get people talking," Amador said. "People will start to speculate what the rush is for."

I knew what she was getting at. Why else would a royal couple hurry to be married if there wasn't a young royal on the way? "I don't have time to care about any of that." My wrists already ached from the iron cuffs, but I had no room for complaint. This was the only way I could keep people safe. The ring on my finger and the manacles around my wrists.

I wouldn't have gotten this far without Nix's or Amador's help.

Now that the excitement of the day was over, a thought was still nagging at me. "Are you two . . ." I didn't know how else to put it. "Are you two together?"

They glanced at each other, and before either of them could answer, I said, "I'm not disapproving. I just want to know."

They stood stiffly, subconsciously mirroring each other, and it actually made me smile. They were waiting for what the other was going to say, and for a moment, I thought maybe I had been reading into things, but Nix turned to me and nodded.

"When did that happen?"

"Since school let out," Nix said.

Amador's face was bright red, but she didn't move to hide it. She was standing like a deer frozen in headlights. But when Nix caught her eye, her shoulders relaxed, like she remembered to breathe. "I sprained my ankle trying on some new wedding shoes, and Nix healed me," she said.

"We started talking more and more, and we just . . ." Nix shrugged. What more could be said?

Amador deflated a little. "My parents don't know, though . . . I'm not sure I'll ever be able to tell them."

Nix asked me, "You're not mad at us? For keeping it a secret?"

"No way," I said. "I'm honestly more surprised that I didn't figure it out sooner. I guess I've been a little preoccupied with my own problems."

"You're turning into a manananggal," said Amador. "I think you get a free pass."

"A lot of things have changed. So quickly," Nix said. She handed me a bottle of sleeping potion, and I drank it. It would keep the worst of my transformation at bay. "And I know Qian is my brother, but I truly believe he's a good match for you," Nix said when she took the empty vial from me. "I just wish all of us were able to be with the ones we want."

Amador nodded solemnly.

"I do want to be with Qian, though," I said. "I really do."

Nervously, I used my thumb to spin the ring around on my finger. It was too loose. My insides churned, and I thought about my future. This was the best choice for my country, for my people. And I had a real chance at being happy. Nix was right: Qian and

I were a good match. But he would never need to know that it was because I didn't want to turn into a monster forever. Maybe someday I would tell him; maybe I wouldn't. I didn't want him to think that my proposal was purely for selfish reasons, but it was, wasn't it? The reason why we were getting married was both to keep myself human and to keep Nix by my side. It felt horrible, knowing that I really was as selfish as I feared. Perhaps I didn't deserve a happily ever after.

But Nix could have one. She could live in Biringan City and be free. I could give her that.

"The tournament will be fun, at least," Amador said. "Lucas will win for sure."

"I wouldn't be so sure about that," said Nix. "He'll be up against Heng. From what I hear, he's unbeatable. He's famous in Jade Mountain for his skill in the ring."

"Lucas is unbeatable, too," I said.

"He's never lost a fight," added Amador.

I knew I shouldn't take sides, but it would be nice for Lucas to win in my honor. At least I'd be able to see him more, especially before my wedding. Any more time I could spend with him was worth it.

For once, even though I knew I was going to turn into a monster tonight, it felt like a weight had been lifted off my shoulders. I could look forward to nights after this without worrying about what I would become.

I wanted to believe this was a step in the right direction toward a brighter future for everyone. But that was the last thought I had before darkness overcame me.

That night when I dreamt, I was flying again. Soaring across the treetops. The chains dangled at my wrists. I was stronger than ever, stretching my wings so wide, it felt like I could eclipse the sky. I was starving, but all I could find was a wild pig. Its screams sounded so human as I tore it apart.

22

THAT MORNING, RUMORS about a monster were abundant again. Edgardo assured everyone it was likely another wakwak. All the staff in the house were talking about it. A pig had been found torn to pieces—what else could it be? Everyone thought Qian had killed the monster and its eggs. Little did they know, the real monster was standing with him, arm in arm.

I'd gotten loose in the night; my worst fear had come to life. Nix was such a deep sleeper, she didn't notice or hear anything. The chains around the tree had snapped as easily as rubber bands. I must have pulled them so hard, they shattered.

I was getting stronger.

Qian wasn't satisfied with killing one wakwak, and he instructed a few of his men to stay behind to find its mate—which had to be the source of the second attack—and kill it. I almost expected him to lead his people, but he was to escort us back to the city, to make sure we all arrived home safely. He had taken it upon himself to see that his betrothed was protected.

I hid all my uncertainty and fear as Qian and I rode together, leading the procession. I could sense his excitement and joy. He looked so regal, sitting atop his horse with his head held high, and he kept glancing at me with a smile so large, I was certain his cheeks would start to ache soon. But he genuinely seemed thrilled to be with me. And I was thrilled, too. I was going to get rid of this curse once and for all, and I believed we could start something great together. I had to.

By the time we made it through the gates of Biringan City, preparations for the wedding had already begun. My royal colors bedecked seemingly every surface in the city. My family's flag hung from windows, banners had been strung across the roads, and purple and yellow sampaguita flowers, the colors of Sirena, blanketed the road.

Commoners flooded the streets to see us coming, and word spread fast, because the longer we journeyed toward the palace, the more people came. They cheered and smiled, calling our names, and Qian reached down from his horse to touch hands grasping toward him.

"The hero Qian!"

"My prince!"

"We love you!"

It was easy for people to like Qian. He had a magnetic charm about him that affirmed I'd made the right decision. He would make a great king, even if it wasn't his aspiration. He was born for it. Merchants and sailors called my name, congratulating me and throwing flowers from their stalls. Qian caught a flower and slipped it behind my ear.

"They love you almost as much as I do," he said, and kissed my knuckles.

Cheers erupted again, and I smiled. It truly felt like something out of a fairy tale.

I felt another pair of eyes on me, and when I looked over my shoulder, I saw Lucas watching me from atop his horse. He broke his gaze to survey the people around us, always on alert for anyone who would want to harm me. My heart felt like it was being torn in two, but I sat up higher on my saddle and waved to the crowd.

Everything was a blur. The moment we set foot inside the palace, Jinky appeared and beckoned to other attendants who would see to my pre-wedding preparations. They were going to turn me into not a bride but a vision.

The delegation from Jade Mountain was still traveling, so some of the other servants in my palace would make Qian presentable for the ceremony, and he gave me one last smile before we were both whisked away to our separate wings.

In the bathing rooms, I was passed between dozens of hands that scrubbed me down, oiled me up, lotioned, lathered, clipped, and trimmed every inch of me until it felt like my whole body had been microwaved. They rubbed my skin raw, brushed my hair so many times, I was amazed I had any left, and massaged my muscles to oblivion. I was getting the real royal treatment and should have been enjoying myself, but I couldn't stop my thoughts from spiraling with worry.

I wanted to be happy. I was overjoyed that Qian had agreed to marry and that I could give Nix the freedom she so desperately wanted, but I couldn't help but wonder if this would really work. Would marriage be enough to fix me? I had two nights left until the full moon.

I had to think positively. It was the only thing I could do now.

From the window, I could see the arena was already being set up for the tournament. Flags billowed in the breeze, and excited voices rose into the air. Tomorrow, Lucas would compete in the tournament, fighting to be my champion. And then I would be wed.

Even though I was going to be married to Qian, I couldn't stop thinking about Lucas.

What was he doing right now? What was he thinking? Did he think about me? Did he imagine himself in Qian's shoes? What would our lives be like if we weren't bound by duty?

One of the handmaidens took my hand and clicked her tongue when she saw the state of my nails, and my stomach twisted as she manicured the dried blood out from my cuticles. She didn't think anything else of it. I knew they must think there was some ulterior motive for me marrying Qian so quickly, that I might have a "surprise" on the way, but those kinds of rumors were the least of my problems.

The whole palace was a flurry of noise and activity as every person was assigned a task for the wedding. I, like the floral arrangements and the cake, was just another wedding decoration. I was carted around, handed off, and made up like a doll, passing between hands for my fitting. It was all a fog, and no matter how much oil they put on my skin, perfume they put in my hair, or gloss they put on my lips, they couldn't disguise the monster that was waiting to come out.

THE NEXT MORNING, the day before my wedding, I awoke alone and chained to my bed. Birds sang outside my window, and I could hear the distant ocean waves lapping on the beach. Sunlight pooled around me, enveloping me in warm morning light. For once, I had slept well. I had no memory of nightmares, no taste of blood in my mouth, no deeply unsettling roil in my gut.

I wondered if I had changed at all, and then, in the next moment, I realized the truth.

My teeth.

I ran my tongue over them, over and over. I put my fingers in my mouth, hoping that I was wrong. But no.

I had fangs.

In a panic, I unlocked the manacles and rushed to the vanity mirror. When I opened my mouth, I saw that my canines had sharpened, elongating well past my other teeth.

A cry broke out of me, and I pinched my fangs with my fingers, trying desperately to pull them out, to break them, to do something, but there was nothing I could do.

"No . . ."

Panic gripped my heart like an iron fist, and I couldn't breathe. Every time I closed my mouth, I nipped the insides of my lips, snagging them on my new teeth. I was turning into a monster. I was already halfway there.

The rest of my body looked normal. My fingers, my face—but what would change next? I paced my room, trying not to cry, but it was difficult. I was running out of time. No one could see me like this.

I went back to the mirror and practiced hiding my fangs, smiling demurely, keeping my lips closed to conceal the truth. I needed to be a queen for a little longer, just a little while longer, and this would all be over. Tears ran down my cheeks, and my lips trembled. On the outside, I looked like myself. But on the inside . . .

No one will ever love me.

No one can.

Shame and despair and fear clenched my throat while I looked at my face in the mirror. This was exactly what Yara had said in her diary. It was a slow transformation until it was complete.

My time was almost up.

My bedroom door opened, and attendants rushed in. One of them had my dress draped over their arms, a handful carried trays full of makeup and accessories, and another had my shoes. It was a procession of pampering and luxury. They talked excitedly with one another, giggling and laughing.

I didn't speak as someone brushed my hair, as another took my hand to polish my nails, as another applied red lipstick. I just stared at myself in the mirror.

THE ARENA ON the outskirts of the Market District was bigger than the ones in the human world, with tiers that stretched so high into the sky that sometimes clouds passed through the upper levels. Proper nosebleed sections. The grassy field below had been painted and divided into sections where each event would take place. Large projection crystals, like the ones I'd used to call my mom, hovered above the arena, magically created by illusionists. Each would get up-close angles and instant replay for the spectators, even the ones in the highest rows. It reminded me of watching professional football games with my mom on Thanksgiving.

Hundreds of thousands of encantos were here. The air in the arena hummed with excitement. Everyone was eating fried lumpia and banana chips, drinking calamansi juice and coconut wine, singing and cheering, celebrating the day. The party was already getting started.

People had a reason to celebrate. I, on the other hand . . . I just wanted today to be over.

The royal box, only a little higher than the field, was the perfect spot to watch all the action.

My heart hammered wildly in my throat when I saw Qian was here, seated on a tall-backed rattan chair, speaking with one of his stewards. When he noticed me, his eyes widened a little, and he rose to his feet.

He looked so dashing in his red Tang suit jacket, and he smoothed out the front as if he was nervous.

"Your Majesty," he gasped.

The crystals turned on me, capturing my appearance and broadcasting it for the masses, and I knew what they would see. They would see my golden gown, a brocade made of some of the finest silk in the hidden world. Rings, including the one Qian had given me, adorned every one of my fingers. Each ring matched the golden crown that sat atop my head like beams of sunlight, holding my veil in place over my face. I was a living sunbeam.

I heard gasps and then cheers when people saw me. They called my name, but all I heard was a cacophony of noise.

With the veil, my entire world was gold. I was grateful that it would at least hide my new fangs.

"You are a vision," Qian said, and held out his hand to me.

I was embarrassed that my hand was shaking when I took his, but Qian didn't seem to mind. He brought me to the edge of the box, where I could see the packed arena. People in the stands jumped and cheered for me, rippling like the surface of water in a storm. They waved their arms or waved flags, crying out my name.

"Queen Mahalina!"

A rush of something, perhaps pride, filled me up, and it took my breath away. All these people relied on me. But they would never really know me enough to truly love me. How could they? Tears pricked my eyes, and I waved to them, and the air buzzed with their voices as they screamed louder.

Qian leaned in close to me, his breath tickling my ear, so he could be sure I heard him over all the noise. "I am the luckiest man alive to have you at my side."

A blush rose to my cheeks, and I couldn't help but smile. Though beneath the veil my fangs caught on my lip and pricked my skin. My breath hitched the moment I tasted my own blood.

Horns blasted, and the champions filed out from a tunnel on the far side of the arena, escorted by pages carrying flags and flowers, dropping them at their feet like a red carpet.

All the champions were tall and strong, and they wore the

same high-necked sleeveless tunic and formfitting pants, ensuring that the competitors were evenly matched. Competitors from both Jade Mountain and the different courts of Biringan were mixed together, men and women encantos alike, all of them looking as tough as the next. Among them was Lucas. He walked with his shoulders straight, his head held high. My heart fluttered when I saw him. His eyes scanned the arena, taking in everything and studying the landscape for the best tactical advantage. I couldn't help but feel a little biased. I wanted him to win.

Qian and I stood at the front of the box while each knight presented me with a gift. Some of them gave me tokens from their own person, like handkerchiefs or necklaces, others gave me flowers, and some gave me fruit. Each of them pledged an oath to me.

"I will win for your honor, Your Majesty."

"I will win for your beauty, Your Majesty."

"I will win for your grace, Your Majesty."

Variations of that continued as the gifts piled up, and I thanked them all for participating.

Heng, broad-shouldered but light on his feet, stepped forward and presented me with a dagger. Qian accepted it and passed it along to me. The blade was cold to the touch.

"I will win for your future, Your Majesty," Heng said. His smile was sharp and confident.

"Excellent, General," Qian said, grinning.

When it was Lucas's turn to come to the box, he bowed. He had nothing in his hands; they were clasped tightly at his waist.

"Do you have a gift for your queen?" Qian asked, mostly amused.

"I have nothing that I can give that would be adequate," Lucas said. "I ask for a gift instead."

Murmurs flitted around the arena. Qian looked at me, then back at Lucas. The crystals zoomed in on Lucas's face, but he remained stoic and unfazed. If he was embarrassed, he didn't show it.

"What do you want?" Qian asked.

"To see Queen Mahalina's eyes."

The arena fell silent, and then murmurs and whispers curled around the stands. The other competitors shifted anxiously, knowing that he was breaking a social taboo.

"You wish to see my bride's face the day before our wedding?" Qian asked, sounding more curious than offended.

My heart pounded so hard, I was afraid I might collapse.

Lucas nodded. "To have her look upon me is the only thing I desire."

Qian turned to me, brows drawn together as if trying to find a reason to say no, but I squeezed his hand.

"Of course, Sir Lucas," I said.

Slowly, I lifted my veil, and the crowd gasped. Not because I was a horrible monster, at least. I could see Lucas clearly now, and I pressed my lips together tightly so they wouldn't tremble. I wanted him to see me, get one last look, before we couldn't do this again.

Lucas's face didn't betray any of the emotions I knew he was feeling. His shoulders rose and fell with each breath, but he looked at me so steadily, it was like I was the only thing in the universe.

His eyes shone with warmth, and all the history we had together was captured between us. Every feeling I had for him welled up inside me like a dam about to burst, but I stood strong and tall. I wanted to tell him how sorry I was, and he seemed to understand that.

With a slight nod of his head, a small smile lifted the corners of his mouth. It was a sad one, though.

The horns blasted again, signaling the end of the opening ceremony, and the rest of the world rushed back to me.

The games were about to begin.

Lucas turned and joined the other competitors to prepare.

I lowered my veil once more in order to hide the tears sliding down my cheeks, and Qian and I took our seats as the competitors met with their opponents. Each event was divided up into brackets, eliminating the losers and moving the winners on to compete against one another until there were only two left vying for the final title of the queen's champion.

I took a steadying breath, and Qian's hand slipped into mine, giving me a reassuring squeeze, and he patted the ring he'd given me with his other hand.

At first, it was difficult to follow everything at once. Each match was taking place simultaneously, so the arena was a flurry of movement as knights battled one another. There was an archery range where competitors fired arrows at targets from farther and farther distances; a net for teams to play sipa, like the match I'd seen at the great house; and even a field for competitors to play kalahoyo, where the goal was to throw a larger stone at a smaller one and knock it into a hole on the other side of the field. I'd watched the Olympics with my mom growing up, and it was very similar to that. The teams were competing for different honors, but the Arnis matches were the ones I paid the most attention to. They were the ones that would crown my champion.

Arnis was a martial art in full meaning. It was a weapons-based duel, each competitor given the same sticks. No blades allowed. Before I had begun training with Lucas, I had never thought of Arnis like an art, but it truly was beautiful to watch. Each strike and parry as swift as it was supposed to be deadly.

Some Arnis matches ended quickly, with the losers lying in the dirt, but other matches went on for half an hour or more. It was reminiscent of a real battle, brutal and fast, even if no one was to be hurt. I couldn't help but be reminded that an actual war had only been narrowly avoided because of our wedding.

From my seat, it was impossible to see whether Lucas had won his bracket or not. I had lost him in the crowd among all the people dressed just like him.

I wrung my hands under the folds of my gown, twisting the rings on my fingers so much, they started to rub the skin raw.

A horn blasted again, signaling the end of the first round, and cheers erupted.

Qian clapped as those who were eliminated left the arena. Among the remaining victors, I spotted Lucas, and my heart leapt with relief. He'd made it through.

I knew I shouldn't be worried, but I couldn't help but feel like something was wrong. The hair on the back of my neck stood on end, and my stomach twisted horribly, but I tried not to let it bother me.

While the remaining victors took a break as the referees reset the field, Qian reached for my hand and brought it to his lips. People cheered for us, begging for more. It was like he knew that the audience would want something to entertain them between fights. But he sensed my uneasiness.

"Are you ill, MJ?" he asked. "Would you like to take a break?"

I shook my head slightly. "I just have a bad feeling, that's all."

"There's nothing to fear. Of course, there's no guarantee no one will be hurt, but that's part of the game."

"I understand. I'd just feel awful if anyone were to be hurt in my honor."

Qian gestured to the eliminated knights now standing around the arena, dirty and beaten. "This *is* an honor."

Qian beckoned for more food and drinks to be served, but I wasn't hungry. The garlic in the lumpia might as well have been radioactive to me. I tried not to flinch every time a plate came near me.

As the day went on, each match got longer than the last as the strongest and toughest put up their best fight. The sun was high in the sky, beating down on our heads when the final contenders for the championship took the field.

"Sir Lucas and General Heng," Qian said, grinning. "Why am I not surprised?"

Lucas and Heng squared up alone in the middle ring. Sweat drenched both of them from head to toe as they eyed each other up and down, scanning for any sign of weakness or for the best point of attack. Lucas's eye twitched, and I could tell something was bothering him.

The announcer's voice boomed across the arena. "The final match is about to begin! Unlike the other qualifying matches, this will be a result of the best two out of three rounds. The victor will be crowned champion."

Lucas looked strong and ready, but I couldn't help the twist of nerves in my gut. He was shorter than Heng by half a head, but he looked faster and more agile on his feet. Heng had size and bulk on him, and I could only hope that Lucas knew what he was doing. I tried to remain composed, but my heart beat in time with the crowd stomping their feet, eager for blood.

I'd trained with Lucas long enough to know what to watch for. Lucas had to make killing blows with his batons, tapping anywhere on Heng's body to get a point. But that meant Heng was going to try his best to counterattack, too.

There was movement at my side, and Nix sat down in the empty seat next to mine, breathless and smelling like astringent. "I've been tending to the wounded. What'd I miss?"

Almost like they were answering for me, the referee blew the horn, and the match started.

Heng made the first move. His footwork was incredible. He stepped in, and Lucas deflected when Heng stabbed at his torso. Lucas was on the defensive, only able to stop Heng for so long until he came at him again.

Lucas dipped his spine backward as Heng lunged as if to slice his neck, and Heng let out a huff of frustration. "Fight me, Invierno!"

Lucas stared Heng down, circling wide. The muscle in his jaw jumped again, and I realized it was because he knew danger was close. But it wasn't just the fact that he was in a sparring match. No. There was more. The hairs on my arms were on end, too. Something was wrong. His power could sense it. But why could I? Was this the manananggal?

I glanced at Qian. His eyes were fixed on the fight.

Cheers rose up, and my eyes shot back to the field just in time to see Lucas find an opening and hit Heng in the side with his baton. The officiant called the strike and raised an arm, declaring Lucas the winner of the first round.

My heart leapt, and I had to stop myself from showing any favoritism, even though all I wanted to do was jump to my feet and cheer his name. The crowd roared in my place, chanting his name so loud, I could feel it vibrating in my chest.

But Lucas looked like he didn't even hear them. His attention was focused purely on the match, zeroed in on starting the second round. Everything else was simply white noise.

Qian clapped for Lucas. "Fine hit," he said. "He's good."

"He's the best," I said. I couldn't help myself.

A smile inched its way across Qian's lips. "We shall see."

I squeezed my hands into fists and watched as Lucas and Heng reset, preparing for another round. The horn sounded, and Lucas was on the defensive again. He was letting Heng make the first move, a strategy to get him to tire quickly, I guessed.

But Heng was fast, faster than I expected. When he stabbed at Lucas, his arm was a blur, and when he stepped forward, it was like he'd teleported. I blinked, thinking I was seeing things, but no.

Heng reappeared behind Lucas. Heng let out a yell and swung, his attack so fast that I barely saw it. If it weren't for Lucas's power, he would have been hit, but he dodged out of the way just in time, knocking Heng's baton away and countering as fast as he could. But Heng was faster.

"Heng's power is his speed," Qian said. "He should not be discounted so quickly."

Heng's attacks grew faster and more precise. Sweat dripped from Lucas's hair. He moved, dodging and deflecting, but I could tell that even though he knew danger was coming, it was still too fast for him to do anything about it.

The horn blew, and it took me a second to realize Heng had struck Lucas on his thigh and ended the round. Heng was so fast, I'd missed it. In a real battle, it would have been deadly.

Qian leapt to his feet and clapped for Heng, who was circling the ring and raising his hand for the crowd. The favorite from Jade Mountain was a popular contender. His face appeared hundreds of times on the crystals above us, showing his victorious smile.

"It's anyone's game now," Qian said, his eyes bright with excitement as he took his seat again. He leaned in close to me and took my hand. I flinched. I'd been so focused on Lucas's hardened expression, Qian's touch jolted me back into my body.

"It's an exciting match, for sure," I said.

"Heng isn't one to lose. This will be over soon."

Qian smiled at me, and I tried to smile back, but my heart was pounding so hard, I felt faint. I couldn't stop thinking that something terrible was going to happen. My skin felt too tight on my body, like I was going to burst inside out, and I tried to take a calming breath. I sent out a silent prayer for Lucas to win so this could be done and over.

Lucas and Heng faced off again in the ring, the air full of excitement and tension, and the horn blew for the final round. Cheers erupted when Heng made the first move, making Lucas race backward.

All the noise turned into a dull drone as the blood rushed in my ears.

Lucas needed to win. If I had any hope of marrying Qian, I needed Lucas to win. That he could still be close; that I could still look at him, even from afar; that I could still know he was there. It was the one thing I could hold on to—the knowledge that he was my champion would be enough. It had to be.

My vision began to darken. My heart beat furiously in my chest, hammering like an iron fist against my ribs, and my breath grew uneven and shaky. I squeezed Qian's hand so tightly, I felt him flinch, but I didn't let go.

Lucas let out a yell when his baton took the full brunt of Heng's hit. If he was going to win, he needed to attack. Now. He shifted his foot, digging his heel into the dirt, and changed tactics. He deflected Heng's hit quickly, and the rhythm of the fight changed, with Lucas now controlling the tempo. The crowd roared when he moved in, and this time, Heng was the one on the defensive.

Lucas was going to win.

I saw a flash of something, a reflection, something shiny glinting in Heng's hand. Then Heng lashed out. Lucas let out a yelp. Heng's hand darted back, and Lucas dropped his baton.

The crowd gasped.

Like a movie playing in slow motion, I was able to see everything so clearly. Lucas leaning back, one arm raised, ready to block.

Heng swinging down, a narrow blade in his fist, his face frozen in a snarl.

Before I knew what I was doing, I leapt to my feet and ripped off my veil.

"NO!" I screamed, and it was like time stopped.

All eyes were on me. And all I saw was red.

Distantly, I heard Qian call my name, but I was already vaulting over the box and rushing into the arena. No one could stop me. My pulse beat in my vision, thumping rhythmically, focusing in on Heng and Lucas.

Heng's eyes widened when he saw me coming.

"Do not hurt him!" I snarled, but it didn't sound like me. It sounded feral and high, like nails on a chalkboard. Heng turned his blade toward me, and something inside me snapped.

Searing hot pain ripped through me. My hands turned into claws, my teeth elongated, and my lips split at the corners. Agony, everything, everywhere. I could see Heng's pulse in the air like ripples on water, felt it quicken, heard it pounding, smelled his terror.

Flay him. Shred his skin. Kill him.

Fury roared through me like a forest fire, burning away every part of me that would have tried to stop. I didn't want to stop. I was hungry. I was starving. I wanted blood.

"What—" Heng gasped, his eyes the size of moons.

Lucas stared at me, agape, but sat frozen in the dirt. The human part of me would have been ashamed, but the monster inside was stronger.

Wings burst from my back, and I rose into the air, leaving my lower half behind.

I was a manananggal.

The crystals captured everything. My transformation, broadcast for everyone to see.

I shrieked and dove for Heng, claws out.

Then the screaming began.

23

I POUNCED ON Heng and dug my claws into his shoulders. He hit the dirt with a scream.

Guards yelled. Spectators fled. It was pandemonium, but I didn't care about any of that.

I bit into Heng's neck, sinking my teeth in. My mind rushed with euphoria when I tasted his blood, drinking it, sucking the life out of him. He scrambled to push me off, but he was too weak. In seconds, his hands dropped limply to the dirt.

I lifted my face off his neck, tipping my head back, savoring the taste of his blood. It filled the pit inside me. But the pit wasn't getting any smaller. In fact, it was growing. I needed more. I wanted more.

With my claws still in Heng's shoulders, I pumped my wings and took to the sky, carrying Heng with me. It was so freeing to fly. I soared through the air, my golden dress trailing behind me like a tail.

I was hideous. I was horrible. I was free.

Guards rushed into the arena as spectators ran for their lives. I could smell their fear. I wanted to taste it.

The guards who had once sworn to protect me were moving below, swarming like ants, shouting orders, and readying their magic. I wouldn't let them stop me.

A nearby guard took aim at me with fire cupped in his hands, and I dropped Heng to the ground just before I pounced. The guard threw the fire at me, but I passed right through it like smoke and tore into his arms with my claws. He screamed, and I licked the blood off my fingers.

There were so many people here, so many beating hearts, it would be foolish to linger on only one.

A woman screamed when I landed on her back and scratched her skin open with my claws, and then I jumped on another man who tried to run away. Their blood was delicious, and I wanted more. With each drop, my vision turned even redder, like my eyes were coated in it.

I took to the sky again, stretching my wings and throwing my arms out to soak up the life that was pulsing around me, when something hot and sharp pierced through my side. Blood spilled over my claws.

An arrow. I'd been shot.

Qian, flanked by guards, had a bow in his hand, his face tight with rage. He took aim at me again with a new silver-tipped arrow.

I opened my mouth wide, baring my teeth, claws out, and soared toward him.

Before my claws could touch him, Qian fell out of my grasp.

Lucas. He'd tackled Qian just before he let the arrow loose. It missed me by a hair, whizzing into the sky, and I reached out for

Qian, but my claws scratched at nothing as Qian and Lucas fell to the ground.

Enraged, I flung my wings out to circle back, but something heavy and cold lashed around my neck. An iron chain. It yanked hard against my throat, snapping my head back, and pulled me down.

I let out a scream, high and guttural, struggling against the chain, but I was weak against it. I hit the dirt, crawling on my hands to get away, but the guards had captured me. I beat my wings, but someone moved in and threw themself on top of me, grinding my wings into the ground.

I gnashed my fangs, searching for flesh to bite, but more and more guards piled on top of me.

Qian shoved Lucas off him and scrambled to his feet. He grabbed his bow again and took aim at me. I hated him. I wanted to kill him. I screamed at him, but Lucas appeared again and stepped in front of me.

"Don't!" Lucas cried. "You're only making it worse!"

Nix walked in, holding my legs in her arms. "Don't hurt her!" she screamed, pale-faced and terrified.

I hated everyone. I hated myself. I wanted to end everything. I wanted to burn everything down. I wanted to incinerate myself. I wanted to tear everything up. I wanted to claw my face off.

Nix laid my legs on the ground, then shoved a guard off me and kneeled by my head. I tried to scratch at her with my claws, but she slammed her hand down on my forehead, and my body seized up. I couldn't move. She had paralyzed me. Her magic enveloped me, and the rhythmic pulse of rage inside me faded.

My claws shrank; so did my teeth. My torso attached to my lower half. My strength left me, and all that was left was a hollowness in my chest and, of course, the pain.

Everyone close by watched as I turned back into myself, covered in dirt and blood.

A sob escaped me. I could barely breathe. I was ashamed and afraid.

All the carnage around me. I heard screams of horror and confusion and saw people stumbling around, gripping bloody body parts, and running away. Terrified.

This was all my fault.

Of all the eyes on me, the ones that hurt the most were Lucas's.

He stared, shocked, and all the color had gone from his face when he saw what I had become. "MJ?" he gasped in disbelief.

I was a monster, and yet he had protected me.

Nix's paralyzing spell had its hold on me, and everything faded into darkness.

The last thought I had was that I hoped I would die.

24

WHEN I AWOKE, my eyelids were still so heavy, I couldn't open them. I heard the sound of a fire crackling, and at first, I was confused about what had happened. Then everything came rushing back. I still tasted the blood in my mouth, remembered how it felt when my teeth pierced skin, how my claws ripped flesh. My heart jolted, and I tried to open my eyes, but every inch of me felt like it had a ten-ton weight on it.

The air was full of incense and almost chewable. It burned my lungs. I moved my hand and felt a cold shackle on my wrist. My manacles. I was chained to my bed. The iron cuffs were so tight, my fingers were numb.

A hand slipped into mine, gentle but callused, and I forced myself to open my eyes.

His face came into focus slowly, but I would recognize the shape of him anywhere.

"Lucas . . ." I cried. My lips were cracked, and my tongue was dry.

"I'm here," he said. He was sitting at my bedside; his hand was warm against my cold skin. He brushed his thumb over my knuckles, grounding me with his touch, and tears blurred my vision.

I turned away so he couldn't see my face. I knew I had changed back to normal, but I was afraid he'd see me for what I really was—the thing deep down. I held a sob tight in my chest, but it hurt. My fangs remained. Maybe I could never go back to normal again.

Lucas reached out and turned my face to his, and he kept his hand against my cheek. His thumb brushed a fallen tear away, and he looked at me so deeply, it was like he was seeing me for what I really was.

"All those people . . ." I said.

"No one was killed."

"Even Heng?"

"He lost a lot of blood, but he'll be fine."

Something like relief worked its way through me, but the guilt remained. I'd still hurt people; I'd still caused all this.

"MJ," Lucas said again. "It's okay."

"It's not! I'm a monster!"

Lucas pressed his full lips into a flat line, stopping just short of frowning at me, when the door behind him burst open. He whipped around, startled, to find Qian, looking furious, marching in, followed by Elias.

"—can't barge in like this," Elias was halfway through saying. "I will call the guards in here at once."

Heng, walking behind them, was still pale and held his arms gingerly so as not to disturb his shoulders. At least he was alive.

"I will go where I please," Qian spat. "Especially when my fiancée is keeping secrets from me."

When Qian's eyes landed on me, the stony determination hardening his jaw tightened. His brows narrowed, and unbridled contempt turned his handsome face into a sneer.

"You," Qian growled.

I held out a hand, pleading. "Qian! I—I'm sorry—"

"What are you?" he hissed. He could barely contain his rage.

Elias moved to step between us, but Lucas got there first. He pressed a hand on Qian's chest and pushed him back. "Calm down. Can't you tell she's cursed?"

"That is no curse," Qian said, pointing a finger at me. "That is a demon. An aswang of the lowest depths."

The horrible truth was that I didn't think he was wrong. I had done all those terrible things—no one else. It was all my fault, and I deserved to be feared. I deserved to be hated.

"She's not an aswang. And you tried to kill her," Lucas said.

"If you hadn't interfered, we could have rid the kingdom of this threat. She nearly killed ten people in the arena, including me."

"But she didn't," Lucas said, his words forceful. "She was provoked."

"It doesn't matter if she was provoked. She deserves to be put down, for the sake and safety of everyone in this kingdom."

My stomach plummeted.

"If you try to touch her, I will not hesitate to put you down first," Lucas said. The fire in his eyes burned so hot, I believed him. "And I won't miss like you did." Qian must have believed him, too, because his glare turned equally blazing. That comment must have hurt. Lucas knew how to get under Qian's skin.

"Gentlemen, violence is not necessary!" Elias barked, but Qian and Lucas were inches from each other's faces.

"Your queen tried to kill my top general," Qian said to Lucas, ignoring Elias entirely. "And if the guards hadn't arrived, she might have tried to kill you, too."

I found my voice, even though it was small and thick with tears. "Heng cheated," I said. "I couldn't stand by and watch that."

"So cheating deserves a death sentence?" Qian asked, turning his eyes on me. Rage had contorted his face. I hardly recognized him. "So this is the so-called safe place my sister has been living in these past few months? Kept hostage by a demon?" The muscle in his jaw jumped while he looked at me. I wondered if all he saw was the bloodthirsty monster I was turning into or if he saw a person who was as ugly on the inside as she was on the outside.

Elias, always reasonable, tried to regain control of the situation. "If I may, sir, I assure you the queen has posed no threat to Nix."

"No threat? She is a monster. She's been feeding for days, killing indiscriminately." He rounded on me again, accusation making his words sharp. "It was you at the great house, wasn't it? The rumors of the monster flying around? It wasn't the wakwak?"

I couldn't meet his gaze. Shame kept me silent.

"How long did you think you could keep this up? How long did you think I wouldn't notice what you really were?"

"I don't know what's happening to me," I cried. "I'm so sorry. Please. All I need to do is marry you to break the curse."

Qian looked stunned, like he couldn't understand why I would even make such a suggestion. "This isn't a curse. You are."

I didn't want to believe that, but a part of me did. Maybe the world would be better off without me. Wasn't I just as horrible as the thing that had killed his brother? Wasn't I just as evil?

Lucas put his hand on Qian's chest again. "Go outside and get some air," he said, pushing him back. "You're not helping."

"Gentlemen—" Elias began.

"You know what would help? Putting a silver blade through her heart," Qian said.

No one had time to move. He signaled to Heng so quickly, I didn't have time to process.

Heng drew his knife and rushed me, but Lucas was ready. He stepped in front of me, grabbed Heng's arm, and twisted. There was a horrible crack, and Heng screamed as Lucas broke his arm. Heng dropped the knife, and Lucas caught it. In one fluid motion, he slashed it across Qian's face.

Qian spun around, hand on his cheek, and howled. When he turned back to us, his face pale, there was a long cut on his cheek where Lucas had sliced him. Qian looked at the blood on his hand and then at Lucas, stunned.

No one that wasn't a monster had ever dared touch him.

"Lucas!" Elias shouted, appalled.

Heng fell to his knees, gasping with pain. He clutched his broken arm to his chest.

"Touch her and you're dead," Lucas said to Qian, still brandishing Heng's knife, fingers flexing on the hilt, ready for another round. "That was a warning. Don't make this worse."

"You spilled blood shared by the Jade Emperor," Qian said. "This means war."

Lucas didn't step aside. He was going to defend me with his last breath.

Qian sneered at Lucas, and then his gaze latched on to mine. "And to think I almost married you."

My last hope was slipping through my fingers. Without a wedding, I would be a monster forever. I wanted to plead with him to stay, but I knew I'd lost him.

"We're finished here," Qian said. And with that, he and Heng left.

"What have you done?" Elias stood, stunned, staring at the both of us. The reality of what just happened finally sank in.

25

RAIN PATTERED AGAINST the glass on my window. I watched it for a while, curled up, still chained to my bed. It felt like I'd already been here for a century. My body ached. I was hungry, but the dinner that was brought for me had gone untouched. Plain rice and water. I wasn't hungry for that kind of food anymore . . . The manananggal was taking over soon. It would be a full moon tomorrow.

I thought about my father, my mom, and my friends, and felt like I'd let them down somehow. At least my mom wasn't here to see what I'd become . . . Though I did wish I could see her one last time. She was safer in the human world. It was better this way.

Lucas and Elias had left me to discuss what to do next. I was too tired trying to stay human. It was as if the last shreds of my humanity were clinging to me by a single thread. I should have locked myself away like Yara had, sacrificed my freedom for everyone else, been brave. But I wasn't brave. I was afraid and lonely, and all I wanted was for someone to help me. And in the end, this was what had come of it.

My room smelled heavily of garlic; talismans dangled from every surface of the room—my walls, my bed, the ceiling. Incense clouded the air and filled my nose, all in an attempt to keep the monster inside me contained, but I knew that it wasn't enough. The healers in the palace didn't know what else to do with me. I didn't know how else to explain it, but I knew deep within me that something was wrong. Anytime I tried to pinpoint exactly what it was, I felt an oily black darkness bubbling in my gut, staining my heart. I was rotting from the inside.

I heard the door open, but I didn't move to see who it was. The sliver of golden light from the hallway spilled across the wall, and a shadow passed across it. At first, I thought maybe it was an assassin here to finish the job, and I didn't fear death. A part of me was resigned to the idea. Maybe it was better after all, for everyone, if I was put out of my misery.

"MJ." It was Lucas's voice. I would know it anywhere.

I felt the bed compress behind me, then his warm body curled against my back while he draped his arm over me. I wanted to shrink away from his touch, but I couldn't. I wanted to be held by him so badly; I was fighting with myself. His breath tickled the back of my neck, and I closed my eyes, imagining this as the life we could have had if things had been different. I imagined this was us on rainy nights, nestled against each other and drifting to sleep.

His lips brushed against my neck, and he gave me the smallest, lightest kiss. For so long, we hadn't been able to talk. The last time he'd kissed me felt like a lifetime ago. And so much had changed since then. *I'd* changed so much since then. I closed my eyes and wished this could last forever.

But it wouldn't.

I sat up, breaking away from him and letting the warmth go. The chains on my ankles and wrists clattered together, a constant reminder that I was a prisoner. A punishment of my own choosing.

"What about Jade Mountain?" I asked. "Is Qian gone?"

Lucas sighed heavily and sat up, too. He brushed his hair away from his forehead, then took a breath, letting his hands drop to his lap. "He's declared war on Biringan," he said. "His army will be here soon to 'liberate the kingdom.'"

"What can we do to stop him? What about our forces?"

"Elias and I had to organize as many encantos as we could, but our numbers are too few. The neighboring courts aren't ready. Usually with war, there's time to prepare. This feels more like . . ."

"Qian is planning a conquest."

Lucas sighed again. He looked tired. The circles under his eyes were dark, and a line had appeared between his eyebrows while his mind, no doubt, raced about all the things we still needed to do. He was wearing a cotton shirt and pants in Sigbin blue, and he looked so mature, even in the dim light of my room. He needed to stand against an army. It was his duty to protect.

"MJ," he said again, turning his dark eyes to me, pleading. "What happened?"

It was time to finally tell him the truth. "I don't know why or how this started," I said. "One night, I had a terrible nightmare. At least, I thought it was a nightmare. But when I woke up, I found out I'd hurt some villagers."

Lucas furrowed his brow in thought. "The monster before we left for the great house. That was . . ."

I nodded. "Me. Nix tried to help me. Amador, too, in the end."

A lot of things started to make sense for him while I spoke, and I could see it all over Lucas's face. "That evening in the cave?"

I nodded again. "I was going to turn. I didn't want to hurt you. I didn't want you to see me like this," I said.

When he looked at me, it felt like my heart was breaking.

"You let me . . . hate you," I said, choking on the words. A sob threatened to escape, but I stifled it. "I know about you and Amador."

Lucas nodded, but he didn't seem surprised. Amador must have told him that I did. "I wanted to protect Amador from her family's expectations, but I needed to protect you, too. I didn't want to choose between anyone, but I had to."

"I know. I realize now. I saw you at the docks with Romulo."

Lucas's eyes went wide, but he let out a breath. "Amador sent me to find a way to break our oath of devotion, and Romulo thought he knew of someone . . . I can't help but feel like I've failed both of you." He stared at the fire, his gaze distant.

"You're noble, and you pretend not to be. You affiliate yourself with thieves and pirates just as much as you do with princesses."

Lucas allowed himself to chuckle. "I never thought I stood a chance with you, though. You're a queen. You're supposed to marry kings—people who are your equal. I'm just a knight."

Lucas's jaw clenched, and he brushed his hand through his hair again. It was a nervous tic, one that made me feel closer to him after noticing. I only wished we'd been able to spend more time together for me to notice even more.

"I guess we're all bound to our titles," he said. "Why didn't you tell me what was happening to you? I would do anything to help you."

"I was afraid—afraid that you would want me dead."

His eyes glistened in the firelight, and he reached out and touched my hand. "MJ . . ."

"I'm a monster. I'm dangerous. How could you ever want to love me?"

Lucas looked ashamed. He lowered his head and swallowed thickly. "I should have told you from the start about my true feelings. But I respected Amador and wanted to protect her, too. Please forgive me. I won't keep any secrets from you ever again."

"We both kept secrets. I don't want to be away from you. I know you are bound to Amador, but I truly do love you."

Lucas's gaze leveled with mine. "I love you, too," he said. And I was ashamed it took me this long to believe it.

"I'm worried I'll never be able to say it again," I said. "Tomorrow night, with the full moon, I'll be a manananggal forever."

"We can't give up. There has to be a way we can stop it."

"I don't know what else there is to do. And even if there was, I'm not sure there's enough time."

Lucas slid off the bed and stood in front of the window, his hands folded firmly over his chest, thinking.

"Nix and Amador tried everything they thought of," I said. "The only history I found was about Yara Liliana."

"Who?"

"Exactly. She was a cursed princess, one of my ancestors, who had turned into a manananggal, too. I found her diary, and . . . she was never seen again."

"Did it say how it happened to her? Any clue we might have that can break the curse?"

"No. Though she did say her heart was broken, and she needed to marry before the full moon or else she would be a monster forever. It didn't happen soon enough for her, though."

Lucas looked guilty. "So it's because I broke your heart that this is happening?"

I pressed my lips together and shook my head. "People get their hearts broken all the time, and they don't turn into monsters."

"You're not like everyone else." Lucas's shoulders dropped, but he still looked pained. "There has to be something we're missing."

"I found Yara's tomb. It was empty. I don't think she was ever buried."

"Or she never died . . ."

"She looked like the lady of the mountain," I said. "I think she became a spirit to stop herself from becoming a monster."

That seemed to frighten Lucas. "You're not dying. I'm not letting that happen." He rubbed his jaw and paced the room. "And with Jade Mountain at our doorstep by tomorrow, it complicates everything."

Time was running out for everyone. I wasn't sure what else we could do.

"I love you, Lucas," I said. "But it's too late for me. You have to let me go."

"What are you talking about? I'm not giving up!"

"Why? I'll only hurt you."

"I don't care! I'll do anything to be with you, monster or not!"

I almost laughed. "Unless you have some magical antidote or something out of a fairy tale, like the power of true love's kiss—"

Lucas swept in and planted his lips on mine, stopping my words. My breath hitched, and my heart threatened to burst out of my chest.

My hands lifted as if by their own accord and rested on his shoulders, pulling him tighter against me. His lips were soft but firm, and he sighed into me. It was like nothing had changed between us. That day in the cave hadn't been magic at all. It was the desire the both of us wanted to act upon but were unable to show.

He cupped my face, his hands warm against my cheeks, and my mouth slipped open, deepening our kiss. The sound of the rain turned into white noise as we embraced each other, caught in each other's touch. His thumbs traced delicately against my cheek; the tips of his fingers brushed the soft skin behind my ears.

"I love you, MJ," he said, breaking apart from me briefly before kissing me again. "I've loved you since I met you."

His words lit something inside me, warm against the cold rot in my chest. "I love you, too," I said.

A cry escaped me, and I crushed my mouth against his. I smiled despite the aching sadness gnawing away at me.

He pressed himself against me, and I fisted my hands against his shirt, unwilling to let him go. I wanted him—I *needed* him to kiss me so I could at least have this moment to remember forever. Even if I forgot who I was when I finally turned, I wouldn't forget this last kiss.

His full lips were pillow-soft, each touch something new. He pulled me impossibly closer to him. Heat flared all through me. I felt like I could fly.

"I love you so much," he repeated against my lips. "I can say it a million times, and I'll say it a million more."

He wrapped his arms around my waist and lifted me to sit on the edge of the bed, then knelt in front of me. He kissed my fingers and my knuckles, eyes closed with such earnestness that it made me ache. "I love you—everything that is you," he said.

"Not how I am now," I said.

"I sense danger every day. And I have never felt it when I'm with you." He touched his lips to the fingers that would turn into claws, that could tear flesh from bones, and he wasn't afraid. He didn't shy away from me, even when I tried to curl my hands away from his mouth. I fought every instinct to hide, and opened my hand for him. He kissed each finger, dragging his lips up my hand, my wrist, my arm, my shoulder, my neck.

His breath was hot and sweet against my body, and it made my skin tingle. When he kissed me again, I placed my hands on his sides, pulling him toward me as I lay down.

He braced himself around my body and kissed me until my lips went numb, then touched me everywhere—my arms, my hips, my thighs. Even with my eyes closed, I could picture him so perfectly, his face hovering over mine, taking in every part that I hated about myself but that he seemed to love.

In the stories, they say that true love's kiss can fix everything, and in that moment, it was starting to feel true.

"Lucas," I said, between kisses. He pulled back slightly and looked down at me. I felt like I could fall into those golden-brown eyes and drown. "I . . . What about Amador?"

Lucas sighed and rolled off me. "Amador and I have an understanding. We both love each other—not like that, but still. I know she doesn't desire me."

"You really care for her, don't you?"

"Different kinds of love can be just as strong as romantic ones."

"And yet you have romantic love for a monster."

He tucked a loose piece of my hair behind my ear and kissed me again.

But I broke away from him, resting my forehead against his, and breathed deeply. The moment was so sweet, I wanted to appreciate every second. We stayed like this, our heads pressed together, his hand cupping my cheek. The rain drummed a beat on the window, reminding me that time was ticking away. I only wished for this to last forever.

"We all have darkness inside us," he said. "Yours is only a part of you, and I love you too much for me to stop because of it."

Even if these were my last remaining days as myself, they would be good ones with him.

The door suddenly opened, and light flooded into the room. Lucas and I peeled away from each other just as there was a surprised squeak, followed promptly by the door slamming again.

"Nix!" I shouted. "It's fine!"

Lucas wiped his mouth with the back of his wrist, color rising to his cheeks, and he lifted himself off my bed to adjust his clothing when Nix reappeared in the room, poking her head in first with a hand over her eyes.

"Sorry to interrupt," she said.

"You don't need to hide your eyes, Nix. Everyone is decent."

Nix lowered her hand and stared at the both of us before stepping fully inside. Behind her was Amador.

"Were you two just kissing?" Amador asked, a grin forming.

Lucas's mussed-up hair was a dead giveaway, but I said, "A little."

"How are you feeling?" Nix asked me.

I adjusted the iron cuffs on my wrists. "I don't feel any *worse*."

Lucas asked Nix and Amador, "You two were helping MJ this whole time? And I didn't know about it?"

Amador, arms still folded over her chest, tipped her chin in my direction. "You kept my secret; I kept hers." It was surprising to think that Amador had actually become my friend despite our history.

Lucas nodded understandingly. He looked at me the way I'd always wanted to be looked at. All this time, I thought we couldn't be together. He had so many reasons to be afraid of me, to run as fast as he could away from me, but he stayed.

"Well, we wanted to come here now because there's one other thing we can try," Nix said. "I'm not sure it'll work, but it's worth a shot, right?"

"What?" I asked.

"Amador and I were doing some more reading about aswangs, and a lot of them talk about the classic warding rituals to either weaken them or kill them. But I've read a lot about antidotes and magical panaceas, like bezoars and toadstones. But there was one that was rumored to be effective against flesh-eating aswang. It's called a coconut pearl."

"A coconut pearl? Like, a pearl from a clam, but inside a coconut?"

Nix nodded. "They're supposed to be incredibly rare, and it could take us lifetimes to find one. But if we do, it could be the cure we're looking for."

Lucas sighed. "But the chances of that are so low, maybe impossible, and by then . . ." He trailed off. He didn't want to say *too late*, but everyone, especially me, knew what he meant.

"But tomorrow will be the full moon," Amador said.

"And Jade Mountain will be here by then."

"Then we have no time to lose," said Lucas.

"It's useless," I said. "It would be too much. I can't ask that of you."

Lucas looked at me, a hard line in his brow, and he fisted his hands at his sides. "I'm not giving up on you."

Lucas went for the door, and I heard him call out to the guards standing just outside.

"By order of the crown, every available coconut is hereby a top priority. Merchants, farmers, and guards from all over Biringan are to bring whatever coconuts they can find here to the palace at once. Halt all other orders. This is for our queen's life."

"Yes, sir!" they said before rushing off.

Before hurrying after them, Lucas glanced back at me one last time and said, "I will move an entire mountain for you if I have to."

26

DURING THE NIGHT, Nix and Amador kept watch over me while Lucas and a team of a hundred of his best men collected all the coconuts in the region.

Elias oversaw the process, keeping the line moving to waste no time in finding a one-in-a-million coconut. I heard his voice carrying through the palace while I remained chained to my bed.

When daylight broke over the horizon, throwing the sky into a hazy pink, I closed my eyes and let sunlight wash over me. This might be the last sunrise I would ever see. I hadn't turned last night, but I had felt it in my body like a lead weight. My eyes ached, my muscles were sore, the bones on my wrists and ankles were bruised, and my skin was rubbed raw. My fangs had grown sharper—my nails, too—even though I had stayed awake all night. I was looking more like a monster with each passing hour.

The manananggal was growing stronger the closer we got to the full moon. A deep, dark pit in my heart was yawning wider, making everything oily and rotten, threatening to eat me from the inside out.

The whole morning, I sat at my window and watched a long

line of people from the city push wheelbarrows or lead donkeys pulling carts teeming with coconuts through the front gates.

By now, word had spread about me, and yet my people had come.

Anything to save their queen.

War was knocking on our door, and yet my people were still trying to help me.

Nix and Amador took turns keeping an eye on me, making sure I didn't lose my mind and escape, but if these were my last hours as a human, I was determined not to let them go to waste. I had to believe there was a cure out there, that I could stop this and save my kingdom from a needless war.

Whenever I walked to my window, cheers from people calling my name rose from below. At first, I thought they were jeers, but the more I listened, the more I realized that people were rooting for me to survive.

"They love you," Nix said, coming to my side. She looked tired, too, from worrying about what was coming just as much as I was.

"Why, though?" I asked. "I've hurt people."

"They want to help you, like you've helped them. You've changed the city, made their futures brighter. No hunger, no one is unhoused, no more human slaves . . ."

Amador added, "Even I have to commend you. You're one of Biringan's best."

Coming from her, that meant a lot. I wondered if I'd done enough, though. I'd had such a short time on the throne. "I hope they can forgive me," I said. "I want to be better."

"They know that," said Nix. "And they'll do anything for their queen."

As the sun stretched across the sky, the line to the palace never grew any shorter.

But with the passing day came Jade Mountain's troops. From my window, I spotted movement to the south of Lake Reyna. At first, I thought it was a warping of the evening light or the wind moving across the palm trees, but the longer I looked, the more I realized it was smoke.

"They're almost here," I said.

Nix came to my side and looked out across the land, squinting. "I don't see them."

My heart pounded. "My vision is getting sharper, then." I could see farther than I had ever done before.

"I have to warn Lucas," Amador said, rushing out of the room.

Nix stayed with me, watching as the army drew nearer—the army led by her brother, my ex-fiancé. He had come to liberate the kingdom from my rule.

She held out her hand for me, and I took it. She didn't flinch away from the sharpness of my nails.

"I'm sorry," I said.

"No, I'm the one who's sorry," she said. "It should have never gotten this far. I should have just gone home when I had the chance."

"It's no use blaming yourself. If you have the chance before Jade Mountain gets here, you should escape with the other civilians."

"I'm not leaving," Nix said, eyes shining. "I didn't leave then, and I'm not leaving now."

"The sooner you go, the farther you'll get away from here."

"But what about you?"

"Everyone's safety matters more to me right now."

Nix looked like she wanted to cry. She wrapped her arms around me and hugged me close.

When Amador threw open the door and came into the room again, she said, "There's a literal mountain of coconuts in the throne room."

"Any luck?" I asked, blinking away tears.

She shook her head. "Lucas is still searching for the pearl. And Elias is gathering the guards—"

"Jade Mountain will be here soon," I said. "We have no time to lose. Get as many civilians as you can to safety. Tell Lucas I want the palace secure. I will not surrender while I still live and breathe in these walls."

"But what about—"

"Forget it. There's no more time," I said. Along with the coconut milk, I could smell Amador's sweat and her blood pumping in her veins all the way from across the room, and I closed my eyes to refocus. I would not let the manananggal take over yet. I had to think of the people who were trying to help me. I had to help them now before it was too late.

Amador rushed out of the room again, her high heels clacking as she ran down the hall.

I called the staff and guards to give them my orders, and they listened. My word was law, but Jinky was the only one who protested. When I called her into my chambers and she finally saw me, she burst into tears. The reality of the situation must have sunk in just then.

"I won't go," she said, sobbing. "I can't leave you here alone."

"Yes, you can. You will go with your family to the tunnels. I relieve you of your duty. A lady-in-waiting has no duties in battle."

"But, Your Majesty," she said, voice cracking. "I cannot abandon you."

"Please, Jinky. Let me do this for you. I can't let you die here. If you won't listen to your queen, will you at least listen to a friend?"

Jinky, chin wobbling, nodded and left. The palace was already quieter, save for the pounding of metal armor and heavy boots of guards rushing to their posts in the palace. Outside my door, there came shouts. Jade Mountain was at our borders. My hands shook when I clenched them into fists. While I would not hide from Qian and the rest of his army, I couldn't stay in my room and wait for him to come.

Nix stood at the window, watching as Biringan City was slowly evacuated. On the streets, floods of people left their homes, carrying what they could on carts or in their arms. Children, being led by their hands, looked around with confusion and a little fear. Elderly people with canes needed help on the stairs, taking to the underground tunnels. There were so many people. I needed to give them time to evacuate before the worst descended upon the city.

When Amador came back, unusually disheveled and winded, she was alone. She had been running all over the palace on my behalf in heels and a long skirt, and she looked frustrated and annoyed.

"Where's Lucas?" I asked.

"He won't listen to me. He's still looking for the pearl," Amador said. She slapped her hands against her sides. "It would seem that he refuses to give up on you."

Nix squeezed my hand, and I squeezed back. It was time.

"I need to get to the throne room."

"MJ, are you sure that's wise?" Nix asked. "What if . . . what if you turn . . . ?"

"And become the thing that Qian knows I am?" I finished for her. "I'm still me right now, I know. We can't risk it. Don't remove the iron. Just unchain me from the bed. Please."

They looked at me, worry making the two of them hesitate.

Nix glanced at Amador, her mouth a thin line, and then she took the key from around her neck and approached my bed. She unlocked the chains tied at the foot of my bed and held them in her hands.

"Lock the chains together," I said, "and I'll carry them."

27

THE PALACE HAD been evacuated. All the lights had been doused, throwing the halls into shadow. Distantly, I heard the sound of armor and shields, barked orders, and calls for action.

The chains were heavy in my arms, but I carried them with my head held high.

Walking barefoot down the stairs, I witnessed the chaos unfolding around me. Guards and soldiers rushed around, hauling wooden barricades and sacks of sand. When people saw me coming, their gazes locked on to me, dread and trepidation in the whites of their eyes. I heard the beats of their hearts, rapid as rabbits'. I could smell the fear. The air tasted of their sweat. The halls quieted when my people saw me, like a hush spread across the palace, as if everyone was holding their breath.

"Your Majesty, it's not safe for you here!" one guard shouted. She was tall and blocked my path easily with her arms stretched wide, but I held out my hand.

"I am not hiding in a tower."

That seemed to be enough for the guard, who stepped aside, bowing slightly. "Clear the way for the queen!" she called.

The guards did as she said, stepping to the sides of the hall and bowing when I walked past them. All eyes were on me. The palace had turned into a fortress, barricaded and barred, supplies stacked meticulously for an invasion.

We would be at war any minute.

The line of people delivering coconuts to the palace had vanished, most of them leaving their carts or wagons behind in the evacuation. I followed the trail into the throne room, where I was met with the sight of mountains of halved coconuts, stacked all around the room.

Alone, Lucas stood, a hatchet in hand, sweat dripping from his brow. He'd left his jacket on the floor, working away in only his undershirt and slacks. He looked exhausted, and when he noticed me standing there, he straightened up.

"MJ," he said, panting. "I—" He looked around at all the coconuts, none of them having any trace of a pearl. "I tried, and I . . ." He fell silent, but I knew he was going to say he failed.

Even more unbroken coconuts surrounded him. It really had been a grand effort. It warmed my heart that he'd tried. His actions alone spoke more than any words.

A calm resolve settled over me. It was a long shot finding a mythical coconut pearl, but somewhere deep inside me, I knew that it was futile. Yara hadn't found a cure, and neither would I. I had gotten all of us into this mess, and it was time I faced it.

I held out my hand for Lucas, and he dropped the hatchet and took it, lifting my hand and pressing his lips to my knuckles. Tears pricked at my eyes, but I smiled at him.

By now, most of the remaining guards had seen what was going on, and some stopped to watch.

We had an audience.

Amador nudged me in the back. "You should say something."

Nix nodded encouragingly.

Lucas squeezed my hand and escorted me out of the throne room.

Jade Mountain must have set fires on their march toward us, because the air was thick with smoke. It softened all noise and color in the garden, turning it into a muted gray. A far cry from the life it once had.

As I walked across the lawn, more soldiers gathered around. No one spoke. It was like they were waiting for me to break the silence.

I needed to get up higher. I went to a wall tower and climbed, emerging on a parapet that surrounded the palace. Below me was a sea of soldiers, their faces turned up to me under gleaming helmets, waiting.

"I . . ." I started, trying to find the right words. If I had known I would be making a speech, I would have been better prepared. "I am an aswang."

A ripple of tension spread through the air.

I continued. "Prince Qian of Jade Mountain is right. Your queen is a monster, and I don't have much time left. In a few hours, I won't be your queen anymore. But I will not use that as an excuse to hide. I stand with you now. It is my duty to protect my people until my last breath."

"We stand with you, Queen Mahalina!" A shout burst up from somewhere near the back, and a flurry of others followed, cheering me on.

I glanced at Lucas, who nodded once, encouraging me to continue.

"An army has come to our door," I said. "If we do not open it, they will try to break it. They claim they want to liberate you. They claim that you are captives. They claim that you are beholden to a demon."

Roars of protest swept through the lawn, and my heartbeat quickened in my chest.

"They will not stop once I am dead. And I will not surrender. This is my home. This is *our* home. I will stay with all of you. Even if they burn Biringan to the ground, I will not abandon you."

A young soldier at the front called out, "We will fight for our aswang queen!"

Aswang queen had a certain ring to it, and other soldiers repeated it until it became a full-on chant.

Voices rose up, and soldiers thrust their fists into the air, crying it over and over again.

No sooner had the chanting started than a voice cried out from the watchtower above. "Incoming!"

There was a tremendous boom, and then the chanting stopped, as it felt like the whole world shook.

A fireball streaked like a comet and hit the side of the palace, sending debris flying. Lucas yanked me back just before a piece of rock fell exactly where I had been standing. He wrapped me in his arms and turned his face to the darkening sky. "They're bombing us," Lucas gasped.

Another series of booms shook the palace, each one so loud, I was amazed the palace was still standing. Overhead, a gigantic shadow flew by, and I distinctly saw it had a rider.

Lucas immediately leapt into action. "Captain Aquino," he screamed over the parapet, to the same guard who had tried to stop me in the hall. Her own fire blazed in her eyes. "You know what to do."

Captain Aquino nodded once, then bowed to me and started shouting orders.

Everyone burst into action. Jade Mountain was here.

Lucas took my hand again and pulled me back as encanto soldiers summoned their magic, light gathering in their palms.

"I'm not leaving them!" I said, pulling against Lucas's grip.

"I know, but we can't stay out of cover. We have to get to a stronghold. You're no good to anyone if you're out in the open."

Lucas rushed down the battlements, but there was a whoosh above us. A winged horse covered in glistening green scales streaked overhead, quick as lightning.

"Longma!" Nix called, pointing to it.

The longma's dragon wings tucked up into its body, and it dove toward us. A masked rider on its back stood on the stirrups, raised a fireball swirling in his palm, and threw it down.

The fire exploded in front of us, drenching the battlement in a wall of fire. Lucas skidded to a halt, and I crashed into him. He held out his arm to shield me. The fire burned so hot and large, the small hairs on my face felt as if they had been singed off.

The wind buffeted around us when the longma and its rider zipped across the sky. An entire cavalry of them circled above, raining down fire while my soldiers below summoned barriers, shielding most of the attacks.

"This way!" Lucas called, turning us around and running back the way we came.

Amador, now in the lead, tripped and fell on her long skirt, and Nix rushed to help her. Amador swore as another bomb exploded close to her, and when she was on her feet, she reached down and tore off the lower part of her dress, leaving it behind. We all took off toward the outer bailey.

A longma landed on the bailey's roof, and its soldier aimed a fireball right at us. Lucas yanked me inside, and the fire whooshed against the stone parapet. Lucas slammed the door behind us, and we were plunged into darkness. Occasionally, bright flashes broke through the arrow slits in the bailey, but everything was pitch-black. At least, it was to them.

"We can't stay here," Lucas said as he blindly felt around for the wall.

"We're trapped!" Amador cried.

Nix froze at the top of the stairs, her hand on the wall. "It's too dark!"

"I can see," I said. I wasn't entirely human anymore.

"What?"

"I'll get us down." I grabbed her hand. "Everyone, hold on."

Lucas and Amador grabbed on to me just before I leapt off

the edge, carrying everyone to the ground floor. Amador let out a shriek as we dropped, and the air rushed around us. We landed, a little harder than I'd intended, but at least we were on the ground and away from the worst of the bombings.

Lucas burst out the door and into the gardens. Fires lit up the sky like it was midday, and smoke filled the air, choking the life out of me.

Lucas led the way, pushing through soldiers rushing toward us, calling orders, and moving troops around for the best defensive positions.

I turned around just in time to see a longma and its rider soaring overhead, but a bolt of fire from the ground shot up and hit the rider in the side. He toppled off the saddle and plummeted to the ground, and the longma flapped its wings, fleeing into the sky.

"Get back to the throne room!" Lucas called, grabbing my hand. "Keep moving!"

"They've breached the gate!" a voice cried out from the wall. Fighting broke out, a clash of metal and shouting. Jade Mountain had broken through. I couldn't tell which side was which, who was fighting for whom. It was chaos.

Lucas sped to the front door of the palace, but it was already barricaded. There was no getting back inside.

Another bomb exploded overhead, and we ducked instinctively. My ears rang, and the air itself felt like it was splitting in two.

"We're stuck here!" Amador shouted.

"I know a way!" Nix said, and dashed along the wall.

She rounded the corner and pressed her hands against the stones like she was playing Whac-A-Mole.

"What are you doing?" I asked.

Just as I spoke, Nix's hand pressed down on one of the stones, and it sank into the wall, melting the stone away to reveal a hidden door. "Secret passages! I found them all over, remember? Came in handy sneaking around, kissing Amador."

"Later, darling," Amador said, breathless.

The moment we stepped through and Nix closed the secret passage again, it was as if the door had never existed. It was perfectly flush with the wall, hidden unless you knew what to look for. I could still hear sounds of the battle—bombs, shouting, and fighting—but the farther we got into the palace, the quieter it got. We reached the end of the tunnel only to emerge behind a tapestry in the grand hall.

Soldiers rushed by, barricading the door. The palace trembled with the sounds of more explosions. Jade Mountain was coming for me, and they would destroy Biringan City to do it.

"They're going to burn this whole place to the ground," I said, barely managing to hear my own words because my ears were still ringing so loudly. Growing louder.

Pain shot through my stomach, hot and all-consuming, and I cried out.

"MJ?" Lucas was at my side in a moment, his hands warm and strong on my arms. "What's wrong?"

The pain worked its way through me, boiling my insides. I was shaking; it hurt so much.

"It's . . . happening," I said. I shrank away from him, turning my head so he couldn't see. But he held on to me and refused to let go.

When Lucas met my eyes, his softened. "MJ . . ."

The pain subsided, easing away like the tide, and in its place came hunger. It filled in the pit that hollowed out my stomach, making the saliva gather on the back of my tongue. *You will hurt him,* that horrible, craggy voice said, echoing in my mind. *You will hurt him . . .*

"We have to get her somewhere safe," Nix said.

"Where else can we go? Jade Mountain is almost inside," Amador said. "How long will the barricades last?"

"Not long," answered Lucas.

Their voices were quiet compared to the ringing in my skull, resonating like a bell. Another voice broke through. *You will hurt them all . . . You want to . . .* The manananggal laughed, and that laugh was mine. I shook my head, reeling.

"You all need to get away from me," I told them.

Lucas, Nix, and Amador turned to me, their expressions equally shocked and appalled.

"We're not leaving you!" Nix said.

There came another thunderous boom, and more fire crashed down on the palace.

I insisted, "Even with the iron, I could still hurt you. I don't have much time left. The full moon is rising."

"We're not going anywhere," Lucas said. His eyes widened, and he threw himself on top of me just before the air exploded.

There came a crash behind us as the front-gate barricades blasted open. Soldiers flew back like rag dolls, and Jade Mountain's soldiers emerged through the smoke.

"Move!" Lucas screamed.

My hunger was excruciating, but I let Lucas drag me down the hall.

"There she is! Monster!" The shouts of the Jade Mountain soldiers followed me.

The ringing in my ears faded, replaced by my rushing pulse. I hadn't realized I'd stopped running until Lucas was tugging on my arms, yelling my name for me to keep going. But his voice sounded so distant. I saw his eyes, his fear, my name on his lips, but it was like I was watching something through a television screen. Like I was so far inside myself, I was a spectator in my own body.

I broke his hold on me and turned.

The soldiers raised their arms, their elemental magic burning in their fists, ready to strike. They must have seen the look in my eyes, because some of them paled with fear.

Let them fear me.

The iron cuffs on my wrists sizzled and steamed against my skin, but I didn't care. I walked toward the army.

"MJ!" Lucas screamed, but I ignored him.

Rage burned through me. This was me, the true me, on full display. A horrible, terrible, unlovable creature.

It was over before it started. I rushed them, tearing my claws into flesh, biting necks. No fire could hurt me. No ice. Nothing at all could stop me. I didn't feel a thing except for the way their skin broke so easily against my fangs and how delicious their blood tasted. Their screams were music to me. When the last scream faded, everything came back to me. I had control of my body again. But for how much longer, I didn't know.

Blood dripped from my claws, down my throat, off my chains.

Smoke curled up my arms from where the iron touched my skin, but it didn't bother me. Everything I saw was red.

My friends stared at me, seeing me for what I truly was. And I hated it.

Pain ripped through my stomach, like my own claws had dug themselves into it and were threatening to rip me in two. Pretty soon, I really would.

"Lucas . . ." I said. But the pain was so intense, I couldn't move. I dropped to my knees, and Lucas rushed to me in an instant.

"Come on!" He picked me up, lifting me under my back and under my knees, carrying me down the hall as he ran toward the throne room. I curled against him, my nose full of the smell of blood, and held on, though I wished he would leave me.

Everything hurt, not just my body. The pain was deeper than that. I was losing myself in it.

More shouting erupted behind us. More soldiers had come in. Nix and Amador hurried behind Lucas, terror stiffening their faces to look like masks.

Amador screamed and lurched forward, clutching her shoulder, when a fireball hit her. Her dress burned, but she didn't stop running. Nix was the first to the throne room, throwing the door open for us and slamming it shut once we were inside.

The mountains of coconuts towered around us. Lucas set me down on the floor in front of my throne. His shirt was covered in blood, none of it his. It was all from what I'd done.

The sounds of the battle were duller, but it would only be a matter of time before Jade Mountain soldiers broke through.

"MJ," Lucas gasped. He brushed my hair back from my face,

but I didn't want him to see. My fangs scraped against my lips. My mouth was peeling wider, splitting at the corners. "It's okay. I'm here."

"Go," I said, my voice a horrible rasp.

"I'm not leaving you."

He held my hand in his, ignoring my claws.

Amador was on the floor, too, curled into herself, holding her burned shoulder. "Nix," Amador gasped. "I . . . I'm hurt."

Nix rushed to her side and worked her magic. "Don't move," she said, tears streaming down her cheeks. "I'll make it better."

A battering ram shook the throne room door, making it tremble with each tremendous boom.

"We're trapped," Amador said. "There's no way out."

All of us knew she was right. The throne room was the most secure area in the palace. There was only one way in and out.

Amador looked at Nix for a long moment, her eyes round and shocked. Nix's hands hovered over her shoulder, healing the burn with intense focus, but the tears in her eyes betrayed her.

"I really wish I could have told you how much I love you," Amador said.

Nix's smile was small. "You just did," she said. And without any hesitation, she kissed Amador fully on the lips. The moment was short-lived and bittersweet. When Nix pulled back, she wiped Amador's tears away. It was almost like a kiss goodbye.

Despair settled over us like a dark cloud.

The floor shook with each boom of the battering ram.

But Amador yelled in frustration and stood up, hands clenched at her sides. The skin on her shoulder was shiny and red.

"It's not fair! I only start to figure out who I am, and then I die?" She let out a wild laugh of frustration. "I can't believe this! I won't! I want to kiss Nix, and I want to love who I choose, and I want my life to be mine!" She stamped her foot and howled to the ceiling.

When she did, electricity arced between her fingers.

Her power—it had come back. Nix must have felt the energy, too, because she leaned back, surprised. Amador stared at her own hands, and her blue eyes lit up with the power crackling in her palms.

Amador raised her arms. Her dress was torn, her hair was wild, and her face was set with determination. Blue electricity whizzed around her body, making her hair stand on end. She looked feral, and dangerous, and beautiful. She reminded me of lightning itself.

A wide, wild smile appeared on her lips, and I realized it was because she finally felt free.

"I'll slow them down," she said. The air in the throne room felt full and smelled like petrichor. "Take cover!"

Dark clouds swirled on the ceiling. Thunder rolled and wind kicked up as Amador summoned a storm. Rain fell, drenching us in a matter of seconds.

"We have to get back!" Lucas shouted. He pulled me away, dragging me toward my throne and shielding me with his body.

The throne room doors burst open.

Lightning crackled and shot out of Amador's outstretched arms. The hair on my body stood on end a split second before a deafening crack and a blinding white light streaked through the air.

Jade Mountain soldiers rushed in.

Nix moved for cover, but she yelped when large hands wrapped around her and snatched her off her feet.

General Heng. He was here.

He was taking her.

"No!" she screamed, her voice lost to the wind. Heng clamped her mouth shut with gloved hands. She thrashed and fought, her eyes wild, as more of Qian's men held her wrists so she couldn't summon her power.

I couldn't get to her. My legs weren't working.

Through the storm, emerging from around a mountain of coconuts, coming for me, was Qian. He was dressed for battle: dragon scale armor, red cloak, knife in hand. He seemed to barely acknowledge the storm raging around us. His eyes were locked on mine.

"Leave the monster to me," he said.

28

QIAN'S MEN POUNCED on Lucas, slamming him to the floor.

Lucas struggled, but they pressed his head to the cold marble and bound and gagged him. He fought to break free, but it was no use, not with five men on top of him. Their knees dug into his back, and he let out a wheeze.

He watched me, eyes wide, fearful, as Qian stepped over him.

Prince Qian towered over me. His eyes were cold and sharp, just like the silver blade in his fist.

"You've shown the whole city what you really are," Qian said. "Look at you. You really thought you could trick everyone into thinking that you weren't a monster?"

The pain in my stomach was so unbearable I could hardly move, even as Qian lifted his foot and kicked me down the stairs leading to my throne.

I yelped when I hit the bottom and struggled to rise, but I was so weak. Everything inside me screamed for this to be over. I wanted Qian to end it so I wouldn't have to go through this anymore.

"The aswang queen of Biringan," Qian said, pointing at me

with his silver knife. "You thought you could hide, but in the end, monsters always reveal themselves."

"You can stop this," I said. I could hardly get the words out. "Stop the invasion. I'm the one you want."

"You will no longer be a curse on this land."

Gani's words came back to me: *There are curses to inflict on one's enemies, but it is a mirrored arrow. What shoots forward must also shoot back.*

Qian closed in, his face illuminated sharply by Amador's lightning while she fought the rest of his men. His focus was only on me. The silver knife in his hand gleamed.

I looked at Lucas, at Nix fighting against her captors, at Amador as her storm raged all around her. Time itself had seemed to slow down to a crawl.

A mirrored arrow.

The vision I'd had in the healing spring. *You can't kill me. I'm you.*

The black tar in my soul that refused to wash away.

I created things.

My power was transformation.

I looked at my hand, the hand I'd used to try to curse Amador that day in the garden. The same hand that had turned into claws. A reflection of my own suffering. A mirrored arrow.

My mind raced. And then it was as if I'd been struck by one of Amador's lightning bolts. No one had cursed me.

I had cursed myself.

All this was my fault. All my self-doubt and insecurities had backfired, rotting my heart from the inside.

I was jealous, and self-hating, and bitter.

I was an alchemist. I could change matter, transform one thing into another.

I was making myself turn into a manananggal.

The reason why I couldn't use my power this whole time was because I had been using it already. I had thought I was so unlovable that I had *made* myself unlovable. I was the only one standing in my way.

I remembered the symbols scrawled in Yara's diary, at the symbol on her mausoleum. It was the symbol of her power. *Change, change, change.* She had been just like me.

I crawled away from Qian, pulling myself across the floor, toward the coconuts. I knew what I needed to do.

"Where do you think you're going?" Qian asked. "You can't escape me."

I reached out, and as I did, something familiar in my chest lurched. Warmth bloomed and rushed through my body when I touched one of the coconuts.

My power. It had come back. It surged through me, filling me to the brim, making my body shake. The cold rot inside me started to thaw. My claws shrank.

Qian stopped in his tracks, watching me with round and fearful eyes.

"What?" he asked, stunned.

I held the coconut to my chest, and the heat inside me exploded. I was bursting with sunlight—my power pulsed, then obliterated the dark void in my chest. I looked up at Qian, and he stared with shock. With a twist of my human hands, I cracked open the coconut shell, and thousands of pearls poured out onto the floor.

Along with the pearls that I had created, light flowed out of my body, blinding everyone, even me. My power swirled around the room like a tornado of pure energy, and it burned all my fear and doubt away.

I closed my eyes and sighed. It was like I'd been drowning this whole time, and only now could I breathe so deeply. A weight had been lifted from my chest, and I rose to my feet. My fangs shrank, and the pain faded.

Thousands of coconut pearls continued to pour out of the shell. My power to change matter was on full display. I was allowed to forgive myself. If no one could give me that grace, at least I could give it to myself.

Qian's surprise passed, and he snarled. He lifted his silver knife at me once again, but I knew how to control my power this time. I raised my hand, and the blade melted like liquid.

Like a pent-up dam breaking, my power was flowing out of me so fast, so strong, I wasn't sure I could control it. But, no—that was the old me. I *could* control it. I was queen of Biringan.

I raised my arms and thrust my light to the ceiling. A deafening boom sounded, and the palace roof blasted apart. Energy burst into the storm, burning through all the rain and clouds. And the silence that followed was like a gasp.

Amador's storm melted away, revealing a clear, starry night lit by the pale full moon.

My power, an essential part of me, receded, and the light faded.

Qian stared at me and then dropped to one knee.

At first, I thought he was bowing to me. Then I heard someone coming, and I turned around.

Dressed in a jade-green silk hanfu was an old man. Jade Mountain's soldiers parted for him as he walked toward me, his cane clacking on the cold marble. The old man took everything in with pale eyes almost as white as his long beard.

"Father," Qian said.

29

THE JADE EMPEROR glanced at the men holding Lucas, and they silently let him go and kneeled. Now free, Lucas got to his feet, shaken and windblown from my power. He removed his gag and stared at me, stunned. We didn't say anything to each other, but he clenched his fists like he wanted to keep fighting. I lifted a hand to assure him that everything was okay. Lucas nodded and backed away.

"My, my," the emperor said, his voice haggard and weak. "What a terrible mess."

His eyes took in all the destruction in my throne room, the mountains of coconuts, the pearls littering the floor. When he saw me, his eyes sparkled, just like Nix's, and he bowed his head. "Queen Mahalina Jazreel," he said.

Remembering my manners, I awkwardly curtsied. My clothes were in tatters and stained with blood, my face and hair a mess, and the chains still hung on my wrists. This was not how I imagined I'd be making a first impression with the Jade Emperor himself. "Your Imperial Majesty," I said, my knees still trembling.

He stood before me, placing his hands upon his cane, and

looked at Qian, who was still on his knee. The Jade Emperor's expression was less than approving.

I found my voice. "What . . . Excuse me, but what are you doing here?"

"I am calling my army back," he said. "No more blood will be spilled this night. I'm sorry I didn't arrive sooner."

"Father," Qian said, "I did what I had—" The Jade Emperor's disapproving glare made Qian close his mouth again. He lowered his head in shame, but his gaze burned while he stared at the floor.

Then the Jade Emperor spoke to me. "Invading an ally's kingdom is an unspeakable act of treachery. I apologize, Queen Mahalina, for arriving so late. I would have liked to introduce myself to you earlier, especially after your father's passing."

I swallowed the lump in my throat. Hearing him speak, I could feel the power radiating off him. It was as if his mere presence was a calming force, the quiet after the storm.

"According to some of my military officials," he said as he looked at Qian's men, who remained on their knees, "there were rumors of a monster. But I see no evidence of such a thing here."

"Father!" Nix cried. She and Amador were arm in arm, hanging off each other, battered and bruised but alive. It was a relief to see them still standing. She gently let go of Amador's arm, but Nix didn't run to him. She stayed where she was, holding Amador's hand. "Have you come to bring me home?" she asked, her voice trembling.

The Jade Emperor stepped toward his daughter, leaning heavily on his cane. She stood tall, despite having gone through so much today. And when the emperor stopped in front of Nix, he smiled. "Is that what you would like me to do?"

"No, I wish to stay here. I needed to figure out who I was outside of the palace," Nix said, tears shining in her eyes. "I want my life to be mine." Amador's eyes widened as she recognized her own words.

The Jade Emperor stared at her for a long moment. For over a year, she'd been on the run, and I had almost expected him to be a hardened ruler to make her do such a thing, but the longer he looked at his daughter, the more it seemed to melt him, and he took a deep, steadying breath.

"I wish you had spoken with me about your feelings sooner," the Jade Emperor said. "You were born into the Jade Mountain empire, and it is your duty to serve your kingdom."

Nix took a step back, her glassy eyes a picture of heartbreak.

Then the Jade Emperor hummed thoughtfully. "It's only now that I realize, to heal our relationship with Biringan, it would be wise to install an ambassador from Jade Mountain here." A subtle smile appeared on his face. "The position can be yours if you so wish."

"Father," Nix said, disbelief and excitement in her voice. "Yes. Yes, please. That would make me very happy." She squeezed Amador's hand.

The Jade Emperor turned to me. "Is that an agreeable arrangement?"

"Yes," I said. My heart swelled with joy. "Most agreeable."

"You're just going to let her go?" Qian shouted. He rose to his feet now, his face flushed with anger. "She's in danger here! Don't let the aswang queen fool you!"

The Jade Emperor raised an eyebrow. "You say there is a monster here, that Phoenix was in danger. It seems that bringing her back against her will would make *me* the monster." The Jade Emperor picked up one of the coconut pearls, tossed it playfully, and caught it in his palm before winking at her.

"I *was* a monster, though," I admitted. Doing so only felt right. "Qian wasn't wrong about that. My magic backfired, and it changed me. It was my fault."

The Jade Emperor puckered his lips and tapped his fingers on the head of his cane. "I've found in my centuries on this plane that, more often than not, those who become the worst versions of themselves often need the most help. It takes great courage to admit our weaknesses. But weakness isn't permanent. Everything in the universe is changing, reshaping, all the time. From the primordial chaos, we emerged. Are we not allowed to change as well?"

"But I hurt people."

"There is yin and yang, a balance of light and darkness, inside all of us, in everything around us, and when an imbalance takes place, the worst in us arises. In my early years, even I was not immune to this. Only with time have I learned that it is a part of living. None of us are immune to change, and it's only when we accept and move with that change that we are truly able to find peace within to become our best selves."

Qian still glared at me with hatred burning in his eyes. No matter what, I'd always be a beast to him. To think we were almost wed. He'd shown his true colors in the end. But was he not capable of change? He'd tried to kill me, and I guess I'd tried to kill him. But could we somehow peacefully go our own ways?

I stepped toward Qian and asked, "Do you hate me?"

He lifted his chin defiantly. "I saw what you truly are."

I bit my lip and nodded, but I took off the ring he'd given me and offered it to him. "Please," I said. "I'm sorry for everything. I want to end any cycle of violence. Here and now."

Qian looked at his ring and then back at me. A dozen expressions flashed across his face, like he was struggling to maintain his composure. And when he met my eyes, I realized he was still afraid. I held no animosity toward him, but he had his own darkness, too, and it was his burden to bear.

Without another word, Qian snatched his ring back and, with a scoff, turned and left the room.

The Jade Emperor smiled at me. "You look so much like your father. And just like him, your qi is strong. Your power is a blessing on the land. Your people are lucky to have you."

"Thank you, Your Imperial Majesty," I said.

"Please." He bowed to me, dipping his head low, then straightened. With another wink, the Jade Emperor left after Qian, and the rest of the soldiers followed.

When the door shut, my knees finally gave out.

"MJ!" Lucas rushed to me and caught me before I hit the floor.

My head felt light. Using so much magic had drained me almost entirely, but Lucas held me close. I felt safe in his arms.

He brushed my hair out of my face. "I'm here," he said. "I'm with you. I love you so much."

Even though I was exhausted, I smiled. "I love you, too. I'm sorry for everything."

"Don't apologize. You did it. You figured it out."

He kissed me, and I realized I was crying when he did. He wiped the tears off my cheeks. They weren't sad tears—I was so relieved and so happy. Everything felt right for once. I had been feeling so terrible for so long, I had almost forgotten what it was like.

I held him, and he held me, and we kissed until our lips went numb.

30

OUR ENGAGEMENT FEAST had become a citywide affair.

Once people returned to their homes after the battle and repairs were made to rebuild the city, a celebration was in order. The banners that had hung for Qian and me had been replaced with the colors of Sirena and Sigbin.

The only person who protested was the most obvious one: Amihan. Amador's mother could be heard bellowing from the grand hall. As I walked toward it, I knew that Elias was getting an earful. When I rounded the corner, I saw her and Elias in the midst of it. He was sitting at the table, and she was standing, leaning close into his face, but he refused to lean back.

Obviously, she didn't want to wait for me to arrive before she tore into Elias.

"We were promised an engagement!" Amihan spat. Elias seemed to be doing everything in his power not to flinch at the spittle flying out of her mouth. "Their betrothal was signed, sealed, and sworn! My daughter was to marry Sir Lucas! Where is the crown's promise? Are contracts worth nothing to you, to the queen?"

Her beautiful face had become a mask of fury and wild-eyed desperation when she screamed. I'd remembered what Amador had said about her family. That her father had made some bad investments, and they were going to lose their house and titles if Amador didn't marry a preeminent member of Sigbin Court. She'd been a political pawn. It seemed like her mother was more upset about losing the promise of better standing than losing Amador.

Elias sounded bored. I think he'd heard enough. "As far as I'm concerned, the agreement is legally null if one member chooses to terminate it. And, correct me if I'm wrong, but I believe it's your own daughter who submitted the request."

"She *what?*"

Elias noticed me coming, and his eyes pleaded for this conversation to end. "I apologize, Amihan. I'll repeat myself for your sake. Your daughter—the grand duchess, if you need a reminder—called off the engagement. It would seem that she has changed her mind about it. She hired a specialist to nullify the oath of devotion. I know no more than that."

That had mostly been my doing. I'd put her in contact with Gani, who was able to lift the oath of devotion for Amador and Lucas. He had been pleased to learn I'd been able to get rid of my curse and applied his own expertise to setting Amador and Lucas free of their own.

"She wouldn't do that to us!" Amihan shrieked. "She knows what's at stake!"

Elias held up his hands. "It's beyond my authority to bind her to a contract that she does not agree to. I am simply a humble councilor to the crown. You may take it up with Her Majesty if you so wish." Elias gestured to me, and Amihan realized I had entered the room.

All etiquette called for her to curtsy, but the moment she saw me come in, her fury turned on me. I tried to keep my face neutral, to be regal, but I felt a pang of sympathy. This was what Amador had had to endure her whole life? No wonder she had been so mean to me at school.

"You," Amador's mother said, pointing a finger at me, "the aswang queen of Biringan! You owe me what is mine."

"You mean Sir Lucas?" I asked.

She stamped her foot so hard, I wondered if she would snap her heel on the marble floor. "You broke a sacred promise! Is this the kind of precedent you want to be setting? After *you* nearly got our city destroyed?"

I put a hand to my chest. "I assure you, Amihan, I would never force two people to be married if that's not something they wish. I am a queen, not a despot."

She bared her teeth at me, much like an animal would. "Sir Lucas and my Amador are to be wed, or else you will regret ever crossing me."

I glanced at Elias, who looked tired and frankly over dealing with her. He just shrugged.

I turned my attention back to Amador's mother and said with all the sincerity I could muster, "I understand the hardship that's befallen your family. I will ensure that you can remain in your palace, that your husband can keep his position in the court and all his titles, so long as you heed Amador's wishes not to marry Lucas."

Amihan stared at me, her eyes so round and her jaw so set,

I wondered if she was trying to summon her magic. But I stood before her, head held high, confident that I was right. Amador didn't deserve to be used this way, and neither did Lucas. It was my responsibility, not just as a queen but as their friend, to see that they were both happy.

"You will regret this," she said, pointing her finger at me again. "I swear it. You will rue this day."

"You're welcome," I said, putting on my best smile.

That seemed to make her even angrier, and she swelled up like a helium balloon.

"Is that all?" Elias asked with eyebrows raised.

Amihan huffed loudly and tugged on her skirt, straightening it out of frustration, before she stomped out of the room.

"You're learning how to play politics," Elias said, amused.

I leaned on his chair, resting my chin on the back of it, and sighed. "Yeah, well, it only took nearly destroying the city."

"Welcome to being a queen," he said.

It was a position I was quickly getting used to. I hadn't heard from Qian since he had nearly tried to kill me that day. I doubted I'd ever see him again, and frankly, I was okay with that. I'd made a lot of enemies, but I guessed that came with the territory.

Elias asked, "And where is your mother?"

"She's organizing the wedding festivities. She's going to make it a night to remember."

My mom had come back to Biringan City shortly after the battle. I had a lot to fill her in on. Admittedly, I was just glad I could hug her again. "I think she's going to turn the whole palace into a party."

"As it should be," Elias said.

It was strange having the palace back. It had taken time to rebuild, but doing it for a wedding lifted everyone's spirits. I had a lot of reasons to celebrate. There had been so many chances for people to turn their backs on me, and they hadn't. I was grateful I was getting another chance to be queen.

Elias inspected me and my well-worn Arnis uniform, an eyebrow raised. "And shouldn't you be getting ready for your wedding as well?"

I pushed off from his chair and gestured to my outfit.

"The wedding isn't for a few months. There's plenty of time," I said. "But I've got more training to do first. Isn't that what you always wanted?"

Elias simply shook his head as I left the room, a slight spring in my step.

I was totally free of the manananggal curse. Gani had visited shortly after the battle to check me over, assuring me that there was no sign of corruption in my body. I had been right in figuring out that I was doing it to myself. It had been a self-fulfilling prophecy the whole time. The manananggal had been a part of me from the start, and the only one who could have broken the curse was me.

Though, if I hadn't had my friends around me, who had never given up on me, I wasn't sure I would have made it that far. Yara hadn't had anyone.

One of the first things I did after the battle was make sure that her name was reinstated in the archives. I made sure that she would never be forgotten again. I even erected a new statue for her in the garden.

Rumors spread about the lady of the mountain appearing all over the island, green and new growth following in her wake. I hoped she could find some peace now, too.

The palace was bright and airy while servants and attendants swept through the halls, decorating for the big celebrations. Parades were being planned, along with feasts in our honor and even a tournament—this time without the threat of a monster swooping in to attack anyone. There were no more surprises lurking around every corner, not even when I stumbled upon Nix and Amador, lips locked while they embraced each other in the middle of the hallway.

"I figured you two were long gone by now," I said.

My voice startled them apart. "MJ!" Nix gasped, then smiled.

Blushes colored their cheeks, but their eyes were bright. They both looked happy, and that was all I could have ever asked for.

"Is my mother gone?" Amador asked.

"She's lurking the grounds, no doubt," I said. "How did you know she was here?"

"Her voice carries," she said with a shiver.

"You better make sure she doesn't see you. Is Romulo waiting for you?"

"Yes," said Amador, "we should go soon, or he might set sail without us."

She squeezed Nix's hand and hurried off to a pair of back-packs on the floor, checking that nothing had been forgotten. I think this was the first time I'd ever seen Amador not in a Maria Clara gown or something just as fabulous. She and Nix were both dressed in brown linen shirts and pants, the uniform of sailors.

Once her engagement to Lucas had been called off, Amador said she needed to disappear for a bit, go where no one would find her, at least until her mother calmed down, and asked Romulo for a spot on his ship when he went on his next excursion. When she told me that she had planned an escape consisting of hard manual labor and no doubt treacherous seas, she'd said it was time for a little change. I knew exactly what she meant.

Nix, of course, agreed to go with her, claiming it was an opportunity to test her healing abilities on the high seas, but the truth was obvious. It was hard for them to do anything separately since the emperor had let Nix stay in Biringan City. They were often sneaking into quiet corners of the library or the garden, spending private time with each other. Even now, she stared longingly at Amador, although they were only a few feet apart.

"So you're officially dating," I said to Nix, failing to suppress a smile.

Nix's own smile appeared, crinkling her eyes. "Yes."

"How does it feel?"

"Amazing," she sighed dreamily.

I knew that feeling all too well. "I'm so happy for you." My chest filled with warmth seeing how full of life she looked, and I grabbed her into a hug, holding her tight. "You promise you'll come back, right?"

"Of course," she said. "We'll be here for your wedding. Besides, Biringan City is my home! Anywhere you are is home."

I squeezed her and let her go. I was so glad to call her my best friend. Even though some things had changed, at least others stayed the same.

"Go on," I said, giving her an encouraging nudge. "You two have a boat to catch."

Without further delay, hand in hand, Nix and Amador ran down the hall and disappeared from view.

If I lingered any longer, I was going to be late, too, so I made my way through the garden, past Yara's new fountain statue and her warm smile, and went down the trail to Sirena Village. The day was bright, the air briny with seawater. Merchants and sailors shouted to one another in the market below, a sign of Biringan City returning to normal.

And I had a feeling he was around here somewhere . . .

I turned down a corner, onto a side street, and heard footsteps behind me.

I ducked into an alcove and pressed my back against the cold stone wall, holding my breath.

The sound of the footsteps grew louder, the soles of boots crunching on gravel, and then silence.

I waited, listening, smiling. He was right around the corner. All I had to do was be patient. Like a predator.

But he always knew when danger was close.

I raised my knife and leapt out, but—of course—Lucas caught my wrist before I could get him.

"Got you," he said, smiling.

I couldn't help smiling, too. "Got me."

I pushed him, and he laughed as he stepped back, light on his feet, and struck out at me with his own knife. I sidestepped and spun, moving in close to him, so when I was right up against him, our faces were inches apart.

"Good," he said. "Wouldn't expect anything less."

I stole a kiss from him, and he laughed against my mouth.

"Is that your strategy? To kiss your opponent?"

"It's not working?" I asked.

With a smirk, he closed the distance between us, and we held each other tight, hidden away in our little alcove, our own world, where we could be together. At last.

—ACKNOWLEDGMENTS—

THE DEEPEST THANKS always to my editor, Polo Orozco; my publishers, Jennifer Klonsky and Jennifer Loja; and the amazing team at Penguin Young Readers, including my hardworking publicist, Jordana Kulak, and copyeditors Kaitlyn San Miguel, Misha Kydd, Cindy Howle, and Ana Deboo. Maraming salamat sa lahat! Thanks always to my book/film/TV family: Richard Abate and Hannah Carande at 3 Arts, and Ellen Goldsmith-Vein, Jeremy Bell, DJ Goldberg, and Sarah Jones at Gotham. Thanks to my friends and family and family of readers. Love you all!